Friday Night Chicas

ST. MARTIN'S GRIFFIN
NEW YORK

Friday Night Chicas

SEXY STORIES FROM LA NOCHE

Mary Castillo

Caridad Piñeiro

Berta Platas

Sofia Quintero

www.stmartins.com

Book design by Stephanie Huntwork

ISBN 0-312-33504-0
EAN 978-0312-33504-5

First Edition: April 2005

1   3   5   7   9   10   8   6   4   2

Contents

My Favorite Mistake

MARY CASTILLO

Chapter One

When you're a failure in Hollywood, that's like starving to death outside a banquet hall with smells of filet mignon driving you crazy.

—Marilyn Monroe

So what are you wearing with my shoes?" my sister barked over the cell phone and straight into my earphone.

Meet my sister. My happily-married-to-her-high-school-sweetheart sister, who recently provided our mother's only grandchild.

When I think of her that way, it's really hard not to hate that bitch.

"These aren't your shoes anymore," I informed her. "You gave them to me."

"I let you borrow them. Now what are you wearing?"

I looked out the window and instantly forgot Lydia's question. Twelve years of living in L.A.—eight of them

wasted in various low-life positions in the movie industry—
had ruined plenty of my illusions and my romance with the
city. Except this. This view of downtown L.A., as my BMW
flew down the 105 onto the 110, still got to me. Ribbons of
red brake lights crept toward the cluster of green sky-
scrapers that rose out of the milky darkness. Downtown
L.A. at night was the closest thing to Oz on this earth.

"Oh, Goddamn it!" Lydia shouted, the force of her voice
tickling my ear. "You're wearing my shoes with the uniform."

Uniform?

"God give me strength," she muttered. "Let me guess.
Black suit with a button-down shirt from the Limited and a
silver necklace. How could you do that to my shoes?"

Not that it's conducive to this story, but I actually have
suits in gray, brown, tan, blue, and black with red pin-
stripes, that I could wear if I had time to work out.

And furthermore, with the way Lydia carried on about
the damn shoes you'd think they were Manolos. Between
us, they're faux designer from Footsie Tootsie.

"Don't you have a child to breast-feed?" I asked her.

"Not for two more hours."

If I hung up on her, Mom would be calling within five
minutes. "I'm wearing a sheer black 1920s dress—"

"Sheer? How sheer, *cochina*?"

"Sheer enough for a nude-colored slip."

" 'Bout damn time you show off that figure you got. Shit,
I'm never gonna get mine back."

Now I shouldn't blame Lydia for thinking I live this

glamorous life up in L.A. She lives back home in Chula Vista where the epicenter of fashion is Toda Moda.

"Where are you?" she asked.

"On the One-ten"

"You got the pass?"

"Yep."

"And your boss let you have it?"

Nerves knifed my insides, which hurt by the way.

"Not exactly."

"You're not going to get fired again, are you?"

For the record, I've never been fired. Well, not that Lydia needs to know, but yes, I was "let go" last week.

"Dale is in Chicago," I answered.

Dale is my boss—sorry, ex-boss—who is unaware that a year ago I optioned a short story with money reshuffled from loans and credit card debt. It was the boldest move I'd ever made and when I think about it, I get light-headed. But this story was the only thing in a long, long time that gave me The Feeling. The same feeling I got when Candace Bushnell was trolling *Sex and the City* to Hollywood. (I made the photocopies at the production company I was interning at.) And again when I read that adaptation of Raymond Chandler's *Lady in the Lake*, which Tyler Banks directed and which resurrected David Duchovny's career.

When I pushed for *Sex*, I wasn't hired after my internship ended. After I insisted on Chandler, my boss axed my position and hired his niece as his assistant. Calling him a moron might have played a factor in that decision.

"I hope you know what you're doing," Lydia sighed.

"I do. I just need to schmooze the right people."

"That's what you've been doing the last eight years. And look where you are."

Here it comes. I moved the phone so she wouldn't hear me sigh.

"Why don't you think about coming home?" she asked. "Tony knows this guy who has a video production company that makes commercials and wedding videos. You could work there."

A shrill car horn sounded behind me and I jerked the wheel back into my lane. "What? Are you trying to kill me?"

"Okay, forget I said that," Lydia insisted. "I never even said it."

"Yes. You did." I felt something catch in the back of my throat. Where was my bottle of water? With the wheel in one hand, my life suddenly depended on reaching across the passenger seat to pluck my water bottle from where it lodged itself between the door and the seat.

"It's just that—"

"I know, I know, I fucking know."

I heard her breathing on the other end. "I just worry about you. All alone up there."

Shit. I slammed on the pedal and the car heaved forward, brakes groaning as the red taillights of the beater in front of me came at my car. Even if my lease payments put me in debt, thank God for German engineering.

"I'm meeting someone tonight," I told her with that mad

dog feeling flaring up inside me as I sat there stuck in a sea of traffic.

"But there are plenty of guys down here," she pled. "And you can still stay in the movies."

Traffic stayed locked in a standstill and I squeezed my eyes shut with frustration. If I had the money to replace it, my cell phone would've been splattered against the windshield.

You see, Lydia wasn't looking into the face of thirty after having jumped from one windowless office to another. I was staring down into a pit of failures.

I'd pitched my project all around town for a year and no one wanted it. There was only one chance left and his name was Tyler Banks. He appeared out of nowhere three years ago with a movie about a con gone wrong, and his second film, the Raymond Chandler flick I mentioned earlier, won him the Palme d'Or and an Oscar for Best Adapted Screenplay. And every subsequent film of his knocked it out of the park at the box office.

Tonight Tyler would be at Que Bella's post-Screen Actors Guild Award party in downtown L.A. Tonight I had Dale's VIP pass in my nifty clutch purse for said party. Tonight was my last chance to pull myself out of the depths of development and unemployment hell and make all these years worth something.

"I gotta go." Or else I was going to say something that would guarantee Lydia wouldn't speak to me for six months. "Give Jody a kiss for me, okay?" I said, missing my little niece.

"Won't you just think about what I said?"

"I'm not that desperate."

"Excuse me but you're wearing my shoes."

Okay. So she had me there.

Chapter Two

You're a lying, conniving human being and all I can say is that karma will bite you in the end. And BTW, would it be okay if I stopped by Friday after work to pick up my stuff?

—Email to Isela from her ex

Hey, excuse me! Who are you?" asked a guy with a name tag that read "Dave," when I stepped onto the red carpet under the glittering marquee of the Orpheum Theatre.

"Isela Vargas, Arabella Productions," I said, pressing my way toward the doors. I really didn't have time for a flunky with a clipboard.

"You're not on the list. Are you someone's date or something?"

A visual scan of his unhemmed pants and high-top sneakers confirmed him as a film school student. I bet he calls famous directors by their first names when debating the difference between movies and films. I should know; I'd been just like him once upon a time.

"I'm attending in Dale Berkowitz's place," I shouted over the screaming photographers and TV show cameras with logos from *Entertainment Tonight, E!, Access Hollywood*, and hundreds of others from all around the world. At the end of the carpet were the faceless, waving, and hysterical fans, most of whom were professional autograph hounds that had spent the night on the sidewalk so they could get Britney Spears's signature to hock on eBay for $500.

Dave pressed a finger against his headset and shouted into his mike, "I have an Isela Vargas in place of—"

Out of the corner of my eye I saw a sex goddess of the early '90s (one really shouldn't name names in this town) shove Christina Aguilera's handler out of the way to present herself and her twenty-year-old boy toy to the screaming paparazzi. She kissed his cheek, leaning on him like a hotel convention hooker, and the flashes pulsated wildly. Word on the street was that when the old girl wasn't bashing the kid on the head with Grey Goose bottles, she was trolling for a role, any role in whatever project she could get her hands on.

No matter how famous or infamous, desperation and age do that to a girl in Hollywood.

A quick side step and I ditched Dave to merge with the passing entourage of the latest teen TV sensation.

"No photos," the heartthrob barked, flipping his glossy black hair over his shoulder. "Fucking people."

While one part of me thought his attitude wouldn't guarantee him a long career, the other blessed him for his sense of entitlement as we sailed past the bottom-feeders waiting to take their turn through the metal detectors. All I had to do was pretend to be hip enough and "somebody" enough to follow them straight into the VIP room.

"Whoa, wait a second, you." I had one foot in the door when someone bigger and stronger than me snagged my arm. I might've heard the word "loser" uttered by someone in the entourage that disappeared into the crowd.

"Excuse me, but who are you?" I demanded.

The guy could've had a career as a double for The Rock, but instead he was stuffed into a black suit with the curly wire thing in his ear and the discreet lapel mike clipped to a no-nonsense black tie.

"Detectors first." He walked me to the metal detectors, glaring at the Colin Firth wannabe in line to step back. He jerked his thumb at me to walk through.

I did. The machine dinged and his crack team descended with their wands.

"Take off your shoes."

"Cindy Crawford lost her shoes in a situation like this," I said.

"Don't care. Take 'em off."

I really didn't want anyone to see the Footsie Tootsie imprint. But what can you do standing in front of a 200-pound black lady in flammable rayon pants?

After they X-rayed my purse and then pawed through said purse's contents, it became apparent I was neither a terrorist nor a reporter for *Tattler* magazine. Security tagged me with a wristband and released me into the party.

There were so many bodies packed tight that I just

flowed with the human current to the center of the main lobby. I was about to find my compact and regroup. But—I know it sounds cheesy—for some reason the smell of the place stopped me short in that moment. Old and dusty yet full of the magic and nostalgia of what L.A. had once been, that was the smell of the Orpheum.

If you imagined hard enough, you could almost see the men in their fedoras and the women dressed in their smart 1940s wool suits and pumps walking in through the lobby for a newsreel, a short, and a movie starring Cary Grant and Ingrid Bergman.

Time and neglect gave it an air of elegant decay. The giant chandeliers burned through the decades of dust on its crystals and the gilded vaulted ceiling had lost some of its shine. But the grand staircase built for the Gloria Swansons and Bette Davises of the world hadn't lost its arrogant sweep.

The last time I'd been here was with my film school buddies, the summer before graduation. We saw *Vertigo*. And we dissected the entire film afterwards at the Grinder on Fig. Over the years my friends—Carly, Paul, Erik, and Stan— left L.A. and our dreams of making Important Films.

And here I was. Another hapless Hollywood bottom-feeder picking up every crumb, scrap, and bit of something I could to survive.

With a snap of my compact, I headed straight for the stairs, roped off in tasteful red velvet, leading to the VIP Lounge. All I had to do was charm my way past the two beefy sentinels who stood watch with hands clasped in front of crotches, gazes straight and feet planted shoulder width apart.

Someone yelled, "Hey!" when I ignored the line.

"I'm meeting a friend," I said, stopping short as if I expected them to let me pass.

One turned his soulless gaze on me. "No hand stamp, no entrance."

"No one told me I needed a hand stamp." Which was true, by the way.

"Not my problem."

"But someone is waiting for me."

"Not tonight." He practically picked me up off my feet with one hand to make room for the current star of another *Melrose Place*–clone show. When the snarling blonde of the moment and her entourage swept into the VIP lounge, Sentinel One stood away from the podium and resumed parade stance in front of the velvet rope.

"Excuse me, but Tyler Banks's assistant called this afternoon to inform everyone that I would meet him here," I insisted, my back breaking out in a sheen of sweat as the other hangers-on watched me.

"Talk to the head of security."

"I really don't have time for this—"

"Neither do I." With one sausagelike finger, he pushed me away.

"I've got forty bucks." I wrested the clasp of my clutch open. If faux authority didn't work, then bribery was the only bow left in my quiver. "I won't touch or harass anyone prettier than I am."

His lips twitched, but he shook his head.

Okay, what was this dude's problem? This is Hollywood. Women, with a wink and a twiddle of the fingers, could get in anywhere. Why wasn't this working for me?

Oh, wait, I'm not blonde, six feet tall, European, or wearing silicone slapped to my chest. Think brown eyes, brown stick-straight hair, pixie-sized boobies, and no butt, and you'll get the picture.

"Ma'am, you can enjoy the party in the main room," Sentinel One said. "Or you can wait outside for Mr. Banks, who isn't here tonight."

Did you hear that? That was the sound of my heart dropping into my stomach.

If he heard it, he didn't give a shit.

Chapter Three

*La suerte de la fea la bonita la desea ("The luck of the plain girl
the pretty girl envies.")*

—Isela's mom to both her daughters

This was a bust.

A loser would skulk back and pose with the wannabes. Not this Mexican bitch.

No. I waited for an hour and a half, hoping Tyler Banks would come out of his self-imposed exile at tonight's party.

But no. He could be anywhere: the Standard, the Miramax party, or still nursing his broken heart in Fiji where he took off with his brother about a year ago.

You have no idea what I'm talking about, do you? Okay, short version: Tyler had been dating Carson Ridgeley, the nitwit they cast as Wonder Woman in that god-awful movie a couple of years ago.

I know, we should just pretend it never happened.

Anyway, she somehow ended up with a role in Tyler's

third movie and then they're on the cover of *People* with a 4-carat Indian sapphire blown up in one of those little boxes. Not six months later Carson was caught kissing some bartender from the Monkey Bar on the balcony of the Chateau Marmont.

After that bomb dropped, Tyler wrapped movie number four and skipped town.

But he was back. Ted Casablanca said so, and Ted, my friends, is never wrong.

I'm telling you, story of my life if Tyler doesn't show. In high school, I had no boobs. Hence no boyfriends. In college I was laughed away from the MEChA table at Freshmen Orientation for not speaking Spanish. I showed them and joined the Latino Business Student Association. And in this industry, I'd frozen in too many lines while one tipsy bimbo after another stumbled out of industry parties with the men who could've given me a job.

So the setback and I weren't strangers. Except next week, I wouldn't have enough money to pay my rent.

I nursed my stale lemon drop martini, knowing that my mark would emerge sooner or later.

My phone trilled. I tried to open my clutch without snapping an acrylic nail. I had to stop gnawing on my real ones.

"What?" Damn it. I shouldn't have snapped my purse shut.

"So what happened?" It was Lydia.

"Aren't you supposed to be getting milked?"

"Not so good, huh?"

"He's not here."

"Then go find somebody else!"

"I'm not moving. I'm just reassessing my game plan."

"Moving back home and getting married to Rodney?" Lydia asked hopefully. Unfortunately obstinacy was a familial trait. "He's single again."

Sorry, but I shudder at the thought of dragging an ice chest to Little League games, overseeing piñatas at birthday parties, and running into the people I went to high school with at Toda Moda. "No."

"Whatever. Is Hugh Jackman there?" Hell if I knew, standing out here in the main room where the current celebrity to civilian ratio was 4,000 to 2. Oh, now that Courtney and David slipped past the sentinels, it dwindled to zero.

Sentinel One, who pushed me around, patted David's shoulder like an old buddy. My eyes narrowed. "No."

"Damn. Well, call me if anything else happens. Tony's passed out and I can't go to sleep."

"You're still not sleeping?"

"No. I don't know what's wrong and I can't take those pills Mom keeps trying to give me because I'm breast-feeding."

My mother's answer to any and every ailment, especially motherhood, was her sleeping pills. I doubt Mom ever had a natural state of rest after she turned eighteen.

"I guess I just worry too much." Lydia sighed and if she hadn't laid it on so thick I might've offered to come down next weekend. "If things don't work out, *m'ija*, you can come live with us."

That was about all I could take. Lydia was probably sleeping just fine for all I knew. Discreetly I pressed the End key. I'd tell her it must've been a bad connection.

I slapped my hand on my purse and then tried to pry it back open. A solid arm brushed mine and I looked over and then up into his eyes. *Cha-ching.*

My first thought was, what did he look like naked? My second was, is that really him?

No. In the pictures I'd seen, Tyler Banks had short hair and this vision standing beside me, *smiling* at me, was Brad Pitt with the *Ocean's Eleven* wardrobe, but with *Legends of the Fall* hair.

"Looks like you need help with that," he said.

My brain flatlined and then blipped. "Oh thanks," I said, handing him, a complete stranger, my purse.

His blunt-tipped finger brushed mine and when he looked down at my purse, a gold strand of hair fell into his face.

I was never this lucky. Something had to go wrong. I couldn't even shut my mouth.

Unlike most directors, Tyler Banks didn't do Steven Spielberg geek chic. His face was all strong lines and hard features, a beaklike nose that was balanced by a stubborn jaw, a broad forehead with a wave of blond hair, and green eyes that saw right through a girl.

"There," he pronounced, holding my opened purse.

"Thanks."

"Welcome."

"I'm Isela," I offered, curling my shaking hand at my side.

"Nice to meet you."

I completely forgot about my phone until it rang again. Lydia. With an eye roll I shoved it into my purse and snapped it shut.

"Your sister?" he guessed.

"Yeah. You have one, too?"

"Cousins, which are probably worse."

I didn't want to be obvious that I knew who he was. "I've still got you beat. Nothing is deadlier than an older sister."

He swiveled his barstool and bumped my knees with his, "So are you—"

"Hey there," cooed a deep British female voice behind us.

He looked over and then forgot what he was saying.

She-Ra smiled at me in that dismissive way girls who know they're prettier than you do. She rested her skeletal hands on his thighs. "What are you doing out here?"

"Just hanging out," he said.

She cocked her head and I swear, her curly highlighted mane did not move. "You didn't wait for me?"

He laughed uncomfortably, glancing at me and then back at her. "Sorry, I think you've got the wrong brother." He moved her hands off him. "I'm Sebastian," he clarified as if she were a slow child. "Tyler's brother."

Both She-Ra and I blinked. She drew her hands to her chest. "Oh."

Maybe I didn't have a Playboy pedigree but as a *mujer de la familia Vargas,* I had centuries of coquetry and manipulating the male mind running in my blood. As I scooted off my stool and wiggled my skirt down, I had what we Mexicans referred to as *cojones.*

American translation: balls.

Tyler Banks's brother was mine. "Honey, how about I send him to you when I'm done," I spoke up loud enough for her not to ignore me.

"Oh," she breathed.

Intrigued, Sebastian grinned at me. "That's right. I was going to show you something."

Even though direct eye contact with those green eyes of his made me just a touch shaky in the knees, I kept my smile beguiling and gaze steady. "That's right."

Unhappy that her excursion among the peasant class had been interrupted by a short, flat-chested girl in vintage and Footsie Tootsie shoes, She-Ra crossed her arms, her hip bone clearly outlined against her dress.

What she didn't know was that my stomach twisted so tight that it hurt. Even though her verbal repartee lacked something, she outclassed me by two Victoria's Secret catalogs.

When Sebastian said nothing to soothe her questioning pout, She-Ra flounced off after tossing a weltering, "Fucking bitch."

"You just cost me a date," Sebastian said, his eyes dancing with amusement.

"And I feel just terrible about that. So what were you planning to show me?"

His eyes did a quick survey. "You really want to find out?"

I must've been having an out-of-body experience. While my heart ran laps in my chest and bells clanged in my ears, I've never sounded this cool before. "How long will it take?"

His eyebrows lifted. "You know, I like a woman with balls."

Somehow I said this with a straight face. "I like a man with balls, too."

He laughed at that one, and I told myself I didn't like his laugh or the fact that he had a sense of a humor. A laugh like his in a package like him could throw me off in this game.

"This might take all night," he said.

Oh God, this sounds like dialogue from one of my boss's movies. All we needed was the heavy bass line. But I matched him. "Are you up for it?"

He watched me, something twinkling in those eyes. "Where've you been all this time?"

In a windowless office with no air-conditioning or heating. "I'm here right now."

His grin widened. "Glad to meet you, Isela. Sebastian Banks."

I took his hand and let's just say that everything south of the border sprang to life.

From now on he would be only known to me as The

Mark. The Mark was a way for me to get to the man who I knew would produce my script. Of course, it got complicated because Sebastian was too damn sexy for my own good.

"So where do we go from here?" he asked.

I took a deep breath. "Surprise me."

Chapter Four

If you ever make a movie about ants chasing stupida white girls running with their boobies out, I'll disown you.

—Lydia to Isela when the family realized
she wasn't moving back home

Now that I had him, I had no idea what to do with him. Sebastian got us up into one of the opera boxes high above the dance floor built over the main floor seats. Standing up there alone with him, I was suddenly the girl I would've envied if I had been stuck down there. Except *that* girl would've made sparkling conversation and then segued into a suggestion that they meet up with his brother for drinks.

"I noticed you earlier," he said after a long silence. "You were staring up at the ceiling."

"Really? Oh yeah," I replied, cringing inside.

He leaned on the back of a seat. "What were you thinking?"

"Nothing. Just . . . about the last time I'd been here."

"And when was that?"

"A really long time ago. They showed *Vertigo*. It's my favor—"

"—ite Hitchcock movie," we said together.

When we stared at each other, the nightclub lights whirling colors against our faces, a recognition sprouted between us. It wasn't love. My heart was zero for three on that score. Just this freakish buzzing thing between us that intensified with each passing second.

A smile touched his face. "How many times have you seen it?"

"Seen what?"

"*Vertigo*."

"Oh. Thirty-four times."

He looked impressed. "You've got me beat by two."

"No one can beat Hitchcock."

"What did you think about the remake of *Psycho*."

My hand sliced through the air. "Never happened. It doesn't exist."

"So I take it you hated my brother's last movie?"

I hit the mouth brakes and asked carefully, "Why would you think that?"

"You know what everyone said, all those comparisons to Jimmy Stewart when he stared at the lady he thought was Kim Novak."

"He didn't swipe from *Vertigo*. He had Brad doing that whole Steve McQueen thing from *Bullitt*."

"*Bullitt?*"

"Yes, *Bullitt*." Even though he was related to the best

filmmaker since Steven Spielberg, Sebastian stared at me a lot like Lydia did when I talked about movies.

I explained, "You know the scene where they're at dinner and the way McQueen stares at Jacqueline Bisset across the table. No dialogue, not even any cheesy romantic music. Just the ambient noise of the restaurant, the people talking, and the camera catches him devouring her with his eyes across the table."

Sebastian didn't say anything. I tried to read the way he looked at me. Truthfully, it was like the way McQueen did Bisset.

Sebastian edged forward, hovering right at the border of my personal space, and I swear I heard the hairs on the back of my neck spear up. "You pass," he said.

"Excuse me?"

"You don't like compliments?," he asked.

Dropping my hip against the seat back put some distance between us, but not enough. "So you're into movies, too, huh?"

He dropped his gaze down to his Bruno Maglis, grinning at some joke only known to him. "Not right now. You're in the business," he said, as if that somehow made me dirty.

"I've produced a couple of movies. Not that they went anywhere. Are you thinking about working for your brother?"

One broad shoulder jerked up. "Maybe. I'm really not sure yet."

"This business is tough. But at least you've got an in."

He didn't blink. If I was standing in the center of a frozen body of water, the ice would be cracking and groaning around me. Apparently our boy Sebastian here didn't mind wearing the VIP stamp on his hand or four thousand dollars worth of clothes. But he radiated a strong inferiority-complex vibe about his wildly successful brother.

Sebastian's hand flattened against his chest and he pulled out a tiny cell phone from his coat pocket. Checking the display, his jaw flexed. "Sorry, but I have to take this."

Long strides carried him into the blackness of the hall-way.

A rush of air heaved out of my mouth and my shoulders bowed forward. What just happened? Did I blow it? And for a second, I worried about waking up tomorrow morning with this guy.

Okay, collect thyself, woman. I was not going to race after him to make sure he came back. Because he was and when he did, I was going to play this game through and end up with five minutes with his brother.

And yes, I admit that I didn't want the clock to strike midnight. I wanted to stay on this fantasy nondate with this very sexy prince.

When Sebastian reappeared I leapt to my feet. Subtle, huh?

"I took a while so I got us these," he said, handing me a glass of champagne before he sat down.

I murmured, "thank you," and looked down into the glass.

"I'm not that kind of guy," he said. "I only use the fast-dissolving kind."

"What are you talking about?"

His eyes widened and then he laughed. "I thought you were— Never mind."

Did I miss something?

With a sigh he shook his head. "You were looking in your glass like I put something in it."

I looked down in the glass. No white pill fizzed lecherously from the bottom. "I thought maybe I said something wrong before you took off with your cell phone and . . . I'm sorry. I feel like there's an elephant in the room and we're pretending it's not there."

"My brother?"

I nodded.

"What about him?"

Oh God. What do I say? "Does talking about him make you feel uncomfortable?"

"No. But tonight I'm not interested in talking about him or the industry or anything else," he said. The wine shined on his lower lip and I wondered what it would taste like if I licked it clean. "But let's you and me start over."

"How do we do that?"

"Want to go dancing?"

"Here?"

He made a face and shook his head. "Nah. Somewhere more . . . classy."

"Like where?"

"Like somewhere down the street from here."

"I'd love to."

"Good. So may I?" I felt his gaze on my lips.

Why the hell not? My smile said yes and his lips, ever so lightly, landed on mine. He was better than chocolate.

"I want to spend the evening with you," he said against my lips, now wet with the taste of him.

Before I could say a word, Sebastian held up a finger and I shut up.

"I didn't say, sleep with me. I said, spend the evening with me. No cheap moves from me and everything out on the table. Deal?"

I was still trying to shush all the clanging in my head.

Clearly amused, Sebastian added, "I'm not a psychopath, rapist, or stalker. Does that make you feel any better?"

I curled my hands into fists. "Sure," I said. "That's what they all say."

Chapter Five

Mas vale de balde hacer, que de balde ser. ("It is better to do something for nothing than to be worth nothing.")
—Advice from Isela's mom

Later in the ladies room with Sebastian's taste mixed with champagne still on my lips, I called Lydia.

"It's me." My voice echoed against the glaring white tiled walls. A toilet hissed by itself and having seen too many movies where the heroine looks in the mirror and sees some crazy-eyed ghost behind her, I kept my back to the dull mirror.

"Why the hell did you hang up on me?" she yelled. "I'm the only one in the family talking to you right now."

That wasn't true! But then I remembered I had little time and a big dilemma, who was waiting outside for me. "I'm sorry but this guy was sitting next to me and—"

"What guy?" She gasped, "Oh. *That* guy, you mean?"

"His brother."

Suddenly all business, "Are you at his place?" I imagined her eyes wide with vicarious delight.

A quick aside: What is it about my married sister, cousins, and friends who think all I do as a single woman is shop, fuck, and worry about my shoes? And when I do any of these things, they want every juicy morsel. *Cochinas*.

"No," I told her. "I'm in the ladies room. He wants to spend the evening with me. What the hell do you think he means by that?"

"*Madre de Dios*. How did he ask? Was he all player or romantic?"

Was Sebastian romantic or was he saying all the right things so I'd trust him? It worked for Ted Bundy.

Or wait, even worse, was he using some reverse psychology on me by not wanting to talk about his brother to lure me to him?

In this town actresses and models can do what we call "dating your manager." But the rules change for executives.

As an executive you have to be smart. You actually have to earn the respect of your male colleagues. And it helps if you're married to one of them or sprung from one of their loins. So for the rest of us, we have to twist the rules to work to our advantage.

"Well?" Lydia pressed.

"Romantic, I think."

She muttered something about knowing my mother had an affair before she had me. "How can you not know?"

"Because what if he's using me?"

"Man, it has been a while since you got laid!"

Why did I even call her? "I can't sleep with him!"

"Is he ugly?"

"No."

"What's his name?"

"Sebastian Banks."

"What is it with you and these white boys anyway?" she asked. I bet she had her fist planted on one hip and one dragon-lady nail waving in the air. "Didn't you learn your lesson the last time?"

I described Sebastian and she made an assessing hum.

"Well, that changes things," Lydia decided, thinking over my problem. "Wait a minute, I'm confused. He wants to spend the evening with you."

"Yes."

"But he doesn't want to sleep with you?"

"Well, yeah I think so."

"Ay, *m'ija*. Didn't we raise you right?"

"You're my sister," I corrected.

"Your older, much wiser sister." Who, I admit, took over for Mom when she went off the deep end after my father died. And since Lydia was the one with a kid and a husband while I was the one leaning against a rust-stained sink in a bathroom that was probably haunted, maybe she was the wiser of the two.

"Would you hate me if I slept with him?" I asked.

"So he'd introduce you to his brother?"

"No. Because . . . I don't know."

"Ay, Isela, why do you make this so difficult? If he's sexy and into you and you're into him, then get it on with him.

And meeting his brother would be a side benefit. But would you hate yourself?"

Yes. No. I don't know. The tricky thing was that I wanted to sleep with him. Sometime after he opened my purse, Sebastian ceased to be my mark and suddenly became the guy I wanted to get it on with, you know. And when Lydia made it sound like he was the free gift from Lancôme, suddenly it didn't seem all that bad.

"But ask yourself this," Lydia said. "Are you sure you're not into him because of what's his name?"

"Dean. His name was Dean."

"Anyone who shits on my *hermanita* don't have no name to me. And don't change the subject."

Until Lydia brought the bastard up, my ex never even entered my mind. Now I was starting to second-guess myself.

"I have to get back."

Lydia made this strangled noise. "You always do that! And don't you hang up on me!"

"I wasn't! You know, you're getting mean in your old age." I wanted her to get mad at me, to stop asking those questions I didn't want to answer.

"Whatever. And speaking of 'mean,' when are you finally going to call Mom?"

"When she gets off her moral high horse and apologizes for what she said."

"She didn't mean it like that."

"Really? Oh, so she must've been talking about someone else when she said something about me driving Dean away."

"Still—"

"Still nothing. I have to go."

"Fine. Call me around three-thirty. The baby will be up then." Click.

I swung around to the face the mirror. My hands were shaking and I half-hoped Sebastian had been snatched up by She-Ra so the decision would be taken from me. But I also hoped he would still be waiting.

Get back in the game. Finish this out, I told myself while flattening out my gown against my thighs and double-checking to make sure the back hadn't hiked up in my panties.

I said to my reflection, "Play this by ear. Be cool." And for good measure I did another lipstick check. "George Lucas didn't sleep with anyone's brother."

I walked out of the restroom and wound my way back to the hall where Sebastian bounced his fist on the marble balustrade, staring down at the party below.

"Ready?" I asked.

His head swung around and he smiled when I stood beside him. "I am."

Keep it steady, old girl. "You ever going to tell me where?"

"You told me to surprise you."

"That was back down there."

"What's the fun in changing the rules?" He walked toward the stairs, his jacket puckered under his hands in his pockets. "Come on."

"Seriously, where are we going?" I followed.

He took one step down. "They've got a combo playing at the Penthouse."

My ex-boss couldn't get into the Penthouse, an ultrachic jazz bar that didn't advertise its phone number.

"Okay," I said as if I could drop in whenever I wanted.

So I took that step down and we ambled side by side down to the main floor. Without any warning Sebastian snatched my hand. Impulse made me tug loose, but he held on tight. "Let's go."

He nearly yanked my arm out of my socket. I put on the brakes to miss someone who looked suspiciously like Keanu Reeves. But because I was being dragged through a crowd of people, I really couldn't tell.

We broke free at the doors and the cold night stung my bare skin. Without the photographers and the limelight, the red carpet lost its glamour. All that remained from the frenzy were the remains of soda cans, fast food bags, and press passes.

He turned, looking like a boy who'd just ditched class after recess.

"What was all tha—"

His hand came around my head and he kissed me again, a wild reckless kiss that in spite of the gummy sidewalk and the trash swirling at our feet was the stuff movies were made of. And the stuff of what could be my undoing.

"What was all that about?" I asked, feeling my eyes uncross as he pulled away.

"I felt like doing it. I like kissing you."

"Oh."

He pulled away until he held on to my fingertips and turned me in a half circle.

"What are you doing?" I asked, laughter at his silly antics getting the better of me.

"Making you walk on the inside of the sidewalk. Sorry, Mom's dating rules."

His hand squeezed mine as we strolled down the street. It was getting to be a habit, but I couldn't help but ask again. "Isn't the parking lot somewhere back there?"

"Don't worry, *querida,* I know exactly where I'm going."

My protests fluttered away when he tugged me to his side and walked the rest of the way with his arm draped over my shoulder.

Chapter Six

*Always look and act like a lady. Never let a boy go to your bed-
room alone in my house. And sit like you have a dime between
your knees.*

—Dating advice from Isela's mom after Isela's *quincenera*

We arrived at the Penthouse, one of those
super-trendy places with a rooftop pool
and servers who think they're better than
you. While Sebastian made a phone call, I settled in our
booth with a lemon drop martini and too much time to
think.

"Is this the kind of stuff you drink when I'm not
around," Sebastian said from behind me as I sipped my
martini.

"Important call?" I asked, watching him take my drink
away. He'd taken another call after we'd torn up the dance
floor.

For a six-foot white guy, Sebastian could move. So well,

you'd never realize I hadn't inherited the Latin gene for salsa or merengue the way he led me.

"Naw," he said. "But I missed you."

His fingertips burned through my dress at the waist and we kissed like there wasn't another soul in the place. And believe me, he was a kisser because I saw Hugh Jackman walk in earlier.

We broke for air. "Here." Sebastian lifted my hand as if it were something delicate and led me from the table.

"I wasn't finished with my drink."

"But you can't drink while you dance with me."

He didn't give me time to protest. There were way too many good dancers out on the sunken dance floor. Beautiful faces appeared around us, lit by candles and the dim brass lights from the muraled ceiling.

For the first time in my life, I was dressed appropriately for the occasion.

Effortlessly, he collected me in his arms and turned me onto the dance floor. "It's okay." He pulled me tight against him. "You're having a good time, right?"

"I am."

"That doesn't sound very convincing."

With each movement, I grew more aware of how powerful his legs felt against mine. "Really I am. I'm just . . . I'm just not used to places like this," I admitted.

His eyes rested on my lips, then back up into my eyes. If I wasn't trying to keep up with him, I would've curled my toes on just that look alone.

He bent his head down so our cheeks pressed together. *"Te gusta bailar?"* he asked me in perfect Spanish.

"Sí. Con tú?" Really, I didn't mean to say it in that smoky Diana Kral voice.

He nuzzled my ear and held me against him. "Just let me hold you."

I let myself fall into the sultry ballad sung by the woman with a gardenia pinned to her hair. A straight English translation made the song seem overly simple. But the poetic sound of a woman begging her lover to kiss her, kiss her more until the night ended, made this dance with him so much more erotic.

In these shadows and in the press of the dancers around us, I could move just a little to the right and taste him again. I could tell him without words that I wanted him.

"Isela, the song is over," he announced, jarring me out of this warm liquid dream. "I'm thirsty."

The new song sounded like a honking horn and jangled noise as he pulled me out of the writhing maze of bodies.

"What do you want to drink?" he asked, tightening his hold on my hand.

"Sparkling water," I said, reality swarming in on me. And when it did, I was twisted and tangled inside. Just one dance and I was lost in fantasies of heart-pumping sex with this man I could've used for my own benefit. I wasn't sure if I could let myself do it.

"You're going in the wrong direction," he said. "Let's go out to the pool."

We threaded our way to the glass doors that stood open

to the pool. Cabanas, some with their drapes shut, and others with candles glowing in hurricane lamps, were placed around the quietly lapping water. White flowers and white candles floated on the surface. Above us the giant Eastern clock glowed mightily.

I sat on a teak lounger and he sat on the one opposite mine.

The conversation had worn thin. All we wanted to do was tear each other's clothes off. "How did you learn to speak Spanish?" I asked him in Spanish.

"I'm Peruvian." He blinked and then laughed. "The blond hair and green eyes threw you off, huh?"

"How can you be Peruvian with a name like Banks?"

"My stepdad adopted us when he married our mom. My birth name is Sebastiano Romero."

"What happened to your dad? I mean, your real one."

"They divorced. He's in Chicago with his family. Are you Mexican?"

"Yeah. But everyone in Hollywood thinks I'm Jewish."

He leaned forward, just shy of kissing distance and said, *"Tú eres preciosa."*

Since I'd dated only white guys in the past, Spanish to me was a language you spoke with your sister at the grocery store or to your elders. I never knew it could be an aphrodisiac.

A server walked in carrying a silver tray with two glasses of sparkling water, a small tureen filled with melted chocolate, and a plate of strawberries.

"When did you order this?" I asked.

He stood up, signed a piece of paper, and then tugged the tent flaps down after the server left. When I reached for my glass, he held up his finger and gestured for me to wait. I'd never met a man, much less a Latino, who not only brought me my drink but made a little plate of dipped strawberries for me.

"Thank you," I said, feeling special.

"What can I say? My mother raised me right."

Damn straight she did. I'd never tasted chocolate as rich as this before. He held a strawberry to his mouth, watching me lick strawberry juice from my palm.

"So what did you mean back at the theater? About me passing some test."

Chewing, he did bashful real cute, escaping my eyes by looking at the pool. "It's nothing."

"Yeah, it is." I nudged his knee with mine. "Come on."

"I don't know. I had a feeling about you."

"Like what?"

"You seem real."

He took my hand and dipped my finger in the chocolate. "Let's just say that I'm glad I trusted my instincts."

I pressed my thighs together when he drew my chocolate-dipped finger into his warm mouth.

"So how much do you trust your instincts?" I asked.

"With everything I've got. Especially when it comes to people. I like this between us."

His fingers played with the beads along the hem of my dress. I tilted my chin up and kissed him. His hand clamped down over my thigh, massaging my flesh and making my knees want to fall apart for him.

"Have I told you how much I like this dress?" he asked against my lips.

"No, you haven't."

He hummed as he traveled down my neck, leaving a trail of shivers by his warm lips and the feel of his hair. Gently he nudged the strap down my shoulder and the hot whisper of his breath against my skin burnt up every one of my mother's codes for ladylike conduct.

I wanted to straddle his lap. I wanted his hands under my dress, on the bare flesh of my thighs where my stockings ended. I wanted to feel his skin that radiated heat through his silk shirt and jacket. I wanted to be pressed against him, naked skin and him inside me.

I nudged to the farthest edge of the lounge, spreading my legs to wrap them around him. "Oh *mami,* that's right," he whispered against my right breast, his hands holding me by the waist. "Imagine me inside you, Isela." That set me off. I saw stars and every muscle seized as an orgasm ripped through me.

Suddenly, my foot kicked over a glass, the water a cold shock against my ankle. He leapt away from me, lost his balance, and his hand caught the strawberries and chocolate that toppled to the floor with a splinter of porcelain. No one had ever done something like this for me and what did I do? I'd literally blown up his sultry scene.

After the silver bowl made its last wobble I blubbered,

"I'm sorry." I reached to right the broken glass, but my strap was down to my elbow, tying my arm to my side.

I looked down. My dress pooled crosswise into my lap, revealing my slip, and my legs were wide open. The heel of my shoe stabbed his hand when I clamped them together.

"It's okay," he said, brushing pieces of glass under his lounge. "It's just a glass."

His forehead ridged with irritation as he slapped drops of water off his pants.

"I'll be right back," I announced, suddenly on my feet and tripping toward the tent flaps.

"Where are you going?"

When I finally fought one of the flaps out of my way, the lights from the patio illuminated our tarnished little scene. Sebastian's long legs sprawled under my lounge. Chocolate dripped down into a murky puddle, and decapitated strawberries had scattered everywhere.

He looked down around him and cracked up laughing. Waving me back, he nearly choked out, "Come here. I need help."

Laughter tickled my lips. We looked pretty ridiculous compared to the elegant couples sipping from long-stemmed glasses and the moonlight sparkling on the pool's surface.

"Will you please help me?" he asked, and I immediately let the flap fall behind me. "Pull it that way."

The lounge chair groaned across the cement.

Sebastian got to his feet, shaking his head at the spilled

chocolate. "They're going to think you kicked my ass in here," he said.

In his arms I felt like the sexiest woman on this earth. Like those Victoria's Secret models who demonstrate lust by gracefully arching their backs with their hair cascading down their backs. But me, I rip the damn place apart.

I plopped down on the lounge chair, wringing my helpless purse.

"Come here, *mi fiera*."

"No, I'm okay."

"Isela, what's wrong?"

Why do men ask the dumbest questions?

He sat next to me when I wouldn't budge. "I think you're great. What's wrong?" he said softly against my neck.

"Oh please don't use me to feed your ego," I snapped.

His hand fell from my arm and I closed my eyes when he sank back away from me. "What's going on?"

I had no idea. I'm not the kind of woman that orgasms with strange men in nightclub cabanas. And yet, I couldn't imagine saying good night to Sebastian.

And even though I was in total lust with him, way back in the corner of my mind I wanted to use him to get to his brother. I'm not proud to admit it but I did. Let's face it. I wanted everything: Sebastian naked and inside me, as well as his brother to give me and my dreams another chance.

"Let's go somewhere quiet," he said gently.

Turning to face him sent jolts of pleasure through me, and I think with the gold candlelight in our cabana, Sebastian saw it, too.

Before I took this any further, I had to lay it all out on the table.

"I came to the party tonight to meet your brother. Not to do this, but to get a meeting with him because I lost my job."

Without moving, Sebastian coiled like he'd spring for the nearest exit.

"I know," he said. "But if I were some guy you met in a bar or at the grocery store or wherever, any guy, would you still have ended up here with me?"

"Yeah," I finally admitted, knowing I sounded fairly pathetic. I didn't touch him, fearing he'd jerk away from all of my psychodrama tonight.

"But how do I know that?" he asked and I heard the uncertainty in his voice.

I let my hand rest on his knee. "See that chocolate on the floor? I'd never kick over chocolate like that even for your brother."

His hand crept out of the darkness and into the light, landing on top of mine. "Come here," he whispered.

He guided me onto his lap, drawing my hand over his heart and my head against his chest. "I want you like this when we wake up tomorrow. Will you come home with me?"

I closed my eyes and nodded my head, yes.

Chapter Seven

So I FINALLY got tired of him rubbing his hands on his pants and did what a woman does when she wants her man's hands on HER. And no matter what Mom says, men like a woman who takes charge.

—Lydia to Isela in an email reminiscing about
her first date with her husband

We stayed silent in the elevator ride up to his loft.

I'd like to think that Sebastian felt what we were about to do was special. But with men, you never ask, which means you hope so without ever really knowing.

Until, that is, Sebastian's hand snuck over from his side of the elevator and took my hand when we passed the floor just below Loft V. We didn't have to look at each other. He squeezed my hand and I squeezed back, like we needed to reassure each other that we were in this together. And then his loft appeared as the elevator doors drew away.

You know that feeling of inevitability when you look down from the roller-coaster car onto earth hundreds of feet below? That's what it felt like when my heels clicked on the hardwood floor.

"This way." He led me down a short hallway to a large living area with bare, floor-to-ceiling windows. My mouth dropped open when I saw the original poster from *The Big Sleep*. Not the cheesy version with Robert Mitchum, but from the real deal with Bogie and Bacall. God, I loved those sophisticated opening credits with their silhouettes smoking cigarettes.

His brother's collection should probably have been in a museum or at least a Planet Hollywood. *The Seven Year Itch* (my favorite Monroe movie), *It*, *She Wore a Yellow Ribbon*, *The Manchurian Candidate*, and, my God, an original *Pyscho* were each expertly lighted and framed on the plain concrete walls.

"Just in case you were wondering, this is Tyler's place," he said behind me.

"I'd never have guessed. What about your place?"

He hid his hands in his pockets. "I'm living here for now. Can I get you—?"

"No, thanks."

"—something to drink?"

"Sorry."

"No, it's OK."

With my track record, there shouldn't be any breakables in the near vicinity. "Great place."

He looked around, his hands in his pockets. "It is."

"Is your brother okay with us . . . with me being here?"

"He's not here right now for me to ask."

"You know what I mean."

"It's fine."

"I don't do this very oft—I mean, at all." Why I didn't keep my mouth shut, I'll never know. "Do you?"

He shook his head.

"So what now?" There was a little voice in my head that sounded like Lydia screaming at me to shut up and kiss him.

Sebastian licked his lips, staring down at the top of the sofa that separated us. "Are you sure you want to do this?"

"Yes," I answered a little too eagerly. I took a breath. "I wouldn't be up here if I didn't."

He seemed to be wrestling with some uncertainty. "You're real honest, you know that?"

Not knowing where he was going with this, I crossed one foot over the other and answered the best I could. "I try to be."

I saw his shoulders rise with the breath he took in and then settle back down. "Hold that thought."

He swiftly turned and crossed the room to one of those sleek CD players mounted on the wall. The sounds of a piano filled the room around us, followed by a tender guitar and a contemplative cello. He came back to take my purse out of my hands and the rest of me in his arms.

Norah Jones's voice sang about a carousel and a clown, as he kissed me back into that sensual place where it was just him and me, a boy and a girl with the music and the city lights glittering beyond the windows.

"I like dancing with you," he murmured.

I shushed him as I slid his hands around my waist.

Sebastian smiled down at me and, my lips tickling with nerves, I smiled back. Taking his time, he slid his hands up my back and with his fingers he gently held my face to the light, kissing my forehead, temples, cheeks, and chin until he arrived at my lips. His savored mine and then I opened them for him to taste my tongue.

A moan slipped out of him and into me.

He backed me away from the living room and I broke the kiss to see where we were going. "Hey." His fingers whispered into my hair. *"Besame,"* he said in Spanish.

I unbuttoned his shirt and then yanked it out of his pants. That brilliant rush of power lit through me as we passed out of the light and into the shadows of his bedroom. I slid my hands over his hot skin and paused over the metal loop around his right nipple.

"Oh," I murmured, drawing a circle around it. "This is a surprise."

"There's a long story where that came from," he said, faceless in the dark. Without those eyes of his taking in everything, I felt even more powerful.

"You can tell me later." Ever so gently I tugged it and his breath hitched. "You like that, huh?"

His hands tightened over the caps of my shoulders.

His nipples beaded and I pinched, teased, and pulled at them until he rubbed himself against me.

"Goddamn," he hissed, fisting his hands in my hair and then giving me an open-mouthed kiss. This was the first time I was making a guy wild for me and the sensation made me hungry to do more to him. But he twisted away when I reached for his chest.

Coming up for breath, he asked, "Are you leaving as soon as this is over?"

I didn't like that he used "this" to describe what we were doing. Then again it was exactly what it was. There really wasn't an "us" or "we."

"Not if you don't want me to," I said.

"I don't want you to."

And then I did what I'd never done before, made love to a man I'd met just a few hours before.

With the men before him—not that there had been many—I always welcomed them on top of me, with promises and expectations on my mind.

But with Sebastian I devoured the man. Not that he complained either time. We met flesh to flesh, moving from moment to moment with nothing on my mind except multiple orgasms.

And when we curled together, fingers intertwined, I fell asleep with a little curve to my lips, knowing that I'd just made love without falling in love.

Chapter Eight

*Men will do and say anything to get you on your back. And when
they're done, you're tainted goods.*

—Lydia to Isela

I rolled out of Sebastian's arms, trying to regain my balance in the murky morning light that filtered through
the sheer curtains. I looked back down at him, curled
up to the indent my body made in the mattress.

My spine bowed as I sighed. I didn't know if I should
congratulate myself for a job well done, or kick myself for
something incredibly stupid.

That would depend if Sebastian woke up as the same
cool guy I'd met last night.

The ding of the elevator echoed in the cavernous loft.
My heart seized to a stop. Tyler.

I smacked one hand over my left breast and peered
over the bed for my dress. It lay on the floor where the
carpet met the hardwood floor, my panties not that far

behind. Only a reed partition secluded us from the living room.

Keys rang against a tabletop and I fled to the bathroom. Leaning against the rippled glass door, I felt a freak-out erupt in full force. I did not want to meet Tyler as the girl Sebastian brought home last night. Shit, *shit SHIT!*

The marble floor felt like glazed ice as I hopped over to the sink. How was I going to do this? My hands shook from the horror of saying hi to Tyler Banks while picking my clothes up off the floor.

The first time I ever broke all of my rules to be with this incredible guy, this is what happens. God was punishing me for this. Unlike Lydia, my one-night stand wouldn't end up as my husband or as the father of my child. Mine would be a catastrophy.

Taking a deep breath against the panic that threatened to strangle me, I leaned against the cold granite counter. On the other side of the door, my cell phone sang from wherever I left my purse.

"Isela?" Sebastian called, his silhouette looming through the glass door. He gently rapped with his knuckle. "I think your phone's ringing."

I twisted one of the towels off the rack and wrapped myself up. The door handle turned. With wild-woman hair and mascara raccooning my eyes, I was about to live my worst nightmare.

"Isela, can I come in?" Sebastian asked through the crack in the door. I twisted on the faucet, gasping when the stone-cold water filled the palms of my hands.

"Hey there," he said. Over the rush of the water I heard his bare feet padding over the floor and stop right behind me.

"Hi," I said between slaps of cold water over my face. "Would you get my dress?"

"Yeah, sure. Look I need to—"

"I'm not letting you see me like this. So go get my dress and I'll come out."

Sebastian switched off the faucet. I looked up but water dripped in my eyes.

"Okay, now you know what I look like in the morning," I joked. But he didn't laugh or even grin. Sebastian just stood there in his boxers. He opened his mouth to say something, but nothing came out.

"My brother's home," he said.

"But it's okay that we're here, right?"

He didn't even look at me. Rejection pierced right through the center of me.

Sebastian wasn't man enough to say that he wanted me to leave quietly. He looked like the guy I'd met last night, except not in the eyes. Unlike last night, his eyes now told me nothing.

"Go get my dress," I said, not letting him see what that did to me. Casually I reached for a Kleenex and rubbed mascara off my skin, like there'd been plenty of morning afters for me.

He reached for my bare shoulder. I jerked away from him.

His eyes met mine briefly. "Stay here," he said. "I'll be right back."

And then he left me alone, closing the door behind him.

After Sebastian wordlessly handed me my clothes and shut the bathroom door, I waited for God knows how long to get the courage to walk out.

But Sebastian wasn't sitting on his bed waiting when I ducked out the bathroom door. I thought about hiding here and then decided, fuck it. I'm not walking down the service stairs or scurrying to the elevator when the coast was clear.

If Sebastian was ashamed of last night, then that was his damn problem.

With shallow breaths, I marched into the main room.

"Oh hi," Tyler said, when he looked up from his newspaper and saw me standing there.

My heart never raced so fast. "Good morning."

His smile was friendly. He was buffer than Sebastian and darker in the way that surfers are. But the brothers had the same sun-streaked hair and green eyes.

And unlike his wimpy brother who I never let be on top last night, there was no judgment in his eyes. "Do you want some coffee?" he invited.

I grinned sadistically, almost eager for Sebastian to walk out and find me making small talk with his brother. "Yes, please."

Sebastian didn't know who he was dealing with, thinking he could woo me and then hustle me out the door like someone whose name he forgot.

The muscles in Tyler's back rippled when he reached for a cup. "Ty should be out in a second," he said. "He had to take a call from his agent or someone like that."

I stared down at the coffee he placed in front of me. Maybe I heard him wrong.

"I didn't know he was seeing anyone," Tyler said. I looked back up and he paused to wipe the back of his hand over his washboard stomach and then held it out to me. "Oh, sorry, I'm Sebastian."

I went completely still.

When I didn't take his hand he cocked his chin up. "Are you okay?"

I couldn't even breathe much less ask if this was a joke. But it had to be a joke. No way could this be for real.

This guy was going to crack any moment and admit he was really Tyler, so that the brother I slept with last night was really Sebastian and—

"Hey, Sebastian, could you give me a moment with Isela?" That came from the guy I'd slept with, who now stood at the other end of the counter from me.

Well, at least he remembered my name.

Chapter Nine

Mom says men and women can't be friends. You know what I think? I think she's full of crap.

— Isela to Lydia when their mom found
out she had a male roommate

I got as far as the entry hall when Sebas—I mean—
Tyler called my name.

I hopped up and down, pulling on my shoe. The
other one I'd aimed at his head when the world finally
righted itself after I absorbed the shock.

"Hold on a second," he said behind me.

I stabbed the elevator button, keeping my back to him.

"Isela, please let me—"

With a quick pivot I snatched my shoe out of his hands
and shoved my foot in it. My throat felt stuffed with the
rage and the humiliation that boiled in me. I couldn't have
asked for the fucking shoe if I tried.

"I meet a lot of people. A lot. And I don't always click

with them. I swear I've never done anything like this and I know I should've told you the truth last night—"

"That's what they all say, you miserable fuck," I said, stabbing the elevator button so it would arrive faster.

He blinked in surprise. "Please don't go like this."

"Just stay away from me."

One moment I was facing the elevator door and then I spun. I jerked to a stop, and he held me by both arms. My purse clattered to the floor. I countered with a left hook, which he dodged and then caught with his strong hand.

"Get off of me!" My voice bounced off the walls around us.

"Just listen to me."

With all of my might I thrust him back. Not caring that all along he was the one who could give my career a second chance, or that his brother listened from the kitchen, or that my voice traveled up two octaves with the strain of speaking past my tight throat. But I really let him have it. Except it might not have come out very clearly because everything just poured out of me: my mindless jobs, my missed opportunities, my embarrassment that I'd thought he was ashamed of me earlier in the bathroom.

The elevator doors whooshed open.

When I was done, I breathed like I'd just run a mile.

"Isela, I tried to tell you but I didn't want it to—" he said in a voice weighted with guilt. "I am so sorry." He bent down, picked up my purse, and handed it to me.

I snatched it back. "So am I." I spun to the elevator and

walked in, holding on to *this much* of whatever dignity I had left.

My back hit the wall of the elevator as I hid behind the panel and punched the lobby button in a frantic staccato.

Just as the doors shut, a tiny blip of hope made me wish he'd slip through and beg for my forgiveness. I blinked back my tears and the elevator gave way to the lobby.

I'd flown so high last night, caught up in the moment of him and all this bullshit fantasy. And for a second there I was so full of myself for screwing that asshole's brains out. Yeah, I was real hot shit.

A piece of my nail flew off and pinged off the brushed metal handrail, but I wrestled my purse open and got my phone.

Lydia picked up on the first ring. "Isela?"

"It's me."

"I've been waiting all morning for you —"

My breath hitched and I clapped my hand over my mouth too late.

"What's wrong?" she demanded. "Where are you?"

"In the elevator," I managed.

"What elevator? Do I need to call nine-one-one?"

"No." I sniffed and wiped my tears away. I wasn't shedding any tears for him. "I slept with him."

"You did —" She gasped. "The brother?"

"No."

"Huh?"

I quickly explained everything.

"Hold on," she said, and I heard her running. Some more rustling and then she came back on. "Okay. Explain that to me again. You slept with the real one, but he said he was his brother?"

"Yeah."

"Was he good?"

"Jesus, I knew I shouldn't have called you."

"Don't hang up! Shit!" Something tumbled in the background.

"Where the hell are you? Do you have me on speakerphone?"

"No," she hissed. "My mother-in-law is here with the baby. I'm in the closet."

I'd met her mother-in-law and if I were Lydia, I'd never come out of that closet. "I'll let you go."

"Don't you dare! So what happened?"

"I threw your shoe at him."

"What!"

"I got it back."

"*M'ija,* you never throw the shoe. You stab them with the heel."

"This isn't funny. I'm hanging up." But I clung to the phone. It was second best to the way Lydia would hold me if she were here, and I really needed something or else I'd fall completely apart.

"Are you going to be okay? Do you need me to come up there?"

"No." The thought of her, my mom, and home loosened a tear down my cheek. No one there would lie to me.

"We can kick that white boy's ass. Key his car," she offered.

My lips trembled as I laughed in spite of myself. We did that to her husband's Dodge Swinger back when they were still dating and I was just a kid in high school. He never knew it was us. If he had, he never would've married her.

"And he's not white," I explained. "He's Peruvian."

She snorted. "I don't know no Peruvians and if I ever do, I ain't gonna like them now."

I opened my mouth to say he wasn't like that but stopped myself. That's what hurt so bad. Sebastian hadn't been like that last night. Last night, he'd been perfect.

"So what are you going to do now?" Lydia asked.

I took a deep breath and the elevator dinged when it stopped. I didn't want to think about it. I'd gambled and lost my only chance. All I wanted was a cab, my Supergirl pajamas, and my own bed.

"Don't say anything to Mom or the family. Please?"

"I won't." I could tell by the gravity of her voice that she wouldn't. "You call me when you get home, okay?"

"Okay."

I stepped out into the lobby that smelled like new carpet and wrapped my arms around my body. The sun felt good on my bare skin and I stood there in the square of light before I started to dial 411. God knows how much a cab in L.A. was going to cost. And I hoped the check card I'd stuck in my purse last night had enough to cover it.

Down the hall a door slammed shut. I turned and there was Sebastian—I mean, Tyler—whipping his head to peer down the hall and back to where I stood. Still barefoot but in his rumpled khaki shorts and Ruby's T-shirt, he stomped over to me with his hair swinging like some grumpy caveman.

"At least let me drive you to your car," he said.

I might have lost my pride, my dignity and my shoe, but I held onto my silence.

"Isela, you have to walk through Skid Row to get back to Broadway."

I hit Send and then told the information operator, "Los Angeles."

"Please, Isela. Let me do this for you."

Clenching my jaw, I weighed a free ride versus a cab ride I really couldn't afford versus walking through Skid Row in a sheer dress with no bra and heels. I mean, come on, when you're broke and Skid Row separates you from your car, a girl has to think long term in these types of situations.

So I let him drive me back to my car and a future that probably included working at some wedding video outfit or hocking flammable polyester clothes at Toda Moda.

"I was going to tell you," Tyler eventually said, his knuckles white as he gripped the steering wheel. "I tried when we were in the bathroom but I couldn't. And I told Sebastian to disappear because I didn't want you to be embarrassed and so you wouldn't find out like that but he . . . Are you even listening?"

I gave him the eye.

"Is there anything I can say that will convince you I'm not a complete asshole?"

"No." Damn. I hate it when they get you to talk.

I turned to stare out the window, watching a Mexican man in a straw hat push a grocery cart filled with roasted corn on the cob.

"I said I'm sorry. I mean it."

"I heard you."

"So that's it? After last night, you're done?"

"You lied to me."

"I didn't lie to you —"

"Oh please. You didn't exactly tell me the truth, either, did you?"

He sighed. "Isela, I'm grasping at anything to make you understand."

My eyes narrowed. Yeah, right. "Glad to know I was that good."

His eyes wide and pleading, he turned to stare at me in spite of the green light. "That's not why."

"You have a green light." A rusted pickup honked behind us.

"I don't give a shit. I spent the night with you because I liked you and you liked me."

The truck swung around violently and before the driver sped off, he screamed, *"¡Pendejo!"*

I couldn't agree more. "Will you just go?"

He switched off, the ignition and yanked his key out. "Get this straight. I was leaving when I saw you staring up at the ceiling and after going back, I found you at the bar. I just wanted to talk to you."

I let him go on, hoping some raving road-rager would bash in the back of his '67 Landcruiser with a pipe.

"I know it was stupid, but I never meant to lie to you. And technically I didn't lie to you. I lied to that blonde chick you pissed off at the bar."

"You should've told me before we went to your place."

"I know. I'm sorry, Isela. I know it sounds stupid but you were there with Sebastian, a guy who couldn't help your career. I just got caught up in the moment with you and I'm sorry."

Well, that made two of us. And the seat groaned as I twisted away to hide the tears smarting my eyes.

"I don't why I'm trying so hard with you," he said.

"Neither do I," I admitted.

He took in a deep breath. "Let's go get something to eat. We can talk."

"You're not wearing shoes and I look like I spent the night with you."

In the side-view mirror I saw him reach for me and then drop his hand back on the gear shift. "Then let me take you back. We can talk and if you don't want me to drive you to your car, I'll call someone and you can have some coffee while we wait."

"You like to give orders, don't you?"

A furious voice exploded behind us and Tyler restarted the engine. "It's what I do for a living."

I held on to the hand brake. "But I didn't say yes."

He looked at me expectantly.

"You need to ask me back," I instructed.

He closed his eyes and then reopened them slowly. "Isela,

will you come back with me to my loft so the guy behind us in the Cucui de Michoacan doesn't drive over my car?"

I looked over my shoulder. Sure enough, there really was a monster truck with six-foot-tall tires, chrome-light racks, and *El Cucui de Michoacan* written in Old English letters across the windshield.

Turning, I folded my hands in my lap. "I don't want to go back to your place."

"Fine. I know where we can go."

I retreated back into myself.

"You aren't going to make this easy, are you?" he asked quietly.

I didn't dignify that with an answer. If he used me, then I needed to do a little using of my own.

Chapter Ten

Give a little thigh, a little cleavage and then make that pendejo
beg for you.

—Many years later, Isela to her niece, Jody, on
giving a man a second chance

I stayed two steps ahead of Tyler so he couldn't open
any doors for me, which wasn't easy by the way since
his legs were about a foot or two longer than mine. But
I kept my distance until he beat me to the double doors of
the Penthouse and with a smirk held the ornate wrought-
iron and glass door for me.

"I'm on to you," he teased, sweeping his hand to let me
enter.

Foolish man. I opened the other door and walked into
the club from the night before.

On the ride over, Tyler explained that he owned half the
place, which made me feel better about breaking the glass
and the plates last night. He walked around the back of the

bar, stuck his head through a door, and argued with someone in the back.

"Be right back," he said and then disappeared behind
the door.

While he did whatever he did, I tried the pool doors. Stepping outside the sun burnt my eyes, but the wind felt good
and clean against my skin. Walking past the pool and the deserted cabanas, I grasped the iron railing. Beyond the refur-
bished lofts and the awakening stores were the abandoned
warehouses and broken up railroad tracks that fringed the
lesser buildings of downtown. A haze lingered as if the city itself recovered from the excesses of Friday night.

Downtown looked different when you saw it from the
inside. At a distance all you saw were the gleaming, aloof
edifices of power. But from the towers themselves, you saw
the scars they bore from the city, the exhaust, and the spray
paint.

"Put it over there," Tyler said to someone behind me. I
turned to the jingling of porcelain against silver. Tyler held
open the door with his foot, carrying a tray of coffee things,
while arguing with some *viejo* who flapped a white tablecloth.

"Es mucho romantico," the old man argued in his gravelly
voice.

"Over by the pool." Tyler jerked with his head. *"Ahora,
por favor."*

"Ay, you finally bring home a lady and you need to—"
The old man saw me lurking out of the corner of his eye and
his whiskered face broke into a grin. *"Buenas días, m'ija."*

Tyler plunked the tray on the table, smiling as this old man hobbled over to kiss my hand. "You speak Spanish, no?"

"*Sí, señor.*"

"You speak very nice, *m'ija.*" Charmed, I let him tuck my arm under his as he walked me to the table.

"Leave her alone, Tío," Tyler laughed lovingly.

"I promise to act like a gentleman," he argued in Spanish. "Sit here. *M'ijo,* pour her some coffee."

While he poured Tyler introduced me to his Tío Mateo.

"*Mucho gusto.*" I smiled as Mateo snapped open a linen napkin and then placed it over my lap. To Tyler, "I like lots of milk and two spoons of sugar."

I watched in case he decided to spit in it, because frankly, that's what I would've done.

"More milk, *m'ijo.* She's skin and bones."

Tyler dutifully added a bit more.

Like an old courtier, Mateo kissed my hand and admonished his nephew to act like a gentleman.

Then, Tyler unwrapped two luscious chocolate muffins that I bet Tío Mateo had personally covered in a white napkin.

"Where does your uncle live?" I asked.

"Up here. I tried to get him a house but he won't let me. He likes the view."

"So are we okay?" Tyler ventured.

Good question. You see, the thing about being a Mexican, especially a female one, is that we never forget and we aren't stupid. Tyler apparently wanted one thing from me and I, another from him. If withholding that meant the difference from me working at Toda Moda and another chance at my dream, I could play this.

On the other hand, the fact that Tyler and his *tío* got chocolate muffins touched me.

"Isela?" he asked.

"We need to start over."

His brow twitched. "How do we do that?"

The Mexican coffee took no prisoners, even with the milk and sugar.

"Where does your brother live?" I asked.

"With me. For now anyway."

"And what does he do?"

The skin between brows puckered. "Why do you want to know?"

"Because when I asked you last night, you said you weren't doing much of anything."

"I wasn't pretending to be him." Staring at the pool, he smiled as if something known only to him was amusing. "I was telling you the truth because I really haven't decided on what I'm doing next. Does that answer your question?"

"Who was calling you last night?"

He counted on his fingers, "My agent and my brother."

"And what about your real name? The one you were born with."

I heard him take in a fortifying breath. "Man, you don't miss a thing do you?"

"Only when I'm lied to." I sipped from my coffee, ignoring the tightening of his fists.

"It's Terencio Romero," he said. "So how do I start over with you?"

I tried to figure out how he went from that name to Tyler. Instead, I focused on the game at hand. "That's up to you."

"How about lunch this week?"

Looking back at him, I took my time to answer. "Fine."

Thinking he had it easy, Tyler grinned and picked up his cup. "I know a good place in Hollywood. You'll like it."

Men. They're so transparent. "We'll discuss business."

"And?"

"And we'll see."

"Are you sure you don't want to speculate?" His eyes did a once-over up my legs. The wind flapped at my skirt which was too short to be blown up, but not long enough to leave much to the imagination if I wasn't careful. "See where this might go?"

I did and I didn't. In one night Tyler unlocked this wildness that made me do something stupid like sleep with a guy I'd just met. And while I think he could be the perfect guy, I wasn't walking back into anything with him blindly, or without wanting something in return.

"Not right now," I said, unable to break these long lingering looks that were starting to become a habit with the two of us. "We'll see each other but only on my terms."

"And what would that be?"

"I want you to direct a screenplay I optioned last year."

Intrigued, he set his cup down. "Yeah?"

Tyler had the senses of a predator because his hand moved across the table, covering mine.

"Are you sure you want to be friends?" His skin against mine nearly did me in. "I'll make it real hard."

"Tyler, I—"

He cocked his head, looking at me with this speculative light in his eyes. "I like the way you say my name."

I did, too. Recovering, I slid my hand out from under his. "Looks like I'll have to get used to saying it."

With a long sigh he sank back into his chair and crossed his arms. "Not that you'll believe me, but I know what it's like when someone you trust lies to you. I'll never lie to you again."

"Why did you lie to that girl at the bar?"

He shrugged and then grinned. "Because I could."

I started to say something and then changed my mind. "So we're set for Thursday?" I asked.

"Yes."

"One thirty at Kate Mantilini's."

Tyler saw that I wasn't letting him call the shots and whisk me off to some romantic Hollywood spot. "Fine."

I handed him my purse. "Open it."

He did and I plucked out one of my cards. That wry grin played on his lips as he caught it between two fingers, brushing mine in the process.

Don't ask me what I felt sitting there with him, staring into those eyes with that hair tied up in a ponytail. However, it did occur to me that Lydia might not speak to me after I told her that I gave Tyler my number.

"Isela?" Tyler asked, tucking my card in his pocket. "I want you to know that I don't give up that easily."

I could see it on his face, the scenarios he'd orchestrate until I let him think he'd seduced me. Against my better judgment, I anticipated every second of it.

With a snap of my purse, I took him up on his challenge and said, "You know what, Tyler? I don't, either."

Hearts Are Wild

CARIDAD PIÑEIRO

Chapter One

Gravity and her breasts were still friends.

Victoria Rodriguez—Tori to her friends— stood before the mirror and took a long, hard look at herself. Breasts. No sag. Downright perky.

Had she just used the "p" word? Even as she told herself she was letting this whole birthday thing get out of hand, Tori turned to the side and perused her butt. No droop. No excess junk in the trunk, like J. Lo.

Tori released a breath she'd been holding and panicked for a moment. *Was that a little belly that popped out?* She sucked her breath back in then released it. Good news— still flat in the one place where it was good to be flat.

Get with it, girl! she chastised herself. What *had* she expected this morning—a total body meltdown? It was just another day. The sun was shining. Birds were singing. And nothing special was going to happen today.

Of course, poor Marie Antoinette had probably felt the same way on the day she uttered her infamous cake quote and had turned her entire world—not to mention most of France—topsy-turvy.

Tori swore there would be no topsy-turviness today, but she definitely planned on eating cake. After all, it was her birthday. Her thirtieth birthday. The Big Three-O. And the eating cake part would hopefully be free of any dire consequences. Other than maybe adding an extra ten minutes on her jog this morning.

But her friends had something else planned as well, Tori reminded herself as she walked away from the mirror and dressed in her running clothes.

Slipping on her jogging bra—best friend to perky breasts everywhere—then an oversized 'Canes T-shirt and fleece shorts, Tori considered her friends' supersecret plan for her birthday night.

She wasn't supposed to know about the overnight excursion, but Tori had accidentally overheard Adriana confirming the reservations on the casino yacht when she had gone by Adriana's restaurant to drop off some papers for a business loan. Tori had been tempted to put a stop to the plan right then and there, only it would have reinforced her friends' belief that Tori was Ms. Uber Anal and unable to deal with a little spice in her life. And the last thing Tori wanted was to add any grist to her *amigas'* mill. They managed to find enough on their own.

With a last little tug on the laces of her Nikes, Tori headed out of her apartment in what had formerly been a tourist hotel on Collins Avenue. The walls of the smallish rooms had been gutted to make more modern-sized dwellings, but a lot of the Art Deco touches had been preserved during the conversion. Those slightly garish highlights were more visible in the lobby and on the front of the hotel, which still bore its former name in glaring pink neon.

A stiff sea breeze blew in off the Atlantic as Tori reached Ocean Drive, jogged across the street, and toward the winding path that ran from one end of Lummus Park to the other.

The gusts pushed at her back as if to rush her along, but Tori didn't want to rush. Not today. She wanted to enjoy this small stretch of solitude on her birthday morning. Few people were out, and what little noise there was came from the occasional screech of a gull or the rustle of the breeze-blown palms.

The headphones of her CD player were draped around her neck, but the CD of the tunes she used to pace herself wasn't playing. She didn't want to let the music intrude this morning.

She flew along, ponytail bouncing with the rhythm of her jog. Her pace as deliberate as she was. In no time she had reached the end of the path, but she continued down along Ocean Drive to where Adriana would be waiting for her in front of her pricey condo facing Fisher Island and South Pointe Park.

From a block away Tori could see her friend, doing

some preliminary stretching and bending. Adriana caught sight of her, waved and jogged to meet Tori.

"*Buenos días* and of course, *feliz cumpleaño,*" Adriana said with a bright smile as Tori slowed her pace. At five feet two inches, Adriana was a few inches shorter, and it was hard for her to keep up with Tori's longer-legged stride.

As their steps fell into sync, Adriana and Tori jogged back toward the main Ocean Drive strip and Lummus Park.

"How was last night?" Tori asked much as she did every other day except Tuesdays, since on Mondays Adriana's restaurant was closed.

In between uneven breaths, Adriana answered, "Busy . . . Thursdays are almost as . . . crazy as Fridays . . . Lots of *turistas.*"

"The snowbirds savoring the South Beach sizzle," Tori quipped, her breathing still as regular as when she had left the apartment.

A street-cleaning machine approached just as Adriana began her reply. Its brushes whirred against the asphalt, picking up the debris of a South Beach night of merriment, obliterating Adriana's words.

As the street sweeper edged away, Tori shot a questioning glance at her friend. "What did you say?"

"I said that you should try some of that night life yourself." It came out a little too loud and a little too harsh.

Tori gave an exasperated sigh. She and her *amigas* had been over this time and time again. Emphasizing the point with her hands as she ran, she said, "See the dictionary.

Under the word 'wild.' Notice there is no picture of Victoria Rodriguez."

"See the dictionary. Under the word 'boring.' Way boring," Adriana said with a roll of her eyes.

"*Sí.* That's me. Boring. Responsible. Connect the dots to successful."

Adriana stopped dead in her tracks, hands braced on her hips. "Hello! Successful, too, only I have a life."

Tori braked to a halt, turned and faced her friend. Adriana's success was blatantly advertised by the tony Fila jogging clothes, the sparkling diamond tennis bracelet on her wrist that matched the large studs in her ears and the perfectly French manicured nails of the hands that were angrily tapping against her hips.

Tori didn't want to get into it. Today was her birthday, and the last thing she wanted was to fight with her best friend. "No, my bad. I didn't mean to imply that you aren't."

Adriana arched a perfectly waxed eyebrow and gave a regal nod of her head. "Apology accepted. But I want you to remember, especially tonight, that we're supposed to have fun."

"Right. Fun. *Mucho* fun." Tori whirled and began to jog again. Adriana fell into step beside her once more.

As Tori received an exceptionally detailed rundown of what they were going to do for dinner that night, seemingly to divert her from learning the real truth, Tori considered that her friends' idea of *mucho* fun for tonight boded for *mucho* major disaster.

She imagined that her *amigas* would spend the bulk of the night trying to get her to be spontaneous, as if spontaneous could somehow be planned. Maybe they would even get on their second favorite topic—Tori's lack of a relationship and start pushing her to meet some guy on the boat. And miles out to sea, there would be little Tori could do to escape, except head to the gaming tables. Or pray that the boat sank.

She was sure that even if the latter were to happen, her friends would continue with their plan, certain that there would be some eligible man on the coast guard ship sent to rescue them.

Funny thing was, none of them were "involved." Adriana had her thing with Riley, which had gone nowhere since grade school. Sylvia had a parade of handsome-model types escorting her. Tori suspected it was a solely a business kind of arrangement—Sylvia wanted to look good and the wannabes needed access to the hottest events in town in the hopes of being discovered. Juliana . . . No, Juliana hadn't mentioned a man in, like, forever.

So none of them really had "relationships." But of course if Tori raised that, they'd say she was getting all lawyerly on them, trying to justify the rut that was her life.

So absent the boat sinking, it would definitely be the gaming tables tonight. Tori wasn't normally a gambler—the idea of losing money just for the fun of it ran contrary to everything in which she believed. But she liked card games and was good at them thanks to an almost photographic memory and innate sense of mathematical probabilities. So at least there was that—a possible diversion to keep her well-meaning friends from driving her crazy all night long.

"Did you hear what I said?" Adriana pressed as they reached the end of the path, turned, and headed back in the direction of South Pointe.

Tori stumbled and fell off her pace, embarrassed that she had zoned out so badly. Recovering, she said, "Sorry, I didn't. I was thinking about . . . stuff."

Adriana blew out a harsh breath, sending an errant lock of dark auburn hair flying, and shook her head. "Probably about work, right? It's always about *el trabajo* with you."

"Right. Work," Tori lied.

"You know, *amiga,* I thought you were wiggy about work before becoming partner. I'd hoped it be a little different now."

Great! Third-favorite amigas' *topic of complaint.* But maybe if she coupled it with talk about a man . . . "It will be, Adriana. I was just thinking about this other partner. The new man in the office, *sabes.*"

"The one you haven't met?" Adriana motioned with her hand for Tori to stop and when she did, Adriana bent over and took a few deep breaths. When she rose, she said, "Sorry, I had a stitch. Don't you ever get them?"

Yes, she did, but she wouldn't stop for one, she thought, but didn't say it since it would be bitchy. "Sometimes when I first start out, but you always meet me after I'm warmed up."

Adriana nodded and took a deeper breath. "Glad to know you're human," she said and started to jog.

Openmouthed, Tori stared after her friend's retreating

back for a moment before chasing after her. She told herself not to let Adriana's comment bother her. Adriana could be curt and insensitive at times. She was just being Adriana.

For a moment Tori wondered why it was okay for Adriana to be herself when she couldn't just be Tori. "I'm a little tired of all the Tori-bashing."

Adriana didn't miss a beat. Didn't flinch or react. "Who's bashing?"

"All of you. All the time," she replied and stopped. Again. Which was so totally going to blow her time for today's run.

Adriana turned, but kept jogging in place. "Come on, Tori. I know how important it is for you to keep the pace." She moved down the path and Tori reluctantly followed.

"Adriana—"

"*Bien.* So maybe we get a little carried away. But we mean well. We're concerned about you," Adriana began, took a deep breath and kept on going. "It's what friends do. Worry about each other. Plan birthday dinners. Even tell their best friends everything, from the nittiest-grittiest details of the latest blow-up with the boyfriend to the wild make-up sex after the fight. *¿Verdad?*"

"Right," Tori agreed, only it had been a long time since she had had anything to contribute in the tell-all department. No Mr. Right or Wrong or even Mr. Maybe. Just no time for it.

No! She stumbled again before picking up her steady pace once more.

Silently Tori admitted that maybe her friends, as annoying as they were at times, were a little right. Maybe she should listen to them, just this once. After all, who knew her better than her best friends? For fifteen years they'd been there for her and if they thought this big birthday event was what Tori needed to add a little excitement to her life, maybe they were right.

It was time for Tori to shake up her *vida* not so *loca.*

Tonight on her birthday.

If the mood was right.

And the cards were running her way.

And the boat didn't sink.

"Listen, Adriana. I promise that tonight I will be All-Fun Tori. No matter what happens—"

"*¿De verdad?* You mean that? No matter what we plan?" Adriana questioned, clearly surprised about Tori's sudden and clearly unexpected capitulation.

"*Sí.* I mean it. Whatever."

They had reached Adriana's South Pointe condo again where they came to a stop for a moment. Adriana reached over and gave Tori a sweaty hug. "*Gracias.* I promise that you won't regret it."

Tori returned Adriana's embrace and forced a smile. Despite her friend's assertion, a slight trace of fear remained about their plans for the upcoming night. But she said nothing. Merely nodded, gave a little wave, and turned to start the return jog back toward her place.

She had gone no more than a few steps when Adriana called out, "And *por favor.* No Ann Taylor or Brooks Brothers tonight!"

Tori gritted her teeth and shook her head, trying to ignore

Adriana's well-meaning but nevertheless bothersome parting words. After all, there was nothing wrong with Ann Taylor, was there? And her friends couldn't possibly expect her to fluff her hair, totter around on three-inch heels, and become some kind of brainless Barbie doll, could they?

A seagull swooped by, its screech sounding suspiciously like laughter.

Tori gritted her teeth and ran on.

Chapter Two

Birthdays were a ritualistic thing in the Rodriguez household—the only thing absent was small animal sacrifices.

Every birthday morning, her *mami* would visit church to light a candle and pray for her *niñas*. Tori had always wondered what *Mami* prayed about. For them to stay out of trouble? Wasted prayers for Tori who had always been downright obedient as a child. Even semiwasted on her sister Angelica who had been a good girl as well—except for that one little incident on prom night.

In fact, everyone on their little piece of *Calle Ocho* knew the Rodriguez sisters were not only good girls, but busy doing all kinds of wonderful things with their lives. Her *mami* made it a point to tell everyone how well *las niñas* were doing. So *Mami's* birthday prayers had been answered for the most part.

Tori assumed that her mother had headed to church that morning. Still praying. Tori didn't want to imagine for what. The thought came unbidden anyway. *So Tori could be more like her sister, Angelica?*

Her *mami* hadn't said it, but Tori knew. Her family had been excited about her promotion to partner for all of about two minutes. Lately, all attention seemed to be directed toward her sister and her new baby. And although Tori didn't want to admit to it, the lack of attention bothered her just a little.

But this was *her* birthday lunch and hopefully her *mami* would be able to rip her thoughts from photos of her slobbery new *sobrinita* and discussions of baby poop.

Her *mami* and *hermanita* were waiting for her in front of the Versailles restaurant. Another Rodriguez birthday ritual. When they were children, her mother would slip something special into their lunch bags—like a *guayaba pastelito*. Once they got older, they would alternate between lunches at Versailles—probably Little Havana's best-known Cuban eatery—and *La Carreta* with its kitschy sugarcane cart exterior.

Tori embraced her Rubenesque mother, loving the rounded mounds of her that somehow always brought a feeling of comfort. It was how *mamis* should feel, not like all those angular tough-as-leather Anglos who frequented her gym.

She turned to face her sister and noticed that Angelica

was almost back to her prebaby shape, although there was something more voluptuous about her, as if pregnancy had smoothed and enhanced her already generous curves. And of course, because Angelica was Angelica, she was wearing a cotton top with a plunging neckline that displayed her amplified cleavage.

Don't look, Tori told herself, resisting the urge to shoot a glance at her own barely Size-B breasts as she hugged her sister. That motherly comforting feeling rose up in her. Could it be a *mami* pheromone? *Was that possible?* she wondered as she drew away from Angelica and they entered the building.

A hostess quickly came to greet and escort them through the crowded restaurant.

As they walked past certain tables, men turned to eyeball her sister and Tori wanted to shout, "Hello, nursing mom!" Instead she gave them her best lawyerly glare and one or two guiltily shifted their gazes away.

Once seated, Tori removed her navy blue blazer and slipped it on the back of her chair. Inside her air conditioned car or office, the *de rigueur* blazer was just fine, but out on the street and in the crowded restaurant, it was a little much.

"This is an exciting day, *mi'jita*," her mother began.

"How does it feel, Tori? The Big One?" her sister added while reaching for a piece of the toasted and buttered Cuban bread a busboy had brought to their table.

It was difficult for Tori to respond. She didn't understand why everyone was making such a big deal about her thirtieth birthday. After all, turning thirty didn't make her eligible to be a card-carrying member of AARP. "It's just another birthday," she replied, although she was starting to worry it was more than that, given how everyone was carrying on.

"*Ay, mi'jita.* I remember my thirtieth birthday. I had just found out that morning that I was pregnant with you, Victoria. Your *papi* and I had just bought our house," her mother said. The joy in her voice was difficult to ignore and yet almost painful at the same time.

"You finally had everything you wanted, *Mami,*" Angelica said with a sigh.

Her mother nodded, her teased and hair-sprayed helmet of Clairol brown hair immobile with the movement. "*Ay, sí, mi'jita.* And you will feel the same way as well in two years, Angelica."

Well, it didn't take long, Tori thought, reaching for her glass of water and taking a bracing sip.

"Just like Tori must be feeling right now, *Mami,*" her sister responded, and Tori choked as she swallowed.

Angelica reached over and patted Tori on the back and again that motherly feeling filled her. As did thankfulness that her *hermanita* had suddenly come to her defense and actually acknowledged her recent promotion.

"*Gracias,* Angie. I'm very excited about becoming partner."

Tori's thankfulness was short-lived as Angelica said, "It's quite an accomplishment. And now that you've done that, maybe you'll find time for other more important things."

The waitress chose that moment to take their orders.

They hadn't opened their menus, but then again, they'd been to Versailles so often that they could likely recite the menu from memory. And of course, since Tori was as predictable as everyone said, she ordered the same thing she ordered every year for her birthday lunch—*bistec empanizado* and a *batido de mango.* And as she always did, she felt guilty about the ultrarich carbo-loaded shake and chicken-fried steak.

Atkins and South Beach be screwed. It was her birthday, damn it, and she was going to enjoy herself. And *Dios mío,* that was what everyone was always telling her, anyway.

She had barely finished returning the menu to the waitress when her *mami* thrust a brightly colored envelope literally in her face.

"Mami?" she asked and shot an uneasy glance at her sister.

Her mother made a shooing motion with her hands and Angelica chimed in with, *"Vamos.* Open it. We couldn't wait until after lunch."

Tori nervously fingered the envelope, turned it around and back a few times before finally slipping her finger beneath the unsealed flap of the envelope. It opened easily and Tori reached in, extracted the birthday card.

It was one of those cards poking fun at being "Over the Hill!" *And what did that mean?* Tori wondered. Over what hill and going where? To buy the farm? And where did all these weird expressions come from?

She grinned at the card despite herself. The young woman on the face of the card—the pre-Hill version— suddenly became the post-Hill someone on the inside of the card and that someone looked suspiciously like her *mami*.

Tori was sure of one thing at a minimum. She looked nothing like her *mami* yet! Not that there was anything wrong with the way her *mami* looked. If you were sixty-something.

But inside as well, taped to one side of the card, was another smaller envelope. Plain white and with nothing to give away what was inside. Tori shot a questioning glance from her mother to her sister. This time it was her sister who motioned for her to open it.

She did and couldn't believe what she was seeing. She glanced from her mother to her sister and then back to her mother again. "You want me to do what with this?"

A second later the waitress came over and served them, giving Tori a brief moment to recover from the shock of the birthday present—a gift card to a sexy lingerie store.

Her *mami* reached for a *tostone*, snagged it delicately from the platter in the middle of the table, and waved it in the air as she said, "We want you to get yourself something special. Something sexy. *¿Quien sabe?* You might get lucky tonight."

"*Mami,*" Tori said a little too loudly and looked around the restaurant, slightly aghast for various reasons. First, her *amigas*—soon to be ex-*amigas*—had apparently clued her mother and sister in to what was actually happening tonight. Second, her mother was suggesting . . . This couldn't be her *mami* talking like this. Not the same lady who had made Tori and her sister suffer through twelve years of all-girl Catholic schools run by nuns as tough as Alcatraz prison guards. And not the *mami* who had probably prayed on every birthday for her *niñas* to remain chaste and pure until married.

No, this had to be a clone. A UFO had abducted her real mother.

"Since you two appear to know about the big plan tonight—"

"As do you, apparently," Angelica jumped in.

Tori glared at her. "My plan is to get lucky tonight—with the cards, since that is where I plan on spending my night."

"Hello. Earth to Tori—" Before Angelica could continue, their mother interrupted, hands held out before her in a pleading motion as she beseeched her daughter.

"*Mi'jita.* You can't be serious. Of course I don't mean cards. I mean, lucky with a man. *Sabes,* a nice respectable and solid—"

"Very solid," her sister, Angelica, said with an exaggerated roll of her eyes, prompting a surprise round of giggles from their mother.

Heat rushed to Tori's face and again she looked around, hoping that no one had overheard. The last thing she needed was for most of Little Havana to think that Victoria Dolores de la Caridad Rodriguez needed to get laid.

"*Mami.*" Tori held the gift certificate in her mother's direction, but her mother just pushed it back and picked up her fork, dug into her plate of steaming *ropa vieja*.

Since her mother was as stubborn as stubborn could get, Tori offered the gift certificate to her sister.

Angelica ignored Tori's outstretched hand. "*Gracias,* but

no. How do you think I ended up pregnant in the first place. I don't need any more *luck* right now."

Tori laid the gift certificate on the table and stared at it, ignoring the steak and the sinfully thick shake that were calling her name.

A moment later, Angie reached out and laid her hand over Tori's. "*Hermanita*. Lighten up. Get yourself something sexy. Just for yourself if there isn't anyone to share it with."

Tori let out an exasperated sigh and scowled at the gift certificate for the sexy little lingerie shop on Washington, just a few blocks away from her apartment. She'd been there before with Sylvia, but the kind of stuff there . . . It wasn't Tori kind of stuff. Brooks Brothers was Tori kind of stuff.

The problem was, her mother and sister knew that Tori hated to see anything go to waste. If they would not take the gift certificate back, she had no choice since a refund wasn't possible. Maybe they'd have something Tori could use. Like some sedate pajamas. Or some nice, almost serviceable underwear instead of the anal floss Angie was fond of wearing.

"Stop frowning, *mi'jita*. You'll get lines," her mother admonished.

"Fine," Tori said. She relented, picked up her knife and fork, and cut into the *bistec empanizado* she had ordered for lunch. A lunch that was turning out to be way more than she had expected. Just as tonight was promising to be something Tori might live to regret.

Her *mami*. *Hermanita*. All of her friends. She was getting tired of fighting all their birthday wishes for her. All of which were remarkably similar. Which bothered her.

Did they all see her the same way? The same unflattering way?
Tori thought, as she reached for the mango shake and took
a long satisfying sip of the sweet drink. Well, they were all
in for a shock, since immediately after lunch she was going
to visit the damn lingerie shop and find something sexy. Tonight she would play along with her friends and go on the
boat. And after? Well, she'd figure out what it was they expected her to do to have a fun night and damn it, she'd do it.

After all, it was her birthday and for this one night, she
was not going to be predictable.

Chapter Three

Tori hesitantly examined one bra-and-panty set after another on the rack. Of all of her friends, except maybe mousy Juliana, she knew the least about sexy underthings.

She moved one *La Perla* bra away and an Alberta Ferretti ensemble caught her eye. Then she dismissed it. The color was wrong for her brunette tones. Snapping the hanger over and moving to the next one, she thought, *What do I know about the getting-lucky kind of sex?* She wasn't that kind of girl normally. Her last few relationships hadn't gone past dinner on the first night and the realization that the guy was definitely not a Mr. Right.

"Easy, *chica*," the shop owner urged as she stepped away

from the counter and came to stand by Tori. "You're bruising the merchandise."

Turning, Tori shot an apologetic smile at Georgie, the shop owner, who was wearing a maraschino red *peignoir* and matching underthings that somehow didn't clash with the warm brown tones of her skin. *Actually, it makes her look like an inside-out chocolate-covered cherry,* Tori thought, suddenly hungry again. "Sorry, Georgie. I'm just not in a good mood today."

Her friend Sylvia had met Georgie, formerly Jorge in another life, nearly six years ago on one of her first magazine assignments. Sylvia had been asked to do a short piece on the gender illusionists that worked at the revues in various Miami hot spots and hotels. Something about Georgie had clicked with Sylvia and they had become friends.

Recently, whenever lingerie was needed as a gift, Sylvia dragged one friend or another with her to Georgie's lingerie shop. Tori had also shopped at Georgie's occasionally—for gifts for others.

"Man problems?" Georgie asked in a falsetto voice while placing her hands on nearly flat hips.

Tori shook her head and continued flipping through the racks of lingerie. "With my friends. They've planned this big *cumpleaño* surprise for me—a night on a casino yacht."

"My, that's a delicious surprise. I'm guessing this is one of the big ones—thirty? And I'm also guessing you need a little something special." Georgie stepped to the rack beside Tori.

"*Mami* and Angelica want . . . Never mind what they

want." Tori stopped, took one set off the rack and held it up before her. "What do you think?"

Georgie waved a manicured hand decorated with a plethora of rings. A dozen bangles clinked together with each flick of her wrist. "Too boring, but are you sure about this?"

Tori wasn't sure about anything anymore except one thing. "It's a woman thing, right? To want your sisters and daughters and friends to be happy? So if they think this surprise and something a little naughty will help me—"

"Well, of course it will help. It will make you feel sexy, even if only you know you're wearing it." Georgie executed another flamboyant wave of her hand, as if she sensed the rising panic behind Tori's words. "Although, you strike me as more of a cotton kind of girl."

Tori found Georgie's candor refreshing. She chuckled and nodded at the shop owner's read of her tastes. But then again, maybe a little surprise kept things lively. She skimmed through a few more outfits until one caught her eye.

She removed the deliciously sinful, tiger print Roberto Cavalli camisole-and-panty set from the rack. Light blue lace edged with black piping trimmed both the camisole and panties. Matching light blue satin ribbons sealed the front opening of the camisole and the face of the panties. The combination screamed Naughty meets Nice. Perfect! And it was in her size. Tori held the outfit in front of her. "Well?"

A broad smile lit Georgie's face. "*Chica,* if you meet a man and that outfit doesn't have the Little General doing a full salute, you're in the wrong kind of trouble."

Tori handed the outfit and gift card to Georgie. "Then let's hope tonight brings me nothing but the right kind of trouble."

Tori smoothed the lines of the figure-hugging brand spankin' new scarlet Michael Kors dress. After buying the lingerie, she recollected Adriana's admonishment of that morning. *Nada*, absolutely *nada* in her closet would pass muster with Adriana.

Bowing to the fashion gods, who would surely smite her dead for combining the Cavalli with her Ann Taylor, she had jumped into her Sebring convertible and driven to the upscale Bal Harbour mall where she indulged herself in the Kors dress.

As she whirled in front of the mirror, Tori decided it had been worth the splurge. She felt . . . sexy. In charge. Powerful. A feeling she usually only got in court.

If a change in clothes could wreak such a change . . . It was no wonder the cult of fashion was so powerful. Tori vowed to reconsider how she'd spend the remainder of her partnership bonus.

She slipped on her solid-gold Tag Heuer, purchased with the first part of her bonus, and paired it with a teardrop-shaped diamond necklace that draped into the deep *V* of her neckline. Adding a few gold bracelets and rings, because she was suddenly feeling more girlie-girl than she had in years, she took one last look at her makeup.

The makeup was another indulgence from her trip to the

mall. Passing by the counters and feeling heady from the mist of a thousand perfume spray testers, she'd decided it was time to trash the Maybelline and move up in the world. The clerk at the M·A·C counter had helped her select a variety of things, including a lipstick that made her lips look fuller and lush, but shy of that bee-stung model look. Tori was often tempted to stick a too-full-lipped fashionista to a window to see if she would cling like one of those '80s Garfield toys that were still glued to the windows of many older-model Miami autos.

The eye shadow, a smoky gray with a hint of mauve, enhanced the green flecks in her hazel eyes, making her look almost exotic. And the scarlet of her dress looked good against her tanned skin and brought out the auburn tones of her dark brown hair.

Not a bad way to hit thirty, she thought, wondering how her friends would react to the change.

They'd wanted her to try something different and she'd definitely taken them up on it. And because she was feeling decidedly naughty—a byproduct of her underthings—if something exciting happened to come her way, she vowed not to turn him away. She'd embrace the moment and not worry about a thing. In fact, just to keep things simple and uncomplicated, she wouldn't even ask his name.

This was a new Tori after all. Sinfully Sexy Tori. Ready for Anything Tori.

Chapter Four

Sinfully Sexy Tori. Ready for Anything Tori. Tori repeated the mantra as she left her apartment, strolled down the block to the Cardozo Hotel, then to the Versace mansion. She increased the tempo of her mantra as she went past the Clevelander Bar, Edison Hotel, and Lario's to the heart of the Ocean Drive strip and her friends' restaurant.

Although Adriana and Juliana had been in business only two years, the restaurant already had a solid reputation that had turned her friends into local celebrities. The success of their collaboration had been featured in a number of local and national papers and magazines. Copies of the articles hung on the wall at the front of the restaurant.

Tori walked up to the hostess who greeted her. *"Feliz*

cumpleaño," the young woman said. "Adriana and Juli will be by shortly. Let me show you to your table."

Saying nothing that would give away that she was aware the dinner at the restaurant was a ruse, Tori followed the hostess and sat down. Almost immediately, a waiter brought over ice-cold *mojitos* and placed one at each seat.

Tori inclined her head and gave him her thanks. She was both pleased and a little surprised that Adriana and Juli would agree to leave the restaurant on a Friday night, usually the busiest of the week. Especially Adriana, who, although she wouldn't admit it, was even more of a control freak than Tori.

Picking up her *mojito,* she took a sip of the sweet minty drink, raised it in an imaginary toast to her absentee friends, and then settled back to savor the sights of a South Beach night as she waited for her *amigas.*

Along the sidewalk before her, tourists and locals streamed along the Ocean Drive strip. Across the way, in-line skaters rolled along the concrete path snaking the length of Lummus Park, while lovers strolled along beside them.

As Tori sat on the open-air veranda of the restaurant, the loud *pachang-pachang* of Latin music from one car fought the machine-gunlike beat of hip-hop from another as the vehicles cruised along the strip. Tori watched the parade, from the classic cars of the fifties to the latest European imports, all waxed to within an inch of their steel-and-chrome lives. As the cars passed beneath the signs illuminating the South Beach night, metal jumped to life and reflected back the neon hues.

She smiled at all the commotion buzzing around her and thought, *Life is pretty good even if . . .*

Tori didn't get a chance to complete the thought as a stretch Hummer limo battled its way into the valet parking space in front of the restaurant. The doors popped open, her friends spilled out and, spying her on the veranda, raced over to envelop her in a tangle of arms and kisses.

Their effusiveness wrapped around her, unblighted until the moment Sylvia whipped something small and black out of her purse. *Dios mío,* something that looked suspiciously like a blindfold!

"Surprise!" Sylvia shouted.

"I'll say." Tori reached for the slip of fabric, but Sylvia moved it out of reach.

Adriana wrapped an arm around Tori's shoulders and gave her a playful little shake. "We've planned something really special for you."

"*Sí.* Nothing that you'd expect," Juli confirmed, a little shyly and almost awkwardly as she stood by Sylvia.

"But we want it to stay a surprise for now." Sylvia jumped in and dangled the slip of fabric before Tori's face once again.

Sinfully Sexy Tori, she reminded herself, thinking that such a Tori would not have any issues with a little blind-fold action. Unlike über-anal Tori, who would confess she knew everything and ruin it. The new Tori was going along with their surprise, even wearing the blindfold. But first . . .

She raised her index finger to stop Sylvia as she went to

put on the blindfold and reached over to the table for her *mojito*. Motioning to her *amigas* to pick up their glasses, she held up the drink. "To life, love and always being friends," she said, repeating the toast that they shared on their regular Monday night get-togethers.

Glasses clinked together crazily and after, Tori took a long sip of her drink, needing the boost of courage that she hoped the rum would give her. *Mojito*-fortified, Sinfully Sexy Tori took a step closer to Sylvia, closed her eyes and said, "I'm all yours."

B eing driven around while blindfolded was a little disconcerting even though she could tell where they were from the motion of the car.

Along Ocean Drive there had been just the jarring stop and go due to the volume of cruising cars ignoring the NO CRUISING signs posted along the length of the road. But as soon as the driver turned onto Fifth Street, the limo picked up speed, as did the conversation of her friends who chatted about how wonderful Tori looked and how she would totally enjoy the surprise they had planned.

Tori murmured her agreement, holding back her own little secret as she felt the rise of the limo that told her they were going up and over the MacArthur Causeway and would soon be turning toward Bayside Marketplace and the many docks adjacent to it.

"Have any idea yet?" Juli asked breathlessly.

"Not a one," Tori lied. A few minutes later, after several more turns, the limo came to a smooth stop.

Silence descended in the car, as if her *amigas* were suddenly having second thoughts. A hand gently grasped her shoulder. *Adriana's?* she wondered, then came Adriana's soft, "Ready?"

"Doesn't the blindfolded prisoner usually get one last request?" she teased.

Sylvia chuckled. "*Chica,* you can ask for anything tonight —later. For right now . . ."

Sylvia slipped her hand into Tori's. "Just follow me."

Exerting subtle pressure, Sylvia helped Tori step from the car and onto the sidewalk. A second later, Sylvia and Adriana eased their arms around Tori's and escorted her along, the ground smooth beneath her high-heeled feet.

"You still there, Juli?" Tori called out, worried their other friend might be falling behind as she often did.

Her gentle touch came on Tori's exposed shoulder confirming her presence, but she said nothing. Typical of her retiring friend.

All was right for now. All would stay right this night. She had to have faith in that.

Tori took a deep breath. The combined smells of diesel fuel and ocean teased her nostrils. There was the *slap-slap* of water against a dock and the low rumbling murmur of an engine. It only confirmed what Tori already knew about their destination, but she was still anxious to see where they were going. "Are we there yet?"

A clanging metal sound announced the presence of the gangplank and her two friends eased Tori to a stop.

"You can take the blindfold off now," Juli said. Tori reached up and slipped it off.

Before her was a large yacht, gleaming almost electric white against the dark waters, thanks to the lights from its berth in Bayfront Park. Four decks were visible above water. The three lower decks were enclosed while the topmost deck was open to the sea air. On that uppermost deck were dozens of people along the railings. The sounds of their merriment peppered the night air.

Tori tried to maintain an aura of surprise and to quell the unexpected rush of excitement. "And this is . . . ?"

"A casino yacht. And we have two staterooms on the top deck for a special overnight gambling cruise. Leave tonight and come back in the morning," Adriana explained.

"But I don't have anything—"

Juli stepped around Sylvia and held up a small overnight bag. "We've got all the stuff you'll need for tonight right in here. And you have one stateroom all to yourself."

Tori eyed her friends and shook her head. "Really? Does the everything include a Mr. Right to share the room?"

Adriana held her hands up and waved off the suggestion. "*Chica,* that possibility is up to you to explore—"

"And explore often," Sylvia suggested with a Groucho-like wiggle of her eyebrows.

"If you meet someone, that is. We haven't arranged that. We promise," Juli clarified and made a little cross-her-heart-and-hope-to-die motion with her finger. A bright stain of pink colored her cheeks. Juli was always the most reti-cent of the three when it came to discussions of sex. For a moment, Tori wondered if Juli was still a virgin. However, there weren't many thirty-year-old virgins in this world.

Shaking her head, she looked at Sylvia and Adriana once more. "Promise, no blind-date setup? Just gambling—"

"And dinner and dancing and drinks. Promise," Adriana replied and held her hand out in the direction of the gang-plank.

Tori eased the blindfold into the side pocket of her small black Prada purse—another product of her splurge at the mall along with the matching high heels that made her feel a little wobbly but did marvelous things for her legs.

The gangplank swayed beneath her feet, forcing her to grab the brass hand railings for support. She worried that the rest of the cruise would be as unsteady. *Remember fun and sexy,* Tori chastised silently and struggled onward until her feet hit the deck of the ship and the floor beneath her steadied.

Laying a hand along her midsection, she breathed in deeply of the sea air and turned to meet her friends as they spilled off the gangplank, chuckling and laughing as if they'd just come off a fun-house ramp. For a moment, Tori en-vied their uninhibited spirit, then she let it wash over her and joined in. "This is going to be quite a night, isn't it?"

"One you'll hopefully never forget," Adriana replied. She looped her arm through Tori's and said, "Let's all get settled in the rooms before we shove off."

"And then that drinking and dancing—" Sylvia added,

slipping her arm through Juli's, who reminded, "After the dinner, that is."

"Agreed. And afterwards, I plan on getting lucky," Tori said, but quickly clarified, "at the blackjack table."

Adriana teasingly shook Tori's arm. "*Ay, amiga.* You know that being lucky at cards means—"

"Being unlucky at love," Sylvia finished, prompting groans from all of them.

Tori glanced over her shoulder at Sylvia. "Well, since I'm not one to believe in clichés or other predictable kinds of things—"

Which prompted even more protests from all of them since Tori was at times a walking cliché about predictability. Tori understood them all too well and how to elicit their fairly predictable response, so she decided to shake them up a little. "You are looking at a new woman tonight. One who plans on being spontaneous—"

"Isn't that an oxymoron? Planned spontaneity?" Sylvia challenged.

Tori raised her hands in surrender. "*Bien.* So you can't plan spontaneity, but for tonight—this is Nonpredictable Tori. Expect the Unexpected Tori."

Adriana narrowed her gaze as she glanced at her friend. "*¿De verdad?* So, if Mr. Right happens to come along—"

"*Carpe diem,* I say," Tori advised.

"And I say, grab something else," Sylvia teased.

Juli chuckled and blushed more profusely before stopping in front of one of the staterooms. "Sylvita, you have a one-track mind."

Sylvia nodded, slipped a key into the door and opened it. "And I hope that one-track leads you here tonight, Tori. With some sweet *Papi Chulo.*"

It had been nearly fifteen years since she and her friends had laid out the requirements for the title of *Papi Chulo,* namely, that the man in question had to be sexy and good-looking with possibly a hint of bad boy thrown in. At fifteen, that had seemed to be enough. In the years since then, the list of requirements had grown.

"So you expect that I'll be lucky enough tonight to meet a man who—"

"Has the face and moves of Ricky Martin," Adriana began.

Sylvia added to the list, "And the body and eyes of Brad Pitt."

"Not to mention Freddie Prinze Jr.'s sexy little-boy grin," Juliana tacked on softly.

Tori rolled her eyes. "Right. And after I find this perfect *Papi*—I will take no names and ask no questions. Just do it."

"And often," Juli finished.

Tori, Adriana, and Sylvia all gaped openmouthed at their friend.

"*¿Que?* You don't think I know about these things? I'm not a naive *virgencita, sabes.*" Without waiting for a reply, Juli handed Tori her bag, then turned, slipped a key into the other door, and opened it.

Adriana shook her head and wagged a finger in Sylvia's direction. "You've been a bad influence."

"Hmm. Maybe it will rub off on Tori here. Maybe she will let loose and then—watch out!" Sylvia stepped into the other room and Tori noticed for the first time that she also had a small overnight bag. Adriana had two, likely one for herself and one for Juli.

"You're all in there together?" Tori asked.

"*Sí.* We wanted you to have privacy, just in case. Meet us back out here in fifteen to watch the ship pull out?"

Tori nodded and entered the room.

It wasn't overly large, but more than adequate for an overnight stay. A queen-sized bed, sumptuously appointed with satin sheets and comforter in deep maroon, took up most of the room. The bed was flanked by a dresser on one side and an entertainment center in front. The latest state of the art electronics filled the entertainment center. By the door to the room there was a large window, with a table and two chairs in front of it, facing the ocean.

There were definite romance possibilities here, she thought as she tossed her bag on the bed and glanced out the window. With the ship docked, the view was of Bayside Marketplace and downtown Miami. The areas were awash with activity, from the people teeming past the various shops and restaurants in Bayside, to the cars and other vehicles cruising along the street behind the Marketplace.

Tori smiled at all the motion and commotion in the city. She loved it and had since she was a small child growing up in Little Havana. Miami had always represented so much opportunity to her. She'd always dreamed of making it big there someday. At thirty, she could happily say that she had. A nice condo in South Beach. A partnership at one of the larger law firms downtown. A great family and incredibly loyal and fun friends.

What more could she ask for?

Chapter Five

People crowded the decks as the yacht pushed off and slowly moved down the Miami River until it had cleared Fisher Island and put out to sea. They were cheering, laughing, and jostling each other excitedly along the railings, ready to enjoy the night and morning at sea.

With the freedom of a longer cruise, the ship had the luxury of sailing along the Miami Beach shoreline once it was on the ocean. Tori felt like a tourist as she and her friends leaned on the railing and pointed out their favorite South Beach haunts, which were highly visible, thanks to the bright neon lights and distinctive architecture. The Park Central and Imperial Hotel with its bright blues. Farther down, Adriana and Juli's place with its classic Mediterranean styling brought to life by strategically placed spotlights.

"It looks great," Juli said excitedly and jabbed Adriana with an elbow.

Adriana smiled broadly. "It does, doesn't it."

There was a hint of surprise and uncertainty in her voice.

Tori eased from the rail, stepped behind her two friends, and wrapped an arm around each of them. "Well, of course it does. My friends have excellent taste."

Sylvia eased her arm beneath Tori's and joined the group. "We hope you'll continue to think so after tonight."

Tori glanced at each of her friends. Each one was as different as the next and yet, there was no doubt about the affection and friendship between them. A friendship that had lasted through high school, college, and the marriages and subsequent departures of others in their circle of friends.

Adriana had been the motivator, a testament to her abilities to both lead and control, even at fifteen. It was after Adriana's *quinceañera* party that they had banded together. The young girls had feared that they would never escape the constraints of their Catholic high school upbringings and the rule of too strict mothers. Not to mention the demands of the men in their lives.

In the years since, Tori had somehow become the mediator and equalizer for the diverse personalities amongst them. The gyro that kept them from sometimes running aground because she, of all of them, possessed a little of each of the personalities of the other women. She was usually unassuming like Juliana, except when in court. Cuban and in control like Adriana, but not as much of a bitch.

Able to enjoy a good time like Sylvia while realizing that life was not just a never-ending party.

Or at least, that was how Tori saw herself. And because her role was not to rock the boat, she grinned and replied, "Of course, Syl. So what's up first? Dinner?"

"Definitely." She urged Tori away from the rail.

As they walked, whiplash occurred as various men noticed Sylvia. She was dressed to kill tonight, in a sapphire blue Dolce & Gabbana dress that hugged the long, lean curves of her body. The color didn't wash out Sylvia like it did many other blondes. The vibrant hue enhanced her friend's green eyes and olive skin, inherited thanks to a mix of genes from her Latino father and Anglo mother. Her long blond hair, artfully highlighted, was pulled back from her face and held in place by a funky clasp. Rather than be severe, the style showed off the classic features of her face.

Sylvia was tall, beautiful, and graceful. Thin. Tori felt like she had to lose another twenty pounds whenever she was around Sylvia. Add Sylvia's sometimes pushy attitude to the mix and it would be easy to hate her. Except that Tori knew she could always count on Sylvia to be there for her.

As they walked along, Sylvia examined Tori's clothes. "Kors? And is that Prada I see?"

Tori held her hands up in surrender. As the "After Dark and Gossip" reporter for one of Miami's upscale magazines, Sylvia never failed to know just what was in and out at any given moment. And the job always kept her on the run. From hip new restaurants and clubs at night, to all kinds of events during the day. "You are amazing, Syl," she advised, but her friend shrugged it off.

"It's just part of the job," she replied, which surprised Tori. Not the words of a happy camper. She'd always wondered how Sylvia had ended up doing such fluff journalism but had figured her friend was satisfied doing what she was doing. Her words belied that, but Tori said nothing else as they walked down two decks to the restaurant.

The host led them to the table where the women settled into the customary places they took on their Monday night gatherings.

Adriana was next to Sylvia, providing a buffer for Juliana in a number of ways. First there was the obvious physical differences between the two women, from Sylvia's fashion modelness to Juliana's schoolmarm sense of style.

Tonight, Juliana was dressed in a flowing dark rose caftan that clashed with the tones of her *cafe con leche* skin and black hair. She looked almost jaundiced. The caftan hung on her like a sack, making Tori wonder if Juliana didn't realize that she was no longer the plump teenager of years ago.

In contrast to Sylvia, Adriana was chic but not flamboyant. Attractive, but in an understated, confident kind of way. It occurred to Tori that Sylvia's style screamed for attention whereas Adriana made a fashion statement in a subtler way.

Tonight, Adriana wore a fitted black Adrienne Vittadini suit that accented her physique. Her auburn hair was cut in a chin-length bob, with not a hair out of place. She was the perfect public face for the restaurant she co-owned with Juliana. But Juliana was the soul of it. *Unfortunately, a soul that hid in chef's clothing in the kitchen and beneath an unflattering caftan out in public,* Tori thought.

And a soul that often couldn't handle Sylvia's sometimes harsh and determined personality, like Adriana could. It wasn't unusual for Adriana to deflect things that Juliana couldn't deal with, although Tori sometimes wondered if that was a good thing.

Still it somehow worked for them as friends, Tori thought.

"So how does it feel to hit thirty first?" Juliana asked.

"It feels . . . the same as it did yesterday. It's just another day."

"And that's the *problema,* Tori." Sylvia jabbed a finger in Tori's direction. "You need to get out of that rut. Do something different."

"Hello. Different here. *No problema* thanks to all of you." Tori lifted her water glass into the air as if in a toast.

"Let's make it official." Adriana motioned to the waiter who hurried over. She ordered a bottle of Cristal and said, "We want this night to be absolutely memorable."

"Well, the blindfold was certainly memorable," Juli said.

Tori chuckled. "Definitely. And I'm sure the rest of the night will be just as interesting."

"It'll be fun, fun, fun, *amiga.* Just let yourself go. Forget all about responsibilities, and party!" Sylvia fisted her hands, did a little party circle motion, and gave Tori a small nudge. "*Vamos.* First step. Just try it. Even if it looks silly. Come on,"

she urged until Tori relented, picked up her hands, and mim-
icked Sylvia, even though she felt a trifle foolish.

"So what's Step Two?" Tori stopped as the waiter came
over, uncorked the champagne and filled their glasses.

"Step Two is . . ." Adriana began as she raised her glass
in a toast, "Whatever you want it to be, *chica*. This is your
night after all."

Tori raised her glass and glanced from one friend to the
next, finally beginning to realize that they were totally serious about this being her night. "*¿De verdad?* Anything?"

"Anything," they all echoed in unison and clinked their
glasses with hers.

Chapter Six

Never ones for card games, her *amigas* opted for spots at the slot machines as Tori watched the roulette wheel for a while, seeing a couple of spins of chips wiped off the tables when the wheel chose to repeatedly hit the zero and double-zero, much to the consternation of the players who had bets placed everywhere else.

Shaking her head at the foolishness of relying on anything as ephemeral as the spin of a wheel, she searched for a reasonably priced table to bet the five hundred dollars her friends had gifted her with as part of her birthday surprise. The baccarat and poker tables were packed and dozens of people lingered around them.

Again Tori watched and waited, but it seemed the players

there were settled for the night and there would be no open-
ings anytime soon.

She turned from the one table and noticed a man standing a few feet away, likewise watching and waiting.

He was dressed in an off-white dinner jacket and black
slacks, much like many of the men at the gaming tables. But
that was where the comparison ended.

Not tall, maybe about five feet ten, but lean, which made
him look taller. And well built. His shoulders stretched the
fabric of the dinner jacket. At the waist, the jacket was but-
toned, accentuating flat abs and lean hips.

He looked up from the table, and their gazes collided for
a moment.

Tori sucked in a breath. *Dios mío* but he was the sweetest
looking *Papi Chulo* she had seen in a long time. High cheek-
bones. A sharp slash of a nose and a strong jaw with just a
small hint of a dimple in his chin. Full, beautifully shaped
lips.

*No, but he's probably one of those model wannabes that flood the
South Beach scene at night, hoping to be discovered*, she thought.

He smiled at her, displaying perfectly white and straight
teeth and blue eyes that glittered with amusement. She
ripped her gaze away, embarrassed that she had been caught
scoping him out. Although Sinfully Sexy Tori, or Sylvia,
would have continued to check him out and maybe even
telegraph a come-and-get-me signal.

But she hadn't yet had enough champagne to be that
bold. Heat bathed her face as she walked toward one of the
blackjack tables. She hoped Mr. *Papi Chulo* didn't see the

blush on her cheeks. Experienced women of the world didn't blush. Risking a quick look over her shoulder, she realized he was no longer at the table and breathed a sigh of relief. And experienced a moment of disappointment that her interest hadn't been reciprocated.

As she approached the ten-dollar blackjack table, a spot opened up. *My first bit of luck,* she thought, as she sat down and counted out two hundred dollars for chips, reserving the rest in case her luck was bad.

Not that she actually believed in luck. Winning at cards was just a combination of knowing what she held in her hand and what was being played by the others around her. Luck . . . well, that was something other people had. She had skill and knowledge and if some chose to translate that into luck, so be it.

It took a few hands for Tori to get a feel for the cards and the other players. After a dozen hands, she had a good sense of what was happening and soon a small pile of chips grew before her.

"You're one lucky little lady," the dealer said as he dealt a fresh hand.

"*Gracias,* but it's not luck." She grimaced as the man next to her asked for another card.

One of the other players was not as reserved as Tori and groaned aloud at the boneheaded play. Not the first for that particular player who had quickly lost a large pile of chips during the time Tori had been seated next to him.

The player drew a nine and busted. "Damn bad luck," he said and as the last of his chips were swept away, he pushed away from the table, complaining loudly as he did so.

Tori breathed a sigh of relief. Being the one who followed him in the draw, he'd made it a little difficult for her at times, taking cards she hadn't expected him to. With him gone the game might improve even more for her.

The dealer turned to her for her next card. She had a two down and an eight showing. Mr. Bonehead had taken the nine that would have put her over the dealer, who had to hold with the sixteen he had dealt himself. But with the cards that she had, it was impossible to bust. She asked for another hit and got what she wanted—an eight that made her a winner again.

As the dealer finished the round, someone slipped into the empty chair beside her.

Tori shot a quick glance at the new player and realized that if there was such a thing as luck . . .

The sweet *Papi Chulo* from before was now beside her. He gave her a small, almost hesitant smile. She returned it quickly before forcing her attention back to the chips the dealer was delivering to her.

But only part of her attention stayed on the game since it proved difficult to ignore the presence of the attractive man beside her. As they laid their bets or reached for their cards, his shoulder occasionally brushed hers. And he smelled like . . . she was sure Sylvia would be able to tell her the aftershave was Calvin Klein or Ralph Lauren or some other expensive designer fragrance. All Tori knew was that he smelled to-die-for yummy.

And his voice was like warm *dulce de leche* over ice

cream—smooth and sweet with just a little hint of the exotic. That familiar singsonginess that said English wasn't necessarily his first language and was confirmed when he used Spanish to thank the young waitress who served him a *mojito*.

As the waitress placed a diet cola before her, he raised his glass in a toast. To avoid seeming rude, Tori copied his motion and then admonished herself to focus on the cards as the dealer gave her two aces. Smiling, she double-downed on the cards and shot another quick peek at her *Papi Chulo*.

He was smiling as well and gave a small nod of his head at her decision. The smile reached his eyes. Marvelous blue eyes flecked with tiny bits of gray. They went well with his hair, which was cut short along the sides, but longer at the top. Those longish locks were a caramel brown streaked with strands of golden wheat.

The work of a skilled stylist, she thought, although his light tan and athletic physique hinted at the possibility those wonderful highlights might have been honestly obtained. But then again, tanning salon! she told herself, trying to find reasons to fight her attraction to the Latin Ken doll.

She turned away from him to watch the hand being dealt and couldn't help grinning as the dealer flipped his cards to reveal he was holding seventeen, improving the possibility of her winning on her double bets.

Shifting her attention to the other players, she watched as they drew or held, glanced at the *Papi Chulo*'s hands as he again checked his cards. He had large hands, with long well-shaped fingers. Strong hands with a hint of a small scar along one knuckle. Capable hands that cradled the cards like . . .

She imagined those hands holding her. Wondered if they would be rough and decided they would be—the slight imperfection of the scar definitely a sign of someone who used his hands.

Heat bathed her face again and she reached for her soda, took a sip, and blamed the slight bit of champagne she had drunk earlier with her friends. Champagne always made her horny. That had to be the reason she was thinking all these things about the hands of the man sitting next to her.

The man who was showing a six and therefore held sixteen at best—making him a likely loser in this round.

Tori looked up from his hand to meet his gaze and something connected. She realized he would hold and lose the hand rather than draw like Mr. Bonehead before him and ruin her game.

He never looked at the dealer, just motioned that he would pass as he kept his gaze locked with Tori's. And somehow, she also couldn't pull away from him as she signaled for a hit.

She didn't really need to look to confirm her first hand had been a winner. It was in *Papi Chulo*'s eyes as they lit up with pleasure.

Signaling that she was done on that hand and moving to the next, she again motioned for a hit. Her *Papi Chulo* smiled broadly and again she knew, motioned for the dealer to move on.

Tori told herself to yank her gaze away from him and

back to the game. The last thing she needed was a distraction. But something went haywire in her brain for she was suddenly saying, *"Gracias."*

"For what?" he asked in that soft, sweet voice.

"Not breaking up my hand."

He shrugged impossibly broad shoulders and worse, gave a hesitant kind of grin. *"De nada.* It was worth it to see you smile."

Which only made her smile broader until the sensible part in her brain screamed, "Player!"

He was just too handsome and too suave, although she sensed something. . . . She didn't know what, only her lawyer's antennae were tingling, telling her that he maybe wasn't what he seemed, just as she wasn't the very collected and chic woman she appeared to be at first glance.

Instead of allowing it to go further, she picked her chin up a defiant notch as if to say, *That little line won't work on me,* and turned her attention back to the game.

And his hands. While she could keep her eyes glued to the green felt of the gaming table, it was impossible not to see his hands. The way they held the cards—sure and confidently. How he moved the pads of his fingers against the soft surface of the table in a calming kind of motion as he played.

She picked up her glass and before drinking took a sniff. There had to be something in there for her to be imagining again how her *Papi Chulo* might use those hands on her. Maybe it had been too long since she had released some of her sexual tension.

Taking a deep bracing drink, which only cooled her

off a little, she forced herself to focus on the cards. He had proven himself a capable player and she trusted he wouldn't blow her game. And if she missed a card or two—well, some would say it had been a lucky couple of hands. So if there was such a thing as luck, she would rely on that luck to make up for not seeing what cards he was playing because that was the only way she could avoid seeing his hands. And therefore ignore how much she wanted him to put those hands on her.

Maybe there is such a thing as luck, she thought, as she won round after round and the pile of chips before her grew steadily, as did the pile of chips beside her. In front of him.

"A lucky night," she said out loud, surprising herself with the saying of it.

There was a long silence after her words, almost as if everything around her had gone into superslow motion.

And then came the brush of his shoulder against hers and the warm spill of his breath against the side of her face as he leaned close and asked, "Just how lucky are you feeling?"

Chapter Seven

Her heart did a funny little lurch in the middle of her chest. She took a deep breath, held it as she turned and found him barely inches away. It would take only the slightest of movements for her to brush his jaw with her lips.

At the realization that this was a major—but intriguing—invasion of her personal space, she pulled back just a fraction, but refused to give any other kind of quarter. "Very lucky," she replied, defiance in her voice.

"All this winning is almost boring. I like more of a contest, don't you?"

The gauntlet had been tossed. She met his gaze and saw the dare there, along with something else: uncertainty. He didn't think she'd take him up on it and normally she wouldn't. But she had promised herself to make this night different. Special. And she suddenly liked the challenge of him. "Definitely."

Facing the dealer, she pushed her chips his way. "Cash me out, please."

"The same," she heard from beside her.

The dealer quickly exchanged the table chips for casino chips. She picked up her winnings as did the *Papi Chulo*, and when she rose and headed to the cashier, he followed. After they had their cash in hand, he said, "What's your pleasure?"

Pleasure? Him in bed. Naked and willing immediately came to mind, but she battled those thoughts away. "Do *you* feel lucky?" she asked.

He slipped his hands into his pants pockets and rocked back and forth on his heels, as if not quite sure of his answer. Of what to do. "Maybe," he said then shrugged.

She chuckled, liking that this gorgeous and seemingly self-assured man was a little wary around her. "Why only maybe?"

"You know what they say. Lucky at cards—"

"Unlucky at love," she finished for him, reminded of the discussion earlier that evening with her friends.

"So maybe I'd prefer to be not so lucky at cards—"

"And improve your luck in other areas," she jumped in once more and felt heat rising to her cheeks. Again.

"Are you game?" he said and held out his hand, opening it to reveal a gleaming half-dollar. "Heads or tails?"

She narrowed her eyes as she glanced at the coin and then back up at him. "And the winner—"

"Gets to pick what we do right now."

"And after?" she asked, a little intrigued by the possibilities in their private game of chance.

"We let the cards decide," he replied, then straightened and patted his pockets. There was a moment of confusion on his face and she asked, "Something wrong?"

"I don't have a deck of cards," he admitted and looked around as if to see where he could get one.

Tori knew. She reached out and laid a hand on the sleeve of his arm. "Don't worry. I believe there's a deck back in my stateroom."

A surprised look crossed his features, as if he couldn't believe what she'd just said. "Your room?" There was a little bit of a croak in his voice and he gulped.

Boldness swept through her, not unlike what she'd felt as she was dressing earlier. "That isn't a problem, is it?"

"N-n-o. N-not at all," he stammered, then said, "Heads or tails?" He flipped the coin in the air and she called out, "Heads."

He caught the coin and turned it onto the back of his hand to reveal tails. "We can do this again," he said and gallantly prepared to flip the coin once more, but Tori reached out and stopped him.

"Your choice. What would you like to do? Right now." She knew what she crazily wanted—for him to lean over and kiss her. Only he didn't. Instead, he nervously fingered the coin before slipping it into his pocket. Again he rocked back and forth on his heels for a moment before he said, "I'm no Ricky Martin, but I'd like to dance."

His hesitation and humility were refreshing. And way more sexy than bravado would have been. And his choice — a nice way not to rush into anything. It told her that he was a patient man. That was good. She stepped to his side, slipped her arm through his, and said, "I'd like that as well."

He was no Ricky Martin, but that was okay because she was no Christina Aguilera. And he was way better than those guys who did the drunk dad dance. Not that it had mattered since after the first couple of pop songs, the band had launched into a set of slow dances.

Wonderful slow dances. At first her *Papi* was charmingly cavalier and kept his distance, but little by little they drifted closer together. Now, you couldn't slip a sheet of paper between them and that was just fine as far as Tori was concerned. She liked the feel of his body, all lean and hard, moving against hers. And his hands, holding her in just the right places. One hand at the small of her back, pressing lightly to keep her close. Another in the middle of her back, his palm rough against her bare skin.

Again her mind drifted to her earlier naughty thoughts and she inhaled deeply to quell them, but instead smelled that sexy scent of his. She inched away and glanced up at him. There was a small smile on his face and as he met her gaze, he asked, "Still feeling lucky?"

"Hmm," she answered. "And you?"

"I won the first toss, remember?"

"Cocky, aren't you?" she teased.

He shifted away slowly, reached into his pants—which did nothing but emphasize the telltale bulge that was getting her attention—and withdrew the coin again. Without waiting for her, he flipped the coin and she stuck to her earlier call. "Heads."

Grinning, he revealed the face of the coin and said, "Heads. You were lucky this time."

"Actually, it's not luck. Given the fact that there are only two possible outcomes, the odds are that—"

She didn't get a chance to finish as he leaned over and kissed her into silence. There was no uncertainty or hesitation in the way he moved his lips against hers or drew her to him.

Tori went willingly, opening her mouth against his.

"It's your call," he said in between small bites of her lips.

"Call?" she murmured while she kissed her way to the side of his face. He shifted his attention to that ultrasensitive spot in the crook of her neck and dragged a moan from her.

"Cards? Another flip of the coin?" he whispered against her ear.

Rational thought chose an inopportune time to return. She pulled away from him and considered that it was impossible that she was actually standing here, making out with a total stranger, albeit a very attractive and obviously willing total stranger. This wasn't her. This was that other Tori. Sinfully Sexy Tori. Having a heck of a time and can't wait to see where it goes next Tori, she decided. "Cards. In my room. If you'd like, that is."

"I'd like very much." He nodded, followed her toward the exit of the discotheque, but as they reached the door, he laid a hand on her arm, stopping her.

She turned to face him. He was dangling something small and black on his finger. Something that looked suspiciously like . . .

"I think you dropped . . . this," he said with a wry grin as his gaze skittered from the small piece of fabric to her face.

"It's not what you think." She vaguely recollected snagging her bracelet on something in her purse. Now she knew what it had been. She snatched the blindfold from his finger and jammed it back into the side pocket of her new Prada purse.

"Really?" he asked and raised one dark eyebrow to emphasize his point. "I think that we're being followed by two . . ." He paused and looked to the side of the club.

She tracked his gaze and noticed that he had zeroed in on Adriana, Sylvia, and Juliana, who were busy trying to appear uninterested in what was going on by the door. Tori grimaced as he continued. "Maybe even three women who are likely your friends and I suspect had something to do with the blindfold. It was a blindfold, wasn't it?"

"I guess it is what you were thinking. And yes, they are my friends. Soon to be ex-friends. May I have a moment?"

He nodded and she walked toward her *amigas*, but as

she did so, it suddenly occurred to her what she was about to do.

Sanity returned.

Then doubt settled in.

By the time she reached her friends, she was wondering how she could gracefully extricate herself from her predicament.

"I need your help," she said and nervously glanced back toward where her *Papi Chulo* waited for her, before turning her attention back to her friends.

Sylvia shot a quick look over Tori's shoulder. "I'd say you're doing fine without us."

Tori raised her hands and insistently waved for her friend to stop. "This is not funny, Sylvia. I don't know what I was thinking—"

"That you were finally going to have some fun?" Adriana interrupted.

"Fun? This isn't about fun, *chicas*. I'm about to take a total stranger to my room—"

Sylvia clapped her hands together. "*Dios*, but that's better than we hoped for."

"This is crazy, isn't it? Tell me it's crazy," Tori pleaded and turned toward Juli, who she hoped would be sensible.

Juli looked toward the door of the discotheque and Tori tracked her gaze as she said, "He seems . . . very nice."

Her *Papi Chulo* was waiting patiently by the door. When he noticed she was looking his way, he smiled, displaying a deep dimple in his cheek. *Does he have to do that?* She liked dimples. They were so "I'm-a-nice-guy, regular-José kind of thing."

"What's his name?" Adriana asked.

"*No se—*"

"You don't know his name?" Juli asked nervously.

"Well, call him Mister Campbells," Sylvia said.

"Why?" Juli asked.

"Because he is 'Mmm, Mmm, good,'" Sylvia finished.

Tori rolled her eyes and faced Adriana. "This is insane."

Sylvia took a step toward the door. "Well, if you don't intend on—"

Tori held a hand up to stop her, annoyed by the possibility that Sylvia would too eagerly exchange places with her. "Don't even think about it, Syl."

"Too late," her friend teased.

Tori examined each of her friends, then shook her head, realizing they would be of no assistance. She turned and walked back to where her *Papi Chulo* stood and strode out the door of the club, leaving him no choice but to follow, but she heard his amused chuckle as she did so.

She shot him a glare over her shoulder to try to regain some aspect of control, but he only grinned back at her, unfazed. Tori vowed to find a way to exact revenge. Delicious, blindfolded kind of revenge.

Which started heating body parts that hadn't gone beyond lukewarm for years and caused her heart to do a funky little mambo beat in the middle of her chest.

And that in turn caused her to begin that mantra again.

The I'm Sinfully Sexy and All Fun Tori tonight. An ask-no-names, take-all-chances kind of Tori. A lucky-at-cards, lucky-at-love kind of Tori. It was possible after all. Who believed in such lame sayings anyway?

She ignored the annoying little voice in her head that said she did.

Chapter Eight

The area by her stateroom was empty, providing a perfect place for viewing the spectacle brought about by the impossibly full moon as it silvered the ocean, creating a shimmering mirror before them. The sea was remarkably calm. Tonight there was barely a breeze and the ship was sailing along smoothly.

Her *papi* paused, bracing his hands on the polished brass of the railing. Tori stood beside him uneasily, juggling the strap of her purse and the stateroom key in her hand. Some of her hesitation still remained and she wondered whether he had any reservations or sensed hers.

Turning, he said, "Beautiful, isn't it," only she knew he wasn't referring to the lunar sensation. She quickly realized that he was grateful for the diversion provided by nature. Her lawyer's antennae again, picking up on his indecision. It intrigued her and dispelled some of her earlier misgivings.

She nodded and he took a step close to her, raised his hand, and cupped her cheek. The palm of his hand was slightly rough. "I know you won the toss, but do you mind if we take a moment before we play our game?"

"No, not at all." Was that her voice sounding so husky? Sexy even? She smiled, and he traced the edges of that smile with his thumb, then slipped his hand down, cupped her chin, and applied the faintest amount of pressure until she was looking up at him.

He was glancing down at her, the blue of his eyes now glittering like the moon-silvered sea just beyond the railing. He lowered his head, coming closer and closer. She was suddenly hearing bells going off. It took her a moment to realize someone had opened a door on one of the gaming decks below them and the bells were from one of the slot machines announcing a winner.

"Someone just won," she whispered.

He grinned, revealing that cute dimple, but didn't retreat from his approach. Nor did he rush. He brushed the tip of his nose against hers then lightly touched his lips to hers as he said, "But you don't believe in luck, do you?"

"No. I—"

"Believe in the odds," he challenged as he finally covered her mouth with his.

His kiss this time was a little more demanding, almost as

if daring her to prove him wrong. The problem was, Tori liked the way he moved his mouth on hers. The taste of him, sweet and slightly minty, like the *mojito* he had drunk earlier that night.

Tori moved nearer, pressing herself to his body, enjoying the strength of him. And the barest hint of a moan that came against her mouth as she shifted her hips against his arousal. That faint sound brought some small bit of sanity back to her.

Forcing herself to withdraw from the delicious sensations he was creating, she said, "Odds are we'll get arrested if we continue this outside."

He chuckled and laid a hand on the railing. It trembled. He stuffed his other hand into his pants pockets, after unbuttoning his jacket as if it were suddenly too tight. "So maybe it's time to continue our game . . . inside."

Tori reached up, cupped his cheek. The start of an evening beard was sandpapery beneath her palm. "I believe we said, cards. Is poker acceptable?"

He nodded, but as she began to walk away, he grabbed hold of her hand. When she turned to face him, he was grinning broadly, the dimple a deep slash on the side of his face. "Hearts are wild, though. It somehow seems appropriate, doesn't it?"

She couldn't control her own smile, nor the slightly erratic beat of her heart as she imagined just where these games might lead. "Definitely," she answered and opened the door to her stateroom.

Her *amigas* had been at it again. Tori should have been angry at their manipulations. Instead, she grudgingly admired their forethought.

A dozen red roses were in a vase on the nightstand beside the bed. Cheese, crackers, and strawberries were on a small platter on the table by the window, along with a standing wine cooler where another bottle of Cristal nestled in a bed of ice.

As her *Papi Chulo* took in the preparations, he crooked one eyebrow again. "An ex-Girl Scout by chance?"

Tori chuckled. "Always be prepared, *¿verdad?* I wish I could say I'd thought of all of this, but I must give credit where credit is due."

He placed a hand on the small of her back as he leaned toward the table, snagged a strawberry, and brought it to her lips. "The blindfold friends strike again?"

"Hmm," she said as she took a bite of the strawberry. Juice dribbled onto her lips and he wasted not a moment to lick them free of strawberry remains.

Her head whirled for a moment and she laid her hand on his chest, urged him away. "Cards, *¿recuerdas?*"

"*Sí*, I remember." He popped the remaining bit of strawberry in his mouth, his tongue darting out to wipe away a small bit of juice on his lips.

Tori's toes curled as she imagined kissing him just then. Licking the juice from his mouth. Somehow she reined in that desire and walked to the nightstand for a deck of cards.

She didn't hear him approach and suddenly felt his

presence behind her as he reached for the cards, held them up. "Your friends, again?"

"Probably, only I don't think it occurred to them how we would—" She suddenly stopped, afraid she was revealing too much.

When she turned to face him, she was surprised. There was . . . Was that a blush on his cheeks? Did she imagine that he fumbled the cards a little as he took them out of the box?

"Poker, right?" He walked to the small table, shuffling the cards the whole time. Clearly avoiding her gaze.

Normally boring and responsible Tori reared her uber-anal head at that moment. She was alone in her bedroom with a stranger. He could be a serial killer. Or worse. And the insanity of that last little concern made her chuckle. *Duh, Tori. What could be worse?*

Except that maybe after they found her body, some nosy reporter would stick a microphone in her poor *mami*'s face. *Mami* would be wailing and crying on television that Tori had been a good girl, while millions of Miamians would think, "*Ay, pobrecita madre*. She had no idea her daughter was a slut."

Then that same reporter would likely head down to the corner where that good-for-nothing Julio would be hanging out in his wife-beater shirt with his crew of fellow ne'er-do-wells. Julio who would crow about how he and Tori had been an item—which they hadn't—and didn't she now wish she'd pulled off his miserable little *pinga* when he'd proudly shown it to her in the seventh grade!

Take a Chance Tori drove those ridiculous thoughts away

and walked toward the window. She closed the curtain, then sat down at the table.

Her *Papi Chulo* had followed her. She gazed up at him and gave him what she hoped was an inviting smile.

He placed the cards he had been shuffling in the middle of the table and joined her.

"Hearts are wild. But what are we betting?" Tori asked. "*Porque* plain ol' strip poker seems so—"

"Obvious? Childish even," he said, clearly on the same path she was following.

"*Sí.* Childish," she repeated, although in the back of her mind, she had kind of been looking forward to the possibility of seeing him naked.

"But playing for money. We decided that was boring, *¿verdad?*"

She met his gaze, trying to gauge where he was going and found it impossible to read him. He seemed calm. His hands were steady as they rested on the top of the table. *He'd make a tough opponent*, she thought, if this was a sample of his poker face. "Bueno. If we've eliminated the strip part and—"

"Who said we vetoed that idea? And do you know you slip into Spanish when you're nervous?"

"*Ño.* I'm not *nerviosa*, just . . . well, maybe *un poquito*." She grabbed the deck because she suddenly needed something to do with her hands.

He placed his hand over hers. "If it helps, I'm nervous, too."

"*¿De verdad?*"

With one finger, he crossed his heart. "Truth. So, what if we say the winner decides the prize."

Tori—Uber-anal Tori—thrust her index finger into the air. "Within reason. I mean, you can't ask for all naked on the first win." *Dios mío* had she just said that? Could she be lucky enough to have a tidal wave swallow her whole right now? Quick, damage control, Tori. "Because that would be way boring and predictable," she speedily added.

That grin came again, unrepentant. "Way boring. Better to take it one thing at a time. Anticipation, *¿verdad?*"

"*Sí*. Anticipation." Time to take it slow and easy and not rush things. Only it was difficult to do so with thoughts of ice-cold champagne running over the ridges of his abdomen.

Hands a little unsteady, Tori laid the cards in the middle of the table. "Your deal."

"Are you sure?" he asked and as she met his gaze, she realized he was giving her one last chance to change her mind. That streak of chivalry only endeared him to her more and convinced her that she wouldn't be making a mistake by continuing their little game. "Five-card stud. Hearts are wild."

Chapter Nine

He dealt the cards swiftly and just as quickly, Tori examined her hand. Her miserable hand consisting of a hodgepodge of low number cards. No possibility of a straight. No pairs in the bunch. No ace to let her draw four new cards. No hearts. She hoped that wasn't a harbinger of the night to come—and not just in the cards department.

She glanced up at him. Did she detect a glimmer of a smile on his face? She was still looking at him, her expression as bland as she could make it, when he lifted his gaze from his cards. "Ready?"

Tori nodded and laid down three cards, hoping he would think she had at least a pair. He dealt her the new cards and she considered them. A little better since she now had a two of hearts. With it being a wildcard, she had somehow managed to end up with a pair of sixes, but as she motioned for him to continue, he gave a small slash of his hand to indicate he wouldn't draw any cards.

"Pair of sixes," she said and flipped her cards over to reveal her hand.

He grinned broadly, the dimple deep in his cheek, and as he met her gaze, his eyes were glittering with delight. One at a time he flipped the cards over to reveal a flush, courtesy of two wildcards. "I guess I won."

"I guess you did. So what will it be?"

Leaning back in his chair, he brought his hand to his face and rubbed his index finger back and forth across his lips, thoughtfully considering his request. Then he grinned again and said, "Tell me your name."

Panic came quickly. Panic and surprise. This very sexy man — the perfect *Papi Chulo* — was sitting in her stateroom in the middle of the night, his inhibitions loosened by the few strong *mojitos* he'd drunk earlier. Loosened enough that they were now engaged in an extremely intriguing game of chance and after his first win . . . He'd asked to know her name? He was suddenly going all Joe Sensitive on her?

Not fair. This was supposed to be about fun. No-strings-attached kind of fun. Which meant no names and no expectations. Men had been doing women like that for centuries and now it was her turn. She was a modern woman after all, with all the benefits of the sexual revolution. And his request. It was just making it all that much harder. She was starting to like him, way too much, and that wasn't supposed to be part of the plan.

"No."

A confused look crossed his face at her answer. "No? Your name is 'No.'"

"No. I mean 'No,' as in no names."

He gave a small wave with his hand for her to continue. "Because that would be . . ."

"Too complicated. This isn't supposed to be complicated." Her hands fluttered in the air as she spoke, awkward in their movements as she tried to explain.

"So, this is a one-night stand for you. I'm just a sex object."

Tori didn't know what she had been expecting, but his tone had a hint of playfulness in it as well as surprise. Possibly even disappointment. "Does that bother you?"

"I've never been a boy toy before. This could be fun." He straightened the cards on the table in preparation for the next hand.

She chuckled and said, "I find that a little hard to believe." And *No*, could she just find some other less embarrassing way of telling him that he was just too handsome for words.

He gave her a half glance and paused his shuffle of the cards, a small smirk on his face. "So. If I don't get my first request, then I guess I can make another choice, right?"

"Right."

Standing, he said, "Take off my jacket. *Por favor*."

Did he have to be a polite hottie? Where was the ruthless kind of alpha male that just expected she do it, like in all those romance novels she sometimes stole out of her mother's and sister's piles of books—just for beach reading, that is. Again she felt the pull of his niceness and worried that tonight was going to turn into more than she had bargained for. But she was committed to the game now.

She stepped toward him and rested her hands on his chest. The cotton was smooth beneath her palm and slightly cool to the touch. She looked up at him.

His jaw clenched slightly, and there was a hint of a tic along one side. Shifting her hands upward, she inched even closer and slipped her hands up to his shoulders.

The muscles of his shoulders shifted beneath her hands, and after she eased one sleeve off, he laid his hand at the indentation of her waist and took the last final step to bring their bodies into contact.

There was no denying the press of his hips against hers as she fumbled for a moment with his other sleeve. Nor the way he raised his hand and idly traced his index finger along the bare skin exposed by the Vee of her neckline. A moment later, he lowered his head to the side of her neck, again finding that *muy* sensitive spot. The one that instantly sent a little tug to her insides.

When he took a quick little bite and then licked her skin, she bit her lip to battle a moan. A little too breathlessly she said, "So I guess this was one part taking off your jacket and one part copping a feel?"

"Hmm. Possibly," he said as he pulled away from her once more, but continued to softly caress the bare skin at her neckline and brush aside the diamond pendant nestled there.

"You won the bet. You could have—"

"Asked if I could do this?" He cupped one breast, lazily ran his thumb back and forth across the hard tip of it.

An exhalation exploded from her mouth and a little shiver of desire danced along her skin. He smiled, clearly pleased by both responses, and leaned close once again, burying his head near the side of her face where he whispered. "But that would be boring. And predictable."

"And you're neither," Tori finished, her voice husky and a little unsteady.

He laughed and pulled away, stuffing his hands in his pockets. "Actually, those who know me would say to the contrary." Amusement colored his words.

"*Yo también,*" she confessed and then bit her lip. *Dios mío,* what was it about this *papi* that had her so loopy? She didn't have time to consider it further, for he held his hand out in the direction of the table, inviting her to return to her spot for the next hand.

She did so, saying a quick little prayer to the *Virgencita* to help her win the hand, then instantly begging forgiveness because of whatever sinful thing she might be doing if her prayer was successful.

But it wasn't going to be her lucky night and he won the next round as well.

Tori clenched her hands into fists, wondering what he would ask for as payment. Again it was a surprise. "*Por favor.* Take my shirt off."

Dios, his shirt. A shirt that she was sure hid a marvelously delicious chest. She had felt its strength beneath her hands before. And truth be told, she had been itching to see his chest. Feel it without the barrier of his clothes. Still she hesitated. "Are you sure you've got the idea of this game right?"

"*Sin duda*. So . . ." He rose once again, held out his arms so she could reach his cuffs.

She began there, quickly removing the gold cuff links and tossing them on the table. Moving her hands to his bow tie and with a slow pull, undoing it until it hung loose at his neck.

Once again he placed his hands at her waist, then moved them upward until they rested just below her breasts.

Tori swallowed hard, slowly undid the buttons on his shirt, then pulled it free of his pants. Mimicking the placement of his hands, she cradled his lean waist, slowly moved upward until she was just below the swell of his pectorals. Gazing up at him, she noted the darkening of his eyes, the way his pupils widened until almost nothing was left of the wonderful gray-blue.

A second later, she touched him, running her hands over all that she had just exposed.

He raised his hands, copied her actions, and she moaned.

"*¿Te gusta?*" he asked, but as he did so, she bent her head and suckled him, ripping a guttural moan from him.

He stopped his ministrations, grasped the back of her head to keep her there, but she gave a quick little bite, rose upright, and moved her hands upward until she had swept the shirt from his body.

Somehow she managed not to groan. Somehow she kept her hands to herself, although the temptation was strong to touch all that warm golden skin and the sharp ridges of his six-pack abs.

Before temptation won the battle, Tori took a quick step away, sat at the table, and then briskly shuffled a fresh round of cards. She perused her own, but shot a glance across the table. His hands were a little shaky as he cradled his cards.

Again they went through the motions of the game, her *papi* drawing two cards while Tori only needed one. The deal had provided her with three of a kind and a wildcard heart.

When he revealed his hand, she knew she had won and smiled.

"Don't gloat." His words lacked any sting and there was an amused look on his face as he tossed his cards down onto the table.

"Not gloating. Just thinking about being boring and predictable."

His head shot up at those words. "You want me to take my pants off?"

Tori examined him carefully. She detected a bit of hesitation, again, mixed in with excitement and, of course, anticipation. It started a corresponding little streak of daring within her. "Not really," she began, rose, and came to stand before him. "*I* want to take your pants off."

There was a sudden flurry of motion as he pushed back his chair and stood before her. He locked his gaze with hers and Tori never glanced downward as she started her task.

As she slipped her index finger beneath the waistband of his slacks and idly moved it back and forth, he sucked in a breath.

Gaze still locked with his, Tori undid the button of his pants and then dragged the zipper down. Slowly. Very, very slowly.

"I gather this is about one part getting my pants off—"

"And three parts copping a feel," she said playfully, but there was nothing playful about the way he cupped the back of her head and brought her close for his kiss. A kiss that demanded her response.

She opened her mouth to his, accepting the thrust of his tongue while she continued stroking him. There was a moan, only she wasn't sure which of them had made the sound.

He moved his hands to her breasts, cupped and teased her, and the only thing she wanted at that moment was for both of them to be naked and making love. Somehow she kept contact with his mouth for just a moment longer as she eased his pants down his legs.

There was an awkward moment as his shoes blocked her progress, but he kicked them off. Then she shucked his pants off and tossed them to the side. Taking a deep breath, she paused to enjoy all that she had revealed. *Men shouldn't have legs that long*, she thought, and grasped her hands before her tightly to keep from touching him. It was a losing battle so Tori did the only thing she could.

Whirling away from the table, she walked to the wine bucket, grabbed the bottle of Cristal and fumbled with the foil. A second later, she felt the press of his body against her back and his arms came around her to grab the bottle and assist her.

It was torture. Sheer torture to have the warm skin of his

chest against the bare parts of her back. His hands deftly dealing with the seal and cork while she inanely gripped the bottle for him.

When he was done, he took hold of the bottle and stepped away to pour, then placed the bottle back in the cooler.

He held one glass out to her and proposed a toast. "To continuing our wonderful little game."

Chapter Ten

Tori's hand trembled as she took hold of the glass and clinked it against his. "To our little game unless . . ."

He raised one eyebrow again in a gesture that was becoming amazingly familiar and she added, "You're impatient."

Spreading his arms wide he challenged, "Do I look impatient?"

For a man who was standing there in nothing but sexy black silk boxers, Tori thought he looked amazingly calm, but . . . "*No se. Are you?*" she said and raised her free hand, laid it in the middle of his chest, and slowly stroked it back and forth in the gap between his pectoral muscles.

"Try and find out." There was only a slight tremor in the

muscles of his chest that gave testament to his possible impatience.

Tori shifted her hand to one of his nipples since they'd been driving her crazy from the moment she'd stripped off his shirt. Granted, it was weird, possibly even insane, to be obsessing about a man's nipples, but his were so perfectly placed on the muscles of his chest. Hard, flat, and nutmeg brown, perfect—

There was that word again and if truth be told . . . He had a perfect face and perfect hair and a perfect body and as she glanced down and noticed that her touching him had made for even more tent action in those boxers, probably a perfect everything else and what was she doing here with a nearly naked man in her room while she still had all of her clothes on?

She moved her hand away, drained the last of her champagne in one big gulp, then set the glass on the table. Shifting her hands behind her she said, "I guess not impatient at first glance, but . . ."

Tori undid the zipper of her dress, letting it slip to the floor and puddle in a heap of scarlet silk before meeting his gaze again.

He bobbled the champagne glass in his hand, spilling some of the Cristal all over his chest.

Dios, just too much temptation for her to resist.

Tori leaned forward, licked off a few of the drops, then stepped away from him once more.

"You're playing a dangerous game," he warned, but despite his words, she had no fear. There was something about him. Something that told her she was safe with him. "I trust you."

"Do you?" her *Papi Chulo* questioned as he imitated her earlier move, slowly passing the tips of his fingers up and down the gap between her breasts, then up along the swells of them. All the time, he watched the reaction of her body and as parts of her peaked against the fabric of the Cavalli lingerie, he grinned. "Are you impatient?"

"Not normally, but . . ." Tori reached up, covered her hand with his and urged it down to cup her breast. *"Por favor."*

His smile broadened, displaying that tempting dimple once more. "Impatient but polite. I love a woman who's a walking contradiction."

Tori had been called many things in her life, none of which came close to his perception of her. She liked that he found her unpredictable. Stepping from the puddle of silk at her feet, she toed off her shoes and took a step closer to him.

He cradled her waist, bringing her flush to his body, then moved his hands up and down her back, before resting them beneath her breasts.

Tori gave a little mew of eagerness. *"Ay, Papi. Bueno,* do you think you can handle me? Impatient as I am?"

"I think I already am *handling* you," he teased as he brought his hands up to cup her breasts. A flash of a quick smile greeted her question a moment before he buried his head between her neck and shoulder, zeroed in on that *muy* sensitive spot which he kissed, then sucked gently. All the time, his fingers teased her until she needed more.

She cupped the back of his head and bumped her hips against his, inviting him into the next step of their little contest. "Ready for another game?"

"Hmmm," he murmured, but did nothing to grab the cards from the table. Instead, he slowly backed her toward the bed and once there, urged her to sit on the edge.

"Definitely," he began, "because I'm feeling incredibly . . . lucky."

Before Tori could guess what he planned, he retrieved the cards from the table and laid them beside her on the bed.

She gave him a questioning look and he replied, "Maybe I'm more impatient than I appear. Hearts are still wild. High cut of the cards gets their choice."

Tori glanced from what she wore to his rather sparse ensemble. "It seems I have a decided advantage, *mi amor.*"

He kneeled before her so they were almost eye level and took her mouth with his in a deep kiss. When they eased apart for a breath, he whispered against her lips, "*Querida,* I'm not afraid of the risk; are you?"

"*Nunca,*" she answered back readily, totally confident that in the ultimate outcome of their battle there would be no losers.

He leaned back and cut the cards. A two of hearts.

After he had replaced the cards, Tori made her cut. A queen of spades. A loser thanks to his wildcard.

Her *Papi Chulo* wasted not a millisecond in easing his hands beneath the waistband of her panty hose and stripping them down her legs. Surprised her a second later as he surged forward and planted a kiss on the gap of bare skin between the top of her panties and the camisole.

Playfully she shoved him back and complained, "Not fair."

"All's fair in love and war," he teased, drew another card. Another heart.

Tori grimaced. "So it's war, is it?" Once more she cut and lost.

She waited for him to reach up and peel her camisole off, but he surprised her. Again. Grasping the minuscule strips that passed for a waistband on her panties, he slowly eased them down her legs, then tossed them aside.

He laid his hands on her thighs, skimming his palms gently along the outside, then to the more tender skin along the inside of her thighs.

Tori thought she knew where he was headed. She didn't.

He continued upward until he bracketed her waist with his hands. Almost playfully, he skimmed his index finger along her midsection, pausing to trace the edges of her belly button. As he lifted his gaze to meet hers, he gave her a dimpled grin and said, "Anticipation, *¿verdad?*"

Her breath was rough. Her body shaking and so on the edge, she surprised herself by saying, "No, *Papi*. No more waiting. It's time."

"I wasn't sure I could wait much longer either," he admitted, confirming his own need.

Tori reached for the drawer of the nightstand, hoping her ever efficient and slightly demented friends had thought of everything. She was not disappointed. Inside the drawer was a collection of all different kinds of condoms.

Chuckling, she grabbed a few and looked back at him.

He stood before her in all his naked glory and her mouth suddenly went dry. He was perfection. And he was hers. And he was laughing as he reached for yet another three or four condoms from the assortment in the drawer. "Let me guess? Your three friends, *verdad*. The ones that are probably in one of the rooms next to us with their ears plastered to the wall?"

Dios, but she liked his off-balance sense of humor. "*Sabes* what that means?"

He arched one eyebrow, tossed back the condoms he held as she selected one and pulled it from the foil. "That we need to use them all?"

There was a slight catch to his words, followed by a groan as she unrolled the latex over him.

Tori smiled. A sexy, incredibly pleased-with-herself smile as she eased into the center of the bed and crooked a finger in invitation. "No, *amor*. It means that you'd better not make me scream too loud."

As he placed one knee on the bed and slowly crawled toward her, his mischievous grin sparked a fire within her. "Sorry, *querida*. But that's one promise I don't think I can keep."

Chapter Eleven

The unaccustomed sway roused her to wakefulness, together with the also unfamiliar warmth of a body pressed to her back and the arm draped over her waist, keeping her close.

Tori slowly opened her eyes. Golden light filtered in around the edges of the drawn curtains. The alarm clock said it was six. They had a few more hours until the yacht docked back in Bayfront Park. Her camisole was draped over the lampshade on the open-drawered nightstand. An assortment of clothes and foil wrappers were strewn along the floor. The empty bottle of Cristal sat punt up in a puddle of water in the cooler. And the playing cards . . .

The cards which had lost her one kind of luck, but

decidedly improved her fortune at love, sat in a neat pile on the nightstand.

She hadn't wanted to get to like him. But she had. And it wasn't that he was absolutely gorgeous and an amazingly skillful lover. Patient and demanding. Funny and yet serious. *Dios mio* but he always kept her guessing, even though he'd confessed to being boring and predictable normally. And during their lovemaking—he'd been caring and tender.

What must he think of her? Did he think she'd just been out for a one-night stand? But then again, what else could he think since that was exactly what she'd told him. And why did it bother her so?

Because she didn't want the night to end.

He moved slightly behind her, tightened his hold on her waist to draw her nearer. His erection nestled against the small of her back and as she shifted to press herself tight to him, the slight soreness between her legs gave testament to just how often they had enjoyed each other the night before.

"*Buenos días,*" he said and placed a kiss on her cheek.

She rolled until she was facing him and laid her hand on his chest. Stretching upward, she placed a gentle kiss on his lips and husked, "Not *bueno*. The *noche* is almost over."

Chuckling, he placed his hand on the middle of her back and brought her flush to him. "We still have a little time," he said as he kissed her more deeply, opening his mouth against her lips.

"*Muy poca,*" she replied as she tugged on his bottom lip with her teeth and soothed the nip with a lick of her tongue.

"Time enough for another cut. Are you game?" he said, but was reaching for the cards even before he heard her answer.

He offered up the cards and she picked one—a jack of hearts. Hard to beat unless . . .

Her *papi* drew the king of hearts. *Somehow prophetic,* she thought. "And you want—"

"To know your name. For you to know mine before we make love again." There was command in his voice. He wouldn't take no for an answer this time as he had the night before.

It went against her original game plan. It would change what she had resolved for her special Three-O night. None of that seemed to matter anymore.

"My friends call me Tori." She offered her hand for a shake.

There was no denying the satisfaction on his face as he took hold of her hand, pulled her full against him and said, "*My* friends call me Gil."

"Gil." She liked the sound of it on her lips and repeated it again. "Gil." Then she repeated his name several times before she said, "I like, Gil. Suits you."

As he rolled to his back and brought her to straddle him, he playfully said, "Don't you think you might get tired of saying my name?"

Tori stretched her hand toward the open nightstand drawer, withdrew a condom and playfully waved it in the air. "Nope. But how about you if you try tiring me out?" She leaned forward, kissed his lips, then worked her way down his body until she was poised right above the tip of him.

"But of course," Gil confirmed.

An hour later, Gil was nestled against her back once more, clearly sated and with no complaints that Tori had uttered his name on more than one occasion. But there was no denying that they soon had to dress and go their separate ways as the speed of the ship registered. They'd be in port soon.

Tori hated that thought even more now. Knowing his name had upped the ante. "We need to get dressed," she murmured and rubbed her hand along his arm as it rested on her waist.

"Five more minutes," Gil grumbled in complaint.

She suddenly could imagine waking beside him in the morning and hearing that gravelly voiced request on a daily basis.

This was not good. After this morning . . .

If she stuck to what she'd planned, she wouldn't see Gil again. But she had already deviated from that plan by giving him her name. Could she just walk away now? For that matter, she was assuming an awful lot, wasn't she? Her *abuelita* had warned her that men were dogs and not long for a relationship after they got what they wanted. Except, of course, for her saint of a husband.

But I was a dog, wasn't I? I acted just like a guy. I saw. I conquered. I planned on leaving.

In her heart, however, she knew she wasn't the kind of woman that could just scratch an itch without caring about it afterward.

Tori tried not to think about that as, a few minutes later, Gil placed a kiss on her shoulder and moved from the bed. For a moment she watched as he collected his clothes from around the room. Then she rose, grabbed a robe from the small closet at the far side of the room, and approached him.

She wrapped her arms around herself, suddenly wary and slightly defensive. Amazingly fearful that Gil would behave as she had wanted to and slip away into the morning light, never to be seen again.

Tori couldn't watch him go. Instead, she stood by the door, staring down at the light blue pile of the rug. A pair of polished black dress shoes came into her line of vision. A second later, Gil cupped her chin and gently urged her face upward.

She met his gaze and saw the reflection of her emotions in the blue of his eyes. Hesitation. Desire. And something different. Determination.

He reached into his back pocket, took out his wallet, and withdrew a business card, which he handed to her. "I'd like to see you again."

Tori glanced at the card and surprise pulled a strangled chuckle from her. "Gil? As in a nickname for Guillermo. As in Guillermo Gonzalez, new partner at Harrison, Morgan and Smith?"

She was babbling, but somehow couldn't contain her amusement at the little joke fate had played on her.

He pointed an index finger at the card and then motioned to her and then back to him, clearly confused. "That's the card from my old law firm, but they'd forward your call to me. How'd you—"

Tori held her hand out to him again in introduction as she said, "Tori. As in a nickname for Victoria. As in Victoria Rodriguez, new partner of same said firm."

He pointed at her. "You were out on Friday. On my first day."

She nodded and smiled. "Took the day off to celebrate my birthday."

"Your birthday, huh? Happy Birthday. Sorry I didn't bring a gift."

Tori stepped up next to him, cupped his cheek and ran her thumb along the outline of his lips. "Oh, but you did. And it's not the kind of gift I'm likely to return."

Gil wrapped his arms around her and began to laugh. A full, rich, happy kind of laugh and she joined in.

"So does this mean I can see you again?" Gil asked.

Tori gazed up at him and grinned. "At the office? In my boring lawyer clothes?"

Gil brought his lips to hers and whispered, "Actually, I was thinking of somewhere else and in something a little more casual. Maybe even without clothes."

Tori chuckled and nodded. "I'd say that's a definite maybe."

"And I'd say I'm a really lucky guy."

Tori opened her mouth and accepted his kiss, thinking she was going to have to find an extraspecial way to thank her friends for giving her a birthday night she'd not forget anytime soon!

And then as he backed her against the door, she stopped thinking and just let herself seize the moment.

And Gil.

Revenge of
the Fashion Goddess

BERTA PLATAS

Chapter One

If a stiff drink is Dutch courage, then a double *mojito* is liquid Cuban backbone. I'd ordered one earlier from room service, and although the mint and the lemon wedge looked kind of wilted, the rum was still strong. Alone in my hotel room, I picked up my glass and sucked down the equivalent of three solid-steel vertebrae. I needed it.

I picked up the invitation and read it again, as if a secret paragraph might have appeared since the last time. My full name, California Esther Montalvo, was front and center, long and shudder-inducing. To me, at least. No one who knew me would be dumb enough to use the whole thing, not even my mother. I think she's embarrassed about it now, as if she'd named me California in a hippie moment. You'd laugh if you knew Mami. She's a Cuban version of Nancy Reagan.

The invitation trembled in my hand. Bad news, since it meant that I was still scared. I could have another *mojito,* but I still had to get to Scooter's—a name that didn't inspire visions of cutting-edge décor—and I didn't want to make a fool of myself on the first night of my reunion weekend.

I was here in downtown Chicago because the words "fifteenth year reunion of North Elmwood Park High School" had stopped me from tossing the envelope in the trash, my first impulse after seeing my horrendous full name spelled out beneath the blue-and-gold North Elmwood Park heraldic crest.

I was amazed that I'd been invited at all. I didn't think my old classmates remembered me, and I sure didn't want them to remember me, not as I'd been. The Cali Montalvo who had worked in the school library, unibrowed and fashion-challenged, who had hidden during PE classes to skip dressing out and had avoided contact with the student body—that person had ceased to exist. I started to kill her in college, bashing her to death with the discovery of people just like me. Latina and literate—not the usual mix at old Elmwood Park, where the only person anything like me had been Rick Capaldi, and that was because he was a borderline social outcast, too. I had the double whammy of also being the school's only Latina.

Rick. *Dios mío,* just thinking his name gave me shivers, years after the hormonal rush of my teenage years, when love and bad self-image combined in a vortex of longing. I wanted to see Rick again.

I wondered where life had taken him. A literature

professor? A writer? Certainly something to do with books. Maybe he wouldn't attend the reunion, ashamed of his humble beginnings, his garage mechanic days. Of course, reunions are a chance not just to revisit your past, but to show off your success. Rick would be there.

That's what decided me. But as the date approached, apprehension seized me. Details that had faded as I got busy with college, internships, and the succession of jobs that led me to the fashion industry came back, like ghastly nuggets floating in a sewer. The paralyzing shyness that ruled my life. The indifferent kids I went to school with.

The shyness was gone, but the memories were returning. I've heard that after childbirth the memory of the pain goes away, until you're facing it again. It's a fitting analogy: if anyone had told my eighteen-year-old self that I'd be a hot New York fashion designer, I'd have laughed hysterically, hard enough to forget to raise my hand to cover the gap between my front teeth, long gone after spending my freshman college year in braces. I had reinvented myself, become reborn.

I put down the drink and picked up my little Prada handbag. It was time to go. The reunion was tomorrow, but tonight was the Friday night mixer, a way to see everyone without committing to the exposure of name badges and whatever horror the planning committee had cooked up.

My girlfriends back in New York were waiting for my report.

Right now they'd be racking up the first balls for our usual Friday night pool game at PeeBee's, Paolo's Billiards, a cheap joint that was all that remained of the 'hood in our revitalized Bronx neighborhood.

They were probably drinking wine and laughing at my strange need to revisit ancient misery. All had agreed that I just needed to get laid, a decision I couldn't argue with, since the stress of Fashion Week had segued into long meetings about the retail lines. Sex was a distant, and not too pleasant, memory, so far in the past that I could almost attribute mystical powers to the act. Instant relaxation. Instant boost of self-esteem. My girlfriends definitely thought it was great. They'd even bet on whom I'd pick. Like I'd pick anyone.

I didn't expect great sex, but I hoped to lay some ghosts to rest. It was a high school reunion. Everybody probably had the same expectations.

I left my room and started down the carpeted hall toward the elevator. I was still about thirty feet away when a woman staggered out of one of the two elevators. I cursed and hurried to catch it, but I was wearing my bronze leather Jimmy Choo stilettos and couldn't run. As the doors slid shut behind her, the woman grabbed the faux-burled walnut console opposite the elevators. Her knees sagged and she bent double, putting her forehead on the table's glass top. It looked like a weird modern dance move. My heel snagged a carpet loop and I almost went sprawling. Good thing I'd drawn the limit at one *mojito,* or I wouldn't even make it out of the hotel.

She heard my staggering footsteps and turned her face toward me, still keeping her head down. In her sober black pants and jacket, she didn't look like the drunk-off-your-ass type. Her shoulder-length hair fell partly across her face, but I could tell she was in her early fifties, and she was looking at me, although her eyes didn't seem to be focused on anything.

"I'm sick," she whispered, as I walked past, trying not to show I was staring.

Damn. Now I had to help her.

"Are you okay?" I asked. *Duh.* Of course she wasn't.

"Flu," she said. "Fever. Can you help me get to my room?"

"Sure," I answered. Torn between relief that she was just sick and not blasted, and fear that she had some contagious, apocalyptic virus, I took her elbow and helped her to stand. She leaned on me as we walked down the hall. Her skin was the color of bad asparagus.

"You look awful," I added helpfully.

"I was okay this afternoon," she said. "Then suddenly I couldn't even think straight." Her words were slurred.

We stopped, and she fished for her key in an oversized black tote bag.

"Is this your room?" She ignored my question as she rummaged, leaning crazily toward the left. I put a hand at her waist to level her.

I took the key card from her and shoved it into the door lock, then pushed the door open.

"Thanks," she said hoarsely. "I'll take it from here." She pushed her hair out of her flushed face. Her eyes were feverishly bright.

"I'm okay. Just need sleep," she said wearily. She squinted up at me. "Thanks, neighbor." She smiled a little.

It made her look more human and less like the Crypt-keeper.

"Hey, no problem. Want me to call a doctor?"

She shook her head and started to close the door. "Sleep," she said. "Everything hurts."

I went back to the elevators, and this time I made it to the lobby without being accosted by any more desperately ill women. I stopped to buy hand sanitizer from the gift shop. Whatever bug the woman had, she could keep.

The doorman hailed a Checker cab for me. I watched the cabbie's face in the rearview mirror as I told him the address of Scooters. No shock, no leer, just a grunt of recognition as he pulled away from the curb. I figured this was a good sign, although it would have been better if he'd been impressed.

Imagine my surprise when we pulled into the parking lot of a three-story entertainment megaplex with an over-sized blue neon sign plastered across the front. Scooters. Not just a sports bar. It was a sports bar on steroids. The parking lot was super *lleno,* full to bursting.

I sat in the cab, speechless, then paid the fare and stepped out into the cold night. I don't know why I expected a nicer venue for the Friday night mixer, but I'm prejudiced against sports bars. I hate talking to people when their eyes are glued to a TV screen above my head. Not that I expected to do much talking.

I wasn't sure what my expectations were, aside from see-ing what had become of Rick, and the girls who had caused me so much grief fifteen years before. I hoped they'd turned into hefty heifers. Maybe I just wanted to prove to myself that I'd made it, that I'd moved beyond my anxiety-driven teenage self.

The cab had dropped me off near the door, but far enough away that I could pull out my compact mirror and freshen my lipstick, which didn't need freshening. It was just an excuse to look at my face again, making sure I hadn't sprouted a unibrow, frizzy hair, and thick glasses. My sleek, razored black hair was the same as before, and my makeup looked just as it had when I'd left my room. I practiced a nonchalant look to replace the wild-eyed apprehension.

Game face on, I pushed through a knot of smokers huddled miserably by the front door, hoping the smoke wouldn't stick to my clothes. The place was huge, and though part of it was indeed a sports bar, the rest was a jumble of cozy booths, pub tables, and dance floors. A deafening mix of '80s dance music blasted through the crowded, dim interior. I stopped just inside the door, letting my eyes adjust enough to recognize faces. Above me, "Frankie Goes to Hollywood" boomed out, "Relax, don't do it, when you want to come to it . . . "

I didn't recognize anybody right away, and I was pretty sure no one would recognize me. I was counting on it.

A couple of guys looked at me curiously as I walked down the long bar. I stared straight ahead, and it was hard to keep a triumphant smile off my face. No guys ever looked at me in high school the way I was being looked at now. Okay, so they weren't exactly *chulo*-caliber, but they were men, and guys think they're hot even when they're bald and paunchy like my Tío Miguel.

Three women and one man were busy behind the bar. The lone male bartender was at the far end, and I headed toward him. I needed a drink to hold onto. I wanted another *mojito* but when I caught his eye I ordered a rum and Coke. A *mentirita*, as my Mom would call it. A Little Lie, a bitter joke on the drink's original name, Cuba Libre, since there was no longer a free Cuba. It was a great business occasion drink since I could later shift to straight Coke and no one would know my glass was alcohol-free.

A pink-cheeked, matronly woman approached me. "Hi, I'm Lydia Stevens, and I know who you are," she said slyly.

"You do?"

Lydia Stevens. I mulled the name, trying to come up with its twelfth-grade equivalent. Finally, I remembered a chubby girl in striped, homemade sweaters, who giggled her way though chemistry class. I'd never figured out what was so funny about atoms, but she'd had a lot of friends who giggled along with her.

"I sure do. We've been wondering when you'd show up." She turned and waved to a group of Lydia clones, who all delivered identical finger waves back to us. I lifted a hand, and then dropped it. Good to see her posse was intact, although there was a *Twilight Zone* quality to their sameness.

"So you're expecting me?" I wondered what fresh hell awaited me. Had Jen Peterson and Alma Marino planned to restage the most humiliating moment of my life? I felt fifteen years' worth of social polish slip away. Panic filled the void. I tried not to show it, keeping my face cool, a small smile pasted to my lips, reminding myself that I wasn't a timid high school geek anymore.

"Hey, is this her?" The chipper, ungrammatical voice behind me hadn't changed at all. My spine hadn't needed Cuban courage after all. It was stiffened by fear. I swallowed, reminding myself that I was thirty-three, not eighteen. My old tormentors were probably all about PTA meetings and amateur tennis now. I turned, and came face to face with Alma Marino, former editor of the school newspaper, the *Elmwood Park Sentinal,* and bully extraordinaire.

She looked terrific, darn it, although the former Miss Perfect's hair showed signs of color and heat damage. She smiled brightly and extended her hand. One inch airbrushed gel claws tipped each finger. The novelty of the moment was lost as I tried not to stare at her garish manicure.

"Welcome to the Elmwood Park Reunion. We've got a great reunion planned. I'm Alma Steuben, the committee chair. I love your work."

"You do?" I was a minor ready-to-wear designer for Kenneth MacBray, and my personal line didn't seem her thing at all. I tried to picture her in one of my skimpy layered-gauze frocks. The effort was too great. She was a Target girl, or maybe Wal-Mart. And what was with the happy smile? Was she on drugs, or had I been wrong all those years ago?

I had a sudden flashback of standing in line at the cafeteria, her cruel words ringing through the room, all eyes on me. And then her friend Jen's hand smacking the bottom of my tray so that salad dressing, milk, and soggy broccoli dripped from my T-shirt, making me as dirty as they'd made me feel. Everyone had laughed, just as they were laughing now.

Whoa. I backed away from that totally Stephen King moment and tucked my inner Carrie away.

Lydia's friends were crowded around, and Alma looked at them triumphantly. "Girls, I am so proud to introduce you to this brave woman. Few people make a difference in the world, but she has." She waved her hand dramatically.

My bewilderment must have shown on my face, because Lydia smiled understandingly and squeezed my arm.

"Girls, I want you to meet Dorothy Kalucheck."

Chapter Two

Dorothy Kalucheck? Who the hell was that? My fear turned to puzzlement, then glee. They had mistaken me for someone else. I smiled and returned the handshakes that suddenly surrounded me, maybe a little more firmly than I should have, squelching the little devil of disappointment that they had not recognized me, that the smiles weren't really for me.

Alma beamed with pride. She must have thought this Kalucheck woman's presence was a real coup. Alma's girlish prettiness had matured, and she was now handsome, although she could have done better than the suede skirt and boots she had on, which made her look clunky. And that hair—who had the frizzed ends now?

Of course, I didn't need to pick on Alma. The whole

room was full of people in need of extreme makeovers.

Off the hook, I felt like taking the offensive and announcing their mistake. Instead I asked a safe question, since they obviously expected me to serve some purpose. I hoped this Kalucheck woman was not a foodie. I totally suck at cooking.

"So, where do I start?" I sounded no-nonsense and official.

Alma and Lydia looked at each other. Still the alpha bitch, Alma took the lead.

"I think you should meet absolutely everybody," she said. "We're all here."

"Everyone?" *How about Cali Montalvo? Oh wait, she's right here, and she's made a huge success of her life despite what you did to her.*

"Some of us have become hugely successful," Alma continued, startling me into thinking that maybe she could read minds. But no, if she could read mine, her brain would be blistered.

I followed her, drink in hand, through the room as she reintroduced me to faces vaguely familiar from the yearbook of the class of 1989. As we walked and made small talk with a succession of accountants, life insurance salesmen, secretaries, teachers, and lawyers, I became aware of my supposed mission.

The documentary filmmaker they'd mistaken me for was checking out the reunion mixer, and maybe returning tomorrow to film the reunion itself. I played along, but as soon as the real Dorothy Kalucheck showed up, *pa' fuera*. I was out of here. And as soon as I saw Rick, I'd declare my mission over, even if I didn't have my dream confrontation with Jen Peterson. And Alma. I owed Alma an invitation to the Guilty Party. Meanwhile, I played the documentary filmmaker.

"Sometimes I like to focus on issues," I said to Alma after talking to a bowling alley manager who had been one of the football team's stars. "Did you have any experience with bullying in high school?"

"No," she said, shaking her retro perm. "That's more an elementary school issue, isn't it?"

"You'd be surprised," I answered, feeling a pang as the old Cali reshaped herself from the ashes. "It takes different forms."

I was about to get more specific when her face darkened. "Here's another success story, but you might not want to meet him." Her eyes were on the bar's front door. "He can be a real booger."

Had she really said booger? It was so high school. Or so mommy. If she excused herself to go to the potty, I'd laugh out loud. I turned to look for this booger person.

I spotted him a second later, and this time my spine melted. Even my fingers felt hot. The ice in my glass clinked softly as my hand shook. Dark hair, chiseled profile, broad shoulders. Rick hadn't changed, not one bit. One hundred percent *guapo*.

"Hm," I said. "Must have gotten a chill. So, who is this guy?" As if I didn't know. It wasn't fear that made my hand shake, it was desire.

"Rick Capaldi. He was one of those really mysterious

guys in high school. Dangerous-looking, too. He was into punk rock, and his friends were just as odd. He had a Mohawk one summer. A blue one."

"But grew back his hair before September," I said, then realized I'd spoken aloud.

Alma nodded. "He sure did. They wouldn't have let him through the school doors otherwise." She looked at me. "Perceptive of you. Or did you have a Rick Capaldi at your school, too?"

"Don't we all?" I spoke lightly, but thought of Rick, hair falling into his dangerous brown eyes, always angry, and so sexy. My one high school friend, if you could call a one-sided crush a friendship. One-sided until just before school ended, when he'd made his surprising confession. My face grew warm as I wondered if he remembered what he'd said, if he remembered me.

Alma led me toward him, and I followed, confident that my disguise was foolproof, although it was disconcerting that I thought of my current appearance as a disguise. This was the real me—confident, put-together, and smart.

Confident, put-together, smart, I repeated to myself, as if it were a mantra. I fought the urge to cross myself.

Rick's eyebrows rose as Alma cut off his progress toward the bar. She pulled me forward. "Rick, so glad you made it," she chirped, sounding as fake as I felt. "This is Dorothy Kalucheck, the filmmaker. She's thinking of doing a documentary about our reunion."

He put his hand out automatically, and my fingers disappeared into his warm, firm grip. He'd held my hand before, and my heart almost broke remembering it. He looked up, about to speak, and instead his gaze stuck to my face as if we were in a staring contest. His mouth closed, and one side twitched. I knew that look. *Busted*.

Out of the corner of my eye, I saw Alma look from him to me and back again.

"Rick. I've heard so much about you," I finally said. I pulled on my hand, which was trapped in his. His grip tightened; not enough to hurt, but I wasn't getting away until he let me go.

"Nice to meet you, too. Dorothy." There was a slight delay before he said the name; then he turned to Alma. "I'd like to speak to Dorothy in private, Alma. Mind?"

"No, of course not." She looked bewildered. "Do you two know each other?"

"No," I said quickly.

"We've met," Rick said, simultaneously.

I stared at him, horrified. I was losing control of the moment. I'd wanted to meet him on my terms.

In my nebulous fantasy I'd imagined that I'd watch him from the other side of the room, and he wouldn't recognize me until I introduced myself. Then I'd bask in his shock and dazzled admiration, allowing myself a little bit of time to gloat before leaving with a nonchalant little wave. Off to be famous, leaving little Elmwood Park behind.

"Well, I didn't know you were a film buff," Alma said. "I'll leave you kids to get reacquainted." She looked at me again, as if maybe I was more famous than she'd thought, then waved at someone across the bar and hurried off.

"Dorothy Kandychuck? What kind of lame name is that?" Rick grabbed my elbow and pulled me into the sports bar. A hockey game was playing in sensurround on twelve different screens. My heart hammered, thrilled that he'd recognized me, worried that he'd rat me out.

"I think the name is Kalucheck, and she's a real person. Alma thinks I'm her. I thought it would be a great way to meet everyone again, incognito."

"That's insane, Cali." He slowed down as we approached the back, a darker area with no TVs. The carpet underfoot was still sticky from spilled beers past. A couple of *viejitos* in their sixties or older were talking, heads together, over beers at a table by the door. They looked like they were about to smooch. Ack.

Rick stopped at an empty booth, motioned me in, and sat across from me. He was gorgeous. Under his leather jacket he wore a collarless black sweater, very in, very spare, that clung to his narrow waist. I approved. As if it mattered.

"You look nice Rick," I said, trying not to sound hungry. My girlfriends' voices sang a Greek chorus in my head. "Him," they chanted. "Pick him, Cali."

"You look —" he looked me up and down, breasts to hairline " —amazing."

"Thanks," I said, and shivered. It's always a boost to the ego to be told you're hot, and I needed every boost I could get tonight. Bonus points that the *piropo* came from Rick. "I didn't introduce myself as Cali. No one's recognized me."

"Not surprised," he said. His words, though true, stung

and made me redden. His next sentence soothed the burn. "They all started drinking around six. Why'd you co-opt this Kaluchick's persona to do it?"

"Kalucheck. It was a mistake, but I didn't want to admit who I really was."

"Why, Cali? You weren't infamous in high school. There are probably some guys here that should have stayed home, but not you." He turned his head sideways, stretching out his neck, then repeated to the other side, popping his vertebrae. It was a nervous habit I remembered, and it made me feel oddly comfortable.

"Because I wanted to see Alma and Jen again."

"Not me?" His eyes twinkled. "Man, that hurts."

"And you, of course."

"Too late," he said. "My feelings are crushed." His smile didn't change, but something in his eyes made me wonder if maybe he really was hurt.

The waitress came by and he ordered a beer and pointed at my glass.

"Coke," I said, preempting his order.

He picked up my glass and sniffed it. "Make that a rum and Coke."

"Are you always this rude?" I snatched my glass back.

"Relax, Cali. You used to be so laid back. What happened to stress you out?" He leaned forward, his eyes warm, and getting hotter.

"Work," I said, trying to ignore the smoldering taking place at the other side of the table. "Success. You have to stay on top of things in my business."

He shrugged and leaned back again. "In any business. No reason to stop enjoying life."

"And you enjoy life?" It was a rhetorical question. He looked as if he enjoyed every second.

"Don't you?" His eyebrows rose as his eyes did another slow inventory. I felt my nipples harden as his gaze locked on my breasts. *Dios mío*, I should have worn a different bra.

"Of course. I thought you wanted to be a poet and live by the sea. I always pictured you that way," he said.

"My high school plans changed when I got to college, and my college plans changed when I hit the real world." I shrugged. "Happens to everybody, I hear."

He looked serious. "It certainly happened to me. So you came to what? Gloat?"

"Gloat? What an ugly word." I squirmed a little. He was right, but it sounded wrong spoken aloud. "I mainly came to see Alma and Jen. I want to lay some ghosts to rest."

His eyebrows rose.

I leaned forward and whispered conspiratorially. "I kind of hoped they'd gotten fat and ugly. Alma looks good, sort of. So I'm pinning my hopes on Jen."

His expression suddenly changed, and I wondered what I'd said to cause it.

"Don't tell me Jen's in a wheelchair and that I'm going to regret my words." I looked toward the bar area, but only a few of the crowd were visible from here. "Because I won't. Regret it, I mean. They were responsible for the worst day of my life."

He laughed shortly. "Mine, too. And no, she's not in a wheelchair. You'll probably run into her tonight."

He didn't explain further. I wondered what Jen had done to account for the bitterness in his voice. I wouldn't put anything past her, the bitch.

"Don't tell anyone who I am, okay, Rick? Please? This Kalucheck woman's bound to show up, and I'll leave then, or tell everyone who I am, but I've got something to prove to myself."

"That you can still run away? Still hide?" He shook his head and sat back, lacing his fingers together behind his head. "You don't need to do this, Cali. Remember when I told you that you were braver than you thought? Look at all you've accomplished. You've got nothing to prove to anyone. Remember that Dead Kennedy song, 'California Uber Alles'? That's still you."

I groaned, remembering the anti–Governor Reagan political anthem. He would sing it to provoke me, and I'd always smile back, unfazed, more concerned by the punk band's near-heretical name than the song. I mean, if I cringed every time anyone said California I'd look like a bobble head. It's a *state*, for Pete's sake. Rick was the only person that I had allowed to say my whole first name out loud, and he'd seldom abused the privilege.

I smiled and struck back, as I remembered something else. "Did you ever tell anyone that you read Kafka and Dickens for fun?"

"Nope. Did you ever tell anyone about your reams of poetry?"

I widened my eyes. "Are you kidding? They thought I was weird enough as it was. You were braver, though. You let everyone see exactly who you were. Except for the book reading part."

"You did, too. But you just stayed in the library, like a little fairy in the forest."

I laughed. "More like a little troll under a bridge."

"You have a nice laugh, Cali. I don't believe I remember that laugh." He straightened and leaned forward to touch my hand. "You should have laughed more."

"Not enough to laugh about, I'm afraid." I smiled to take the edge off the words, not daring to look at his hand on mine. It felt great, all warm and comforting. "All that teenage angst. But things have changed for me. I'm not a famous documentary filmmaker, but I'm one of Kenneth MacBray's lead designers."

"The fashion guy?" He slapped the tabletop with his open palm. "That's great. So half these women are wearing clothes designed by you?"

I rolled my eyes in mock horror. "Oh, I hope not. But in two years they'll be wearing bargain store knockoffs of the clothes my clients wear."

"All that, and humble, too," he said, smiling. His fingertip circled a mark on the table. "So, did you ever marry?"

I watched his lightly tracing fingertip, thinking of how it would feel on my skin, caressing my breasts. I shivered and my nipples reacted, tightening again. He didn't miss the show, but made a brave attempt to keep looking at my face.

It occurred to me that I was reacting like my high school

self, a shy prude, the pride of my old-fashioned Cuban parents. Not allowed to date, not allowed to pluck my eyebrows until I was sixteen, and by then I was too embarrassed to admit to anyone that I didn't know how. I spent four years in perpetual embarrassment.

Boy, had things changed in college.

So Rick was staring at my breasts. So what? I was here for a weekend. It was Friday night, the traditional party night. Why shouldn't he enjoy himself? Why shouldn't I? I sat up straight and threw my shoulders back. He reeled slightly, then recovered.

His finger continued to go round and round, and when his eyes met mine, the message was clear.

Somewhere in the Bronx, my girlfriends were going to scream.

Chapter Three

I'd been waiting for this moment for fifteen years—almost half my life. My heart was beating in time to Rick's circling finger and I swallowed, mouth dry. My drink was empty and I clinked the ice, thought about sucking on a cube, then decided it would be either provocative or annoying, and I didn't know which.

"Earth to Cali," he said. He touched my left hand, stroking my bare ring finger. He raised his eyebrows in a silent question.

"Too busy," I said. "It takes time and commitment to ramp up to marriage. I date occasionally." I didn't mention that my dates were male coworkers, mostly gay. We served as each other's escorts as needed for business dinners, weddings, and other family occasions. It saved a lot of headaches. My little black book was full of numbers for fellow designers, fabric shops, pattern makers, and embroiderers.

Alma's radar must have been set on high. She appeared at our table, fake smile pasted on, eyes switching from Rick to me.

"Rick, you're hogging Dorothy. She hasn't had time to circulate yet."

Rick ignored her and smiled at me. "How about another drink?"

I'd planned to stop at one, but now my second drink was empty and my backbone still needed reinforcing. "Just Coke this time, really," I said.

His smile was crooked, sardonic, and totally adorable. "Girly drink." He stood and stretched backward a little. "Sorry," he said. "I put a new head in a Tahoe this morning and I'm stiff all over."

Stiff. I held back a vintage Lydia Stevens giggle, but it faded when I thought of what he'd just revealed. As he headed toward the bar, disappointment killed my burgeoning lust. He was still an auto mechanic. He'd worked in his dad's car repair shop after school and during the summers, but he'd been headed to college and a teaching career. He wanted to teach in inner city Chicago. I was sure he'd left suburbia and the auto shop behind.

Just like me, he'd longed for escape. What happened to being a teacher, to making a difference? He'd played the rebel, but then bought into the Elmwood Park life. His black leather jacket, cool black sweater—his whole bad boy look, was all a disguise.

Despite being Dorothy Kalucheck for the night, I didn't feel like a hypocrite. I was answering to a false name, but underneath, I was the real me, with real accomplishments.

That reminder freed me. I was here for two days, not a lifetime, so why not play? It didn't matter what he was. I wanted him, and he seemed to want me. This opportunity would never come again. Of course, I could be fooling myself. In high school, we'd done little more than hold hands in the library until that moment just before graduation, and that episode might have been a fluke.

We'd both been individualists, loners, although that word's gained a bad reputation lately. We'd kept each other's secrets. They were tame secrets, as high school lives go, but his literary bent would have labeled him a joke, a nerd ten years before the dotcoms made nerds cool. High school was tough enough without handicapping yourself, especially when you're already different. Like being the only Cuban in a predominantly Italian high school.

Alma watched Rick leave, then turned to me. A little wrinkle between her eyes signaled her displeasure. No Botox here. "I've made a list of some of the people you need to speak with. This will give you a cross section of Elmwood Park High's most interesting stories." She handed me a sheet of paper.

"Thanks, Alma." I took the sheet between thumb and forefinger, and read what looked like a who's who of the popular kids in our class. Bland, white, and respectable. Not a single really interesting person had made the cut, and no one of color. Of course there had been few of those.

I wondered how much I could admit to knowing. Would Dorothy Kalucheck have researched the class? Would she know more than what Alma told her? I gave it a try. "I don't see Jane Boskin, the chef, Or Evan Tiswell, the guy who was nominated for a Pulitzer in journalism." Just because I didn't come back to Elmwood Park didn't mean I didn't read the *New York Times*, and those two were nationally known.

"Oh, why—" Alma seemed flustered. "Of course, we're very proud of them. Evan isn't here, and Jane, well." She leaned forward and whispered. "Jane's not what you're looking for."

"She has her own cooking show on TV." This was true. I'd watched it a couple of times. She was big into cooking meat, and I was a sometime vegetarian, not to mention totally cold on cooking, so I didn't watch it much, but there were plenty of people who did. "Is she here?"

"Yes, but—" Alma pursed her lips. "She's brought her significant other with her."

"So?"

"She has a, oh, how can I say it?" Alma blinked rapidly. "She has a wife," she finally said.

"Jane's a lesbian?" She was more interesting than I'd thought.

"Yes," Alma hissed, looking around as if I'd said a dirty word in front of the preacher.

"Here's your rum and Coke, Cal—" Rick had turned the corner and held the drink aloft. "Calvin. Calvin's at the bar and I think you should talk to him, too."

I breathed again. For a second I thought he was going to give me away, but he was quick.

"Calvin," Alma frowned. "I thought the bartender's name was Zack."

"If my name was Calvin, I'd change it to Zack, too," Rick said.

I took the drink Rick was holding out and said, "Excuse me, I have to go to the ladies' room. I'll talk to, er, Calvin on the way back." I dashed away before Alma could chirp that she was joining me, in that restroom-inspired solidarity women sometimes have. Behind me, I heard her chiding Rick because Calvin had not been in our graduating class.

"The focus here is on Elmwood Park," she said behind me. As if anyone could forget.

Beyond the bar, carpeted stairs led up to the second floor. A huge illuminated sign read LADIES in pink neon, with a beribboned finger pointing up. I climbed, hoping for a roomy bathroom with a lounge. I needed to sit for a while and figure out what to do next. The evening was not turning out the way I'd hoped. There were no bald ex-crushes, no fat cheerleaders. And as far as I knew, the only fake in the room was me.

I would have said that things weren't going the way I'd planned but there had been no planning for my impulsive trip back in time. My presence here was totally unlike the methodical woman I'd become, and it showed. I started to hope that Dorothy Kalucheck would show up soon. If I left now, Alma would follow me, asking why her pet filmmaker was leaving. The arrival of the real Dorothy would draw a lot of attention, and not the good sort of attention if I got caught, but I was a fast runner.

The music changed as I went upstairs, going from nostalgic to techno. At the top of the stairs I blinked as my eyesight was assaulted by dazzling colors and lights. I stared at the glass and mirrors that ringed a huge space filled with pool tables and whirring, pinging, singing video games. Totally different from downstairs, it was almost empty. The Elmwood Parkites hadn't discovered it yet.

Not my style, but at least it was livelier than the pseudo-Irish pub look downstairs.

I found the bathroom at the far side of the room. A woman held the door for me as she exited. As I'd hoped, there were lounge chairs, a long counter with makeup mirrors, and a separate room with stalls. It smelled like lemon disinfectant.

My face and hair looked okay, or at least nothing was wrong that I could fix without an appointment. I went into the first stall, hung my Prada bag on the door hook, pulled up my dress, and was just sitting down when a nearby toilet flushed. I'd thought I was alone, not that it mattered.

A door creaked open and I briefly heard the music outside. Someone else coming in. The bathroom scene was picking up now that people's drinks had percolated through their systems.

"Who've you seen?" a woman asked over the noise of water running in the sink.

"Oh, lord, everyone," another woman answered. "Not that I don't see them all the time. We could have saved a lot of money by holding the reunion at the PTA fish fry last week." They both laughed.

Hidden in the stall, I shuddered. I wouldn't put it past them. The sports bar suddenly seemed like a palace.

"You know who else I saw downstairs?" The first woman's voice lowered. "Rick Capaldi came in. By himself."

"I'm not surprised," the other woman said. "Jen's here somewhere. She came straight from work or at least that's what she said."

I froze. I don't think I even breathed. *Jen*. How many could there be at this reunion? Maybe someone's wife had the same name as my archenemy.

"Yeah? Well she probably doesn't know that Rick's down there schmoozing that documentary lady."

I sat straight up.

"Jen probably wouldn't care if Rick was screwing her on the bar," the other woman said. "If I was married to a hunk like that, I'd pay attention to him."

"She's too busy putting the Peterson whammy on Chip Alstead."

"Mmhmm. Yummy Chip."

They both laughed again, and then moved toward the door. I heard music again.

And then I was alone.

Jen Petersen. Married to Rick.

I wanted to run away, back to New York. I wanted to

kill Rick for not telling me. I wanted to kill him for marrying the bitch queen of Elmwood Park High.

For a second, I remembered her at the Homecoming Parade before the football game our senior year. She wore dark blue velvet with big sleeves, and a long, bouffant pleated skirt that made her waist look tiny. Her golden hair fell to her waist, held back from her face by a glittery tiara. It had started to snow, and she'd looked like something out of a fairy tale, a snow princess.

As unhappy as I was with my own appearance, she had seemed magical, and despite who she was, and how horribly she treated me, for a moment I had desperately wanted to be her. There was no escaping who I was, short and dark, near-sighted, scraggly-haired, and Latina. I hated her for being beautiful and popular and blond, for driving her own car and being allowed to go to parties. She was a star. I was the last lump of coal in the bin.

I'd come to rid myself of these memories, not to relive them. Now, ten years later, I hated her all over again, for bringing back that ugly time, and for taking away my hope. I couldn't even confront her without admitting that I wasn't Dorothy Kalucheck. Talk about getting off on the wrong foot—I'd have to first admit I'm a liar.

Rick was married to Jen, and I was in the bathroom, alone and feeling foolish, panties around my ankles, tears smearing my mascara. My triumphant return was *so* not following my fantasy script.

I pulled myself together, quickly rubbing the mascara

from under my eyes before anyone else came in. I threw my shoulders back and raised my chin. Fearless, and a little drunk, I stepped out of the bathroom, new plan in place.

I was going to confront Jen, slap Rick for leading me on, and teach Zack how to make a killer *mojito*. I needed one.

Chapter Four

I crossed the big room again, looking around in case Jen and Rick had come up here. I felt small and weak, but mostly I was mad. It was not fair that the life I'd built for myself had melted away so quickly when confronted by my past.

Remember who you are, I told myself. I recited my successes: improved appearance, ideal job, successful new fashion line. It didn't seem like enough. It wasn't easy to pump up my self-esteem with evil Jen lurking somewhere in the building. So far, my big Friday night sucked.

Maybe I could kill Alma, Jen, and Rick. Then I could sell my story to the Coen brothers and carve a new niche for myself with the fashionista Death Row crowd.

A blonde in sparkly Spandex rushed past me and

slammed through the bathroom door. I didn't recognize her, but she made me think that anyone could be Dorothy Kalucheck. She could already be here, observing me, and I'd end up as a surreal footnote in her documentary. Uneasy, I went down the stairs. The music changed as I descended the steps, morphing back to the '90s. It was like going through a time tunnel to the past. I so didn't want to go there.

Before I stepped on terra firma again, Sue Ann Lemke, the valedictorian of the class of 1989, started toward the stairs. I remembered her because although we never spoke much, she'd been nice to me. She'd changed very little. No nonsense and plain then, she was an older, more sophisticated version of her teenaged self. She glanced at me, and instead of a perfunctory smile as our eyes met, her eyes brightened and she stopped. *Uh-oh.*

"Cali, it's great to see you," she said.

I felt sick. How could these people recognize me? I looked nothing like I did in high school. Or did I? That made me feel worse. "Hi, Sue Ann. How'd you know it was me?"

"I saw you in New York during Fashion Week, and I kind of hoped you'd be here. I've been following your career." She paused, face full of concern. "Are you all right? You look a little pale."

I stared at Sue Ann, more in shock that she'd recognized me than in fear that she might reveal my secret. "I'm okay. Just had a little surprise upstairs. Where are my manners?" We air-kissed like civilized women.

"I'm glad you're all right. You scared me for a second."

"Thanks. It's something I'll take care of soon. Sue Ann,

I'd have recognized you anywhere. You haven't changed." It was true. She still had dark chestnut hair, wide dark eyes, and a tall, lanky figure. "What were you doing at Fashion Week?"

She grinned. "I cover fashion for the *Chicago Tribune,* and caught Ken MacBray's runway show. You work for him, don't you? And I was at your trunk show, too, for your line, Cali E. That's how I recognized you, 'cause, girl, you are totally changed."

That was gratifying. Better than a *mojito.*

"You were at my show?" The night was a blur of faces in a crowded room, exciting but chaotic. "I am so sorry I missed you, Sue Ann. Why didn't you talk to me?"

She smiled. "Are you kidding? You were mobbed. And your designs are divine. I love that layered, casual look. And the way you mix natural tones with blues is terrific. I've been reading about you since you left Miriam Zimmerman to work for MacBray. But you know, Cali E is so strong, you should ditch MacBray and open your own shop."

"Thanks. That's my dream, but it's a scary one." The recognition was flattering, but bad. I didn't want to tell her that I was pretending to be Dorothy Kalucheck. I smiled at her. "Most people outside the trade don't know my name, or my tiny little private label."

"They will. So, is this a vacation? Fashion Week was grueling, wasn't it?"

I agreed, looking over her shoulder. Although I wanted to talk longer about the insane world of high fashion and ready-to-wear, I wanted to find Rick.

Alma walked past and smiled approvingly at us, and I realized that Sue Ann must have been on the list. Sue Ann, who knew my real name. Suddenly, the room felt stuffy.

"Uh, Sue Ann, I need to tell you something."

She tilted her head. "True confession time?"

"What do you mean?" My heart thumped loudly.

She shrugged. "Isn't that what people do at reunions? Forgive and forget? Or there's revenge, of course."

I tensed, wondering if she was going to bring up Rick and Jen. My teeth ground together at the thought of their names strung together, as if they belonged that way. Except they did. They were *married*.

She noticed my expression and grinned. "You know, hoping the cheerleaders are fat and the football players are bald."

I relaxed, remembering the time that Sue Ann loaned me lunch money in fifth grade, when I'd lost mine on the bus. She had been one of the kind ones. Trust is built on simple things when you're a kid. Betrayal, too.

"Do you remember Rick Capaldi?" I kept my voice casual.

She rolled her eyes. "Brains, looks, and bad attitude. Yup. He's here, you know."

"I've spoken to him." I kept my voice neutral.

"Oh yeah?" Her eyes sparked with sudden interest. "A new acquaintance, or revisiting history?"

"He used to come to the library, to talk."

Sue Ann's brows rose. "About?"

"Stuff. You know, kid stuff." It sounded lame to me, too.

Back then, it had seemed intense and sexy. Anything but kid stuff.

"And you had a crush on him?" Her smile turned cynical.

"Was it obvious?"

"No." She laughed. "Cali, everyone had a crush on him."

Everyone? Suddenly my special feelings felt bargain store. I wanted to yell, "Nuh-uh. I saw him first."

"He was so dangerous," she continued. "I would never have dared bring him over to meet my parents. He was a punker."

"Punk," I corrected. "And he wasn't, not really. He liked the music, and some of what the punks stood for, but he was too, too—" I wanted to say, too real, too grounded.

"Too Elmwood Park?"

I laughed, a little too loudly. "Perfect. Yeah, too Elmwood Park." And he still was.

"You know he's married." Her tone was cautious, as if I might slap her at the news. Okay, I wanted to slap someone, but it wasn't Sue Ann.

"I heard."

She opened her mouth to say something else, then shut it again. Wise girl.

"Another rum and Coke?" Zack the bartender grinned at me from the end of the bar.

"You know how to make a *mojito*?"

"Mint crushed into sugar, rum, ice, fresh lemon juice. I don't have fresh mint, though."

"Make it without, I don't care."

His brows went up. "Rum lemonade, then. Any brand of rum?"

"Bacardi." I handed him the empty glass I'd been carrying around like a good luck charm.

"That sounds good," Sue Ann said. "Make me one, too." She turned to me while we waited for our drinks. "What did you want to tell me? Just that you had a crush on our bad boy?"

After looking around to be sure no one was listening, I shook my head. "It's me, Sue Ann. I haven't told anyone who I am."

Her eyebrows rose. "Incognito at your own high school reunion? Cali, that's just weird."

"Don't call me Cali out loud," I said, shushing her.

"Did you register under a false name?" She looked confused.

"I didn't register at all. I thought I'd get my business done and leave. Lydia grabbed me at the door. She thinks I'm Dorothy Kalucheck."

"The documentary filmmaker? Oh, that's rich. You don't look anything like her."

"You know her?" This was great. "What does she look like? If she's here, I'm so gone."

"Relax. I don't think she's coming tonight—she would have been here by now. We've emailed back and forth for a while. She contacted a friend of mine at City Hall about filming a high school reunion, and we hooked up. Our class is so strange, she couldn't resist."

"Keep my secret?" I crossed my fingers.

"Are you kidding? This is a hoot. I'll be able to talk about it afterward, right?"

I shrugged. "Why not?"

"Hey, you want these drinks or not? The ice is melting. Found some mint, too." Zack held out two tall glasses. I took my drink and Sue Ann got hers. She tasted it and licked her lips.

"Damn, that's good."

I smiled and gave Zack a thumbs-up. He smacked the bar gleefully and raced to the other end of the bar, where faded football heroes needed beer. When I turned back, Sue Ann had wandered off to mingle some more. I'd wanted to quiz her about Rick and Jen.

I sipped my drink at the bar, watching the action on the dance floor. Whatever else you could say about them, the class of '89 was not inhibited. I wondered how I'd find Rick in the mass of gyrating suburbanites. There was no balcony like any decent dance club would have, so I'd have to circulate. Totally *primitivo*.

Zack danced by, two beers held aloft, and passed them over the crowded bar to waiting hands.

Someone tapped on my shoulder, and I turned to find Lydia's face only inches from mine.

"Earth to Dorothy," she chirped. "I've been calling your name for about a minute."

"Sorry." I didn't even pretend to come up with an excuse. "What's up?"

"Alma's looking for you. She's by the front door."

"On my way." Alma probably wanted to check out how

many people I'd spoken to. Amused at my painless pseudo-relationship with my former enemy, I slipped off the stool and started to thread my way through the increasingly rowdy crowd, still looking for Rick and Jen. Around me, old Elmwood Parkites were sliding back into adolescence, lubricated by Zack and his merry alcohol-slinging coworkers.

Someone grabbed my elbow, nails digging into my flesh. I turned. "Ow, Lydia, quit grabbing me —"

I stopped, horrified.

Jen Peterson was clinging to me, a cosmopolitan clutched in her other hand. From the lopsided smile on her lovely, evil, face, it wasn't her first.

Chapter Five

Dorothy Kaluchnik? I need to talk to you." Jen
looked angry. With her lean, elegant, body she
could almost be one of my models.

I felt inferior and suddenly tongue-tied.

"Kaluchick," I said, then cursed inwardly. "Kalucheck."
Just being next to her was making me *loca*. I banished all
self-disparaging thoughts that immediately flashed into my
mind, reminding myself that I was a curvy Latina, and that
I wasn't short, I was petite.

She waved her drink. "Whatever. Come on, let's get private."

It was like being in a car wreck; I was a participant, but
had no control over the outcome. We made our way back toward the bar, moving as if in slow motion. Around us, faces

flashed by, smiles turned questioning, probably wondering what Jen had to confess to the filmmaker. I couldn't hear the music anymore, just the throbbing bass. Ahead of me, at the other end of the tanned and shapely arm that held me, Jen's blond shoulder-length hair swung in time to the beat.

I attributed the Fellini-movie atmosphere to my empty *mojito* glass. In a symbolic gesture of sobriety, I handed it to a surprised redhead by the bar as Jen and I started up the stairs to the game room.

Relax, I told myself. *No es nada.* It's nothing. She thinks I'm Dorothy Kalucheck, and she wants to talk. My thumping heart was so not listening. I pictured my grieving mother's face. I couldn't have a heart attack from a simple confrontation. I had arguments at work all the time with my temperamental boss. Ken MacBray was an animal. He even threw things. Jen didn't look the book-heaving type, though she could sure sling the hurt.

There were leather sofas at the other end of the pool tables. I'd missed seeing them when I came up earlier because the tables and their low-hanging industrial lamps hid them from view. Very cozy. Very private. Absolutely terrifying, if it involved Jen and me, *mano a mano*.

Jen fell onto one of the red sofas, pulling me down next to her. "Let's talk, Dorothy."

"Okay." I steeled myself for the confrontation. "What do you want to talk about?" As if I didn't know.

"Me, of course. Aren't you interviewing the class of 'eighty-nine?"

My mouth opened and closed. I'd been ready to talk

about Rick. Or about when she attacked me in the cafeteria.

"Alma gave me a list. I'm not sure who's on it."

"I'm on it," she said. She sounded confident. I envied that natural confidence. I'd worked hard for mine. Not that it was anywhere in sight. "I was very popular in high school. It was the best time of my life," she added.

Not mine. "Really? Tell me about it."

She looked over at me. "Aren't you going to take notes?"

Concho. I didn't have anything to write on. Then I remembered what Lydia has said. "I'm just checking you guys out. I'm not sure I'll be doing your reunion or another one. If I decide to do yours, then I'll come back tomorrow with my film equipment."

"Oh. I think Alma mentioned that." She watched a nearby game of pool. The upstairs was almost crowded, but most of the people clustered around the pool tables and the video games.

"You must have a lot of friends here tonight." That should get her talking, I thought.

"Absolutely. I was one of the more popular girls." She actually preened as she said it, like a peacock with breasts. Artificially augmented ones, from the looks of it. I know. Meow.

I nodded. "Can you define popularity? What does it take to be popular?"

I was trying to fake being Kalucheck, but I couldn't miss the opportunity to hear it in her own words. It almost made me wish I were really a filmmaker. I was treated with respect and could ask personal questions and get an immediate, almost eager answer.

She flipped her hair back and smiled. Her teeth were white and even, but she still managed to look like a barracuda.

"There were people who were just naturally popular, you know? They were great at sports and cheerleading. Others wanted to be popular. Some of them tried really hard, and it was pitiful. But others did their own thing, like the musicians and drama people. They hung around together, not with us."

So far, she hadn't said anything I didn't know. She was conceited, but truthful. I listened as she spoke, mixed feelings roiling in me. I hated her, or I had, fifteen years ago, but even up close, she was still beautiful. I wondered what it would be like to grow up lovely, admired even by strangers. A model once told me that school had been effortless due to her looks. Good looks buy goodwill, from teachers, other students, and later, possible employers. It was a lesson that I learned in college. Too late, in some ways.

My parents had told me to be strong, to love myself. They'd been right, but I needed more detailed instructions. Of course, they also didn't let me date or go out with friends. Are there Cuban Amish? I'd felt like one.

"What do you do now, Jen?" It was hard to say her name without wanting to spit to clear my mouth out.

"This and that. I don't have kids, so I'm not part of the PTA crowd. And my husband absolutely forbids me to set foot in his offices." She laughed nervously.

I had been almost getting comfortable in my role, but I felt my back stiffen again. Her husband. My Rick. "What does your husband do?"

What was I doing, asking that question? Maybe I really was a masochist. I needed another *mojito*. That way, I could have a drink and still have the lemon slice to rub all over my raw wound. It would probably hurt less than this conversation.

"Rick's another Elmwood Park success story. He owns ten car repair shops and two BMW dealerships," she said.

I stared. "I talked to him earlier. I thought he did auto repair."

She rolled her eyes. "I've told him a million times not to get his hands dirty. He's a CEO, not a mechanic. Not anymore. It's part of our problem. He needs to oversee the operations, but still he's out there, changing spark plugs."

A waitress in black slacks and a silly little white apron came by. "You ladies set for drinks?"

Jen waved her empty martini glass. "Get me two more cosmos, will you?"

"Not for me, I've been drinking rum," I said.

"The two cosmos are for me," Jen said, looking peeved at my interruption. "This girl hasn't been around in ages. I figure I'd better get my drinks lined up."

The "girl" in question was about our age, and Jen didn't notice her eyes squint into little slits. The waitress turned the little slits to me. "What can I get you, then?"

"Rum and diet Coke," I said. Diet because sugar would make the alcohol go straight to my head. Jen's cosmos certainly seemed to have affected her. At PeeBee's my girlfriends and I don't hesitate to cut each other off, or to confiscate car keys, either. I didn't qualify for that post in

Jen's world, although I wondered how she'd gotten to Scooters. Briefly, but I wondered.

The waitress left with our order. I didn't think we'd see our drinks before the end of the evening; Jen didn't exactly encourage good service.

The second she was out of earshot Jen grabbed my arm again. "That's what I brought you up here to talk about."

"The service?"

"No. Rick and me. I don't know how to break it to the guy. He's crazy about me, but—" She stopped and started chewing her lip, staring at her French manicure.

It's just as well. All I could hear was a buzzing in my head, from "He's crazy about me" on. The table in front of us was low slung, made out of some dark wood. It wasn't bolted down. Maybe I could brain her with it.

I stood up. "Thanks for talking to me, Jen. It's been edifying, but I've got to run."

"But I wasn't finished."

"Catch me later, then." *If you can,* I added silently.

"Sit down, this is important." She grabbed my dress and tugged.

"Let go." I'd had it with her. "I said I'd talk to you later."

Tears filled her eyes. This was so unexpected that I stopped trying to pry my dress loose from her fingers.

She whispered hoarsely, "My husband doesn't know."

"Know what?"

"Sit down."

I sat. She was drunk, but she was also upset. A teeny-weeny, mean part of me was really glad. The rest of me put on a concerned face.

"Rick and I got married when he came back from college, after his father died. He loved me so much. Still does. It's that puppy dog kind of love, you know? And he wants kids." She shuddered. "So it's really hard on me."

"Sounds tough," I said. I was all choked up too. Different reason.

"So I met this guy, Chip Alstead. He teaches tennis at the Y. And he's so buff, you know? Really takes care of himself. He understands me."

I nodded, thinking that Rick didn't deserve to be treated like this. Hell, I didn't deserve to be treated like this. Dorothy Kalucheck owed me one.

"Chip knows the real me, more than Rick ever did, even after seven years of marriage."

"Why are you telling me this? Do you think it should be part of the film?"

"I had to tell someone, and everyone else here knows me. Although come to think of it, maybe it would make a good part of your movie. Star-crossed lovers." She hugged herself. "Do you think I should tell Rick?"

"I can't tell you what to do. I'm not an attorney or a psychologist. Are you going to stop seeing Chip?"

Her eyes widened. "No, I love him. Well, sort of. He's great in bed. He's got lots of money, too."

TMI, I thought. *Way too much information*. It made me wonder how Rick's performance rated. I was not going to ask.

"He acts rich, too, instead of hanging out with poor peo-ple and writing poetry."

I straightened. Rick still wrote poetry? My heart, calmed after my initial fear, started thumping hard again.

"It doesn't matter, either way," she said. "I've got the pa-pers filled out, and my lawyer's filing for a divorce on Mon-day."

My emotions had taken a beating, and now they'd been tossed into a blender. Divorce meant Rick would be free. But what did I care? I was here for a weekend.

I stood up again. "Seems you've resolved your situa-tion," I said. "I need to talk to some other folks. I'll see you around."

She seemed to ignore me, staring across the room, a lit-tle smile on her lips. I glanced toward where she was look-ing. The guy headed our way had to be Chip Alstead. He was Ken to her Barbie, all blond highlights and rippling muscles, with the kind of definition you can only get at the gym. Nothing like Rick, who was rock hard from work, and dark as a gypsy.

Heading toward the stairs I passed the waitress, her tray loaded with drinks, including two cosmos. I tossed a ten on her tray, took my drink, and wished Jen a colossal headache tomorrow.

Downstairs, Ted the bowling alley manager grabbed my elbow. "Come on, Dorothy, let's boogie." He started to tug me toward the dance floor. I'd been pulled around enough.

"Oh, no, please. I don't dance." I tried to pry his fingers loose. He wasn't gripping me hard, but he was tenacious.

"Sure you do."

The loudspeakers started to blare "Rhythm Dancer."

Someone yelled, "Electric Glide," and seats all around emptied as my former classmates turned into hopping, gyrating, cowboy animatronics. I gave up and started to dance next to Ted, trying vainly to keep up with the shimmying and walking in step. Ted was surprisingly good, and I told him so.

"Marching band, after I wrecked my knee junior year," he yelled over the deafening music. "I played the clarinet." Honestly, it explained a lot.

As we turned and swayed in unison toward the back of the room, I caught a glimpse of a rawboned blonde talking to Alma by the front door.

My heart pounded, not from fear, but from apprehension. If Alma was talking to Dorothy, I'd just walk right past them and hail a cab. Who me? Chicken? You bet. The old, nonconfrontational Cali had leaped to life again.

Except for Rick and Sue Ann, no one had recognized me, but it was two too many. I realized that I was planning an escape route, and it made me stop. I was back on the edge of the dance floor, where bad dancing held sway.

Twenty years from now when the survivors met again, arthritis might keep some of them on the sidelines, or at least calm some of the offbeat flailing that was going on. For now, good taste took a beating as my classmates boogied. The Electric Glide was beyond the skills of a lot of the folks there, probably more to do with alcohol consumption than lack of dance ability.

I was no dancing queen, but I'd picked up some low-key moves in New York, enough to get me through dancing situations without looking like an idiot. A little shuffle, a hip swivel, a shoulder roll, and I looked nonchalant and sophisticated, if no actual dance steps were involved. My Cuban DNA had somehow omitted the Cuban rhythm gene, and I tried not to show off what I didn't have.

I was close enough to the front doors to see the wreaths of smoke from the exiled tobacco addicts. Alma stood by the waiter station podium at the front door, speaking to the tall blond woman.

Kalucheck, I was sure of it. My party was over, not that I'd had any fun. I wished Sue Ann had told me what the filmmaker looked like.

I danced on, trying to keep the woman in view. If any accusatory glares came my way, I was ready to vanish. The line dance turned out to be a pretty good hiding place.

Warm hands encircled my waist, growing hotter as body heat penetrated the thin silk of my dress. I glanced to my side, but Ted had boogied into a different line.

"You didn't used to dance, but baby, look at you now." The words were spoken next to my ear, hot breath caressing my jaw. I didn't have to turn to know who'd spoken. Knowing that he was married didn't keep my body from reacting. I felt my nipples harden, and my knees felt weak.

I forced myself to keep moving. To the right, to the left, swivel my hips. Except that the hip swivel brought my ass up against him as he danced close behind me. *Basta*.

I turned around. He was laughing, enjoying the silliness

around him. His hands stayed at my waist, forcing me to lift my arms. Curious eyes turned our way. Someone was bound to recognize me. I had to lay low, not make a spectacle of myself. *Basta ya.* Enough.

"Why did you stop?" He didn't seem concerned.

"Let's go somewhere private," I said. My voice, pitched higher so that it would carry over the noise of the dance floor, rang out in the sudden silence. The song had ended.

The dancers' wide eyes went from me to Rick and back again. This was just as good as a fat cheerleader, as far as they were concerned. Ricky Lake—caliber drama on the reunion dance floor.

Laughter pealed from the bar. Jen staggered to the edge of the dance floor, a cosmopolitan in each hand. She sipped from one.

"Gotta hand it to you, Rick, you make it too easy."

Rick's face looked like a granite carving. "Jen, you're drunk."

"Damn straight. I'm drunk, and you're putting the moves on Dorothy Kalucheck." She laughed again.

"You're wrong," he said quietly. He reached forward to take one of her drinks, but she held it back, out of his reach. He would have had to rub against her to get it. Instead, he stood back and dropped his arm.

Jen's drunken smile turned cruel. "Is he good, Dorothy? Did he get you there?"

"Nothing's happened, Jen. I was just upstairs with you. Remember what we talked about?" I kept my voice level, but loud enough that everyone else could hear, too.

Her eyes focused on me, and her smile faltered. As I'd hoped, she was remembering that she confessed her divorce plans to me. She frowned.

"That was confidential, right?"

"Of course, it was," Alma said, sweeping her friend up in her arms and moving her off the dance floor. "Everyone dance, it's still party time!" She shot me a look and jerked her head sideways. *Follow me.*

"Excuse me, Rick. I'll be right back." I hurried after them, wondering what in the world I'd gotten myself into.

Alma had stuffed Jen into a booth and was bullying a waitress into bringing black coffee. Jen had collapsed into the booth, her head lolling back, eyes half-opened, and a triumphant smile on her face.

"Gotcha," she said. "Weren't you surprised, Kalucheck? Screwing Rick. Ha."

"I sure was surprised, Jen. What made you say that?"

"Shush, Jen, you don't have to answer." She turned to me. "Dorothy—I can call you that, right?"

I nodded.

"Dorothy, Jen's under a lot of pressure. She's not herself tonight. I'm sure I can trust you not to use this to make some kind of point in your documentary."

"I can't promise anything, Alma."

Her eyes widened. She hadn't expected me to say no to her. "Well," she said, her smile faltering. "Well."

"I'll talk to you later. I still have that list you gave me." I gave her a little wave, turned on my Jimmy Choos, and walked back to the other room. Rick quickly turned and pretended to talk to Zack at the bar.

"Too late," I said. "I know you were eavesdropping."

"All taken care of?" he asked. His eyes held a million questions, but he kept them to himself. Discreet, unlike his wife. I corrected the thought. Soon to be ex-wife.

Rick didn't know, and it wasn't my place to tell him, but the words were like poison ivy in my throat. Itchy and toxic. I longed to get them out.

Chapter Six

I was only worried about you, beautiful." His hands, large and capable, were at my waist, fingers splayed, pressing my ribs and holding me in place. I wanted to stay there and enjoy the feeling, but I was aware of being watched, and that the bitch queen was only thirty feet away and would enjoy catching us like this.

Beautiful. He'd called me beautiful. My heart lurched. "Jen's just drunk. Alma's got it under control."

Sue Ann walked by, then stopped, eyes fixed on Rick's hands at my waist.

"Well, you two didn't waste any time getting reacquainted," she said.

"We have a lot of catching up to do," Rick said.

"Hush, both of you," I said.

Sue Ann laughed and moved on.

I watched her disappear into the crowd. "She recognized me earlier. She's been to my shows in New York."

"Ah, I see. She can tell everyone who you really are." He grinned. "Like that's a sin."

"You don't get it, Rick. I'm supposed to be this Kalucheck woman."

"Right, but you're not, so Sue Ann is actually a problem, because she knows that you're a real success, not a phony, but that you're a phony, because you're hiding your real success. Did I get that right?"

"Are you drunk?"

"Nope. Are you?"

"No, of course not." I remembered the bet made by my friends back home in the Bronx.

"Then why keep your success a secret? I'd be bragging all over the place." He looked at the crowd of thirty-somethings that now filled the bar. "Want me to make an announcement? I'll brag for you."

"Don't you dare."

I followed him back around the bar and stopped myself from wringing my hands. Why still pretend to be Dorothy Kaluchek? Why be scared of two average women? I was disappointed at my lack of courage—okay, my knee-knocking fear—but it didn't make it any less real. I was here to get over it.

It didn't help that Rick was standing very close, filling my senses. The scent of his leather jacket mixed with a soapy, just-showered aroma and a hint of pure man. My libido, at war with my cowardice, offered a mutually agreeable solution. Escape. Well, escape and sex, except that he didn't know about Jen. He thought he was still happily married.

"Let's go upstairs and talk."

His eyebrows climbed. "What's upstairs? First you want to know if I'm drunk, then you want to drag me upstairs." He shook his head, his eyes wide with feigned innocence. "Cali, are you trying to seduce me?"

"Get over yourself," I said, laughing. But the laugh didn't sound sincere. It sounded nervous as hell. "And don't call me—that name."

Two women pushed past us, recounting a story about their junior year cheerleading tryouts.

It occurred to me that time might be my best revenge. The girls who had tormented me in high school had fallen, hard, from their pedestals. The cheerleader goddesses were Wal-Mart moms, wearing enough eyeliner and dark shadow to supply a Goth nightclub for a month. I couldn't say the same about the guys. Then, I'd been invisible to them, and now they were invisible to me.

Except for Rick. He had come to the school library every afternoon to do homework. When he tired of math or chemistry, he'd lean on the counter and talk. Once, he'd looked for me and found me shelving next to my book-laden cart. My heart still pounds, thinking about it.

When I noticed the books he'd chosen to check out, he put a forefinger to his lips, requesting my silence, and touched that fingertip to my lips. It was intimate, and the warmth of his finger on my mouth featured in my fantasies to this day. Not to mention what happened later.

The bartender put another *mojito* before me, unasked. He met my eyes and smiled, then spoke to Rick. "Hey, man. Can I get you a drink?"

He nodded. "Whatever you've got on draft, Zack." He gestured toward the departing bartender. "His older brother works at my garage."

"So the garage is yours now?" No need to tell him that Jen had filled me in.

His eyes darkened. "Dad died five years ago."

"I'm sorry. He was a nice guy." My hand moved to touch him lightly, as if to reinforce my sympathy.

He watched my finger touch him and draw back. "Thank you," he said.

I couldn't tell whether he was thanking me for the touch or the expression of sympathy.

"So, where are you now?" he asked. "Paris? Milan?" A beer appeared in front of him.

"I work in New York."

"As in the city?" He reached into his pocket, withdrew a slim wallet, and placed a couple of bills on the bar. Zack swept them up as he walked by.

"As in the city."

"You one of those bridge and tunnel people?"

I rolled my eyes. "You're pretty snobby for someone from Elmwood Park, Illinois. I live in the Bronx."

He frowned.

"It's not all Fort Apache and burnt-out buildings, Rick.

I live in a really nice neighborhood. Trees, houses, friendly neighbors."

A lazy smile crawled across his face. The kind that used to make me stop breathing. I inhaled. Just making sure.

"Sounds like here. Like home," he said, drawing my hand into his. It felt really good.

I glanced around nervously, sure someone would notice, but the dancing had degenerated further. I didn't recognize the mob's steps anymore.

"For me, home is New York. Last time we spoke, you wanted to leave Elmwood Park."

Rick pushed a hand through his hair, giving him an uncharacteristic, nervous look. Or maybe it was anger, so in keeping with his high school persona.

"I did want to leave, but not as far as New York. After college, I was offered a teaching position in Cleveland. Almost got there, too."

"Was that when your father got sick?"

He nodded, his mouth a grim, straight line. "Yeah. I took care of him, and then when he died, and I tried to close the shop, I realized that his employees would be out of work. Some of them had been working for my old man since I was a little kid."

"I'm sorry." His compassion had kept him from selling the shop. I should have known.

"I figured that if I had to keep the place, I may as well make it profitable. Dad wasn't one for computers or marketing ideas, so it didn't take much to make a big difference in the bottom line."

I laughed.

"What?" He scowled at me.

"You. Saying 'bottom line.' It doesn't fit the kid I knew."

"It does, believe me. I live and breathe the bottom line."
He stared into space. "You know, I never thought I'd end up
like this. You're right. I wanted to leave Elmwood Park. But
I play a role in this community. People look up to me." He
shook his head. "I never thought that would be important,
but it is."

I bit my lip, thinking of how little I enjoyed my success.
Fulfillment eluded me, except for my work on Cali E Designs, which wasn't successful. Yet.

"I turned Dad's little shop into a chain, and added two
car dealerships," Rick said. "People look up to me."

I pondered this new Rick, evaluating his clothes, shoes,
and haircut. I didn't know why I'd missed it earlier, since he
was dressed expensively. He didn't act or dress like an un-
derachiever. Somehow, it made me sad.

"I love your new look, but I sort of miss your Mohawk,"
I said.

Overhead, Culture Club's Boy George warbled, "Do
You Really Want To Hurt Me."

He ran his fingers through his hair. "It was cool in the
summer, but I don't think my customers would understand.
Besides, there's a new generation of kids getting into the
old music. They'd think I was strange. A has-been."

"You're hardly old," I said, irritated. If he was old, what
did that make me?

His smile said he knew exactly what I was thinking.

"Let's go upstairs. You were there earlier, weren't you? What's up there?"

I shrugged. "Pool tables, video games. The restrooms are up there, too."

"Ever shoot pool?"

My eyes widened. "Me?"

"What was I thinking? Little miss dress designer wouldn't be caught dead with a cue in her hands. Come on, I'll teach you."

Why ruin his enthusiasm with the truth? I kept my mouth shut and climbed the stairs, admiring his backside and ignoring the weight of the stares drilling into my back. I was probably being sized up as a possible Jerry Springer contestant. First Jen, then Rick. What's that Kalucheck woman up to?

The pool tables were all in use, so we strolled around the room, joining the knots of people playing video games.

When we'd made a circuit of the entire room, Rick headed purposefully toward one of the corners, I followed, and was surprised when he opened a door marked EXIT. Inside, narrow concrete steps led up and down. A bare lightbulb provided enough light to read a small metal sign on the wall. It read ROOFTOP ACCESS, with an arrow pointing up.

"Let's see what kind of view we've got from up here." Rick started up the stairs, then returned and took my hand in his. "Come on, California. It's an adventure."

"It's probably against the law to go up there."

"I didn't see a sign saying so, did you?" He tugged on my hand, but I didn't need convincing. We almost skipped up the short flight, and then we were through the door, and onto a gravel-topped flat roof. I took my shoes off and picked my way over the gravel. It was windy up here, and colder than it had been earlier.

A small park bench and round glass-topped patio table with four wrought-iron chairs were proof that this was a regular destination, maybe for the restaurant staff.

Rick dragged the bench close to the roof edge and we sat side by side, feet propped on the low wall. The view wasn't so great, just more buildings and the night sky, but it was quiet. Rick pulled me close, his arm around me, and I snuggled into his warm, masculine chest.

I shivered a little and he sat up, releasing me briefly while he took his jacket off and draped it over us. For a moment after, we enjoyed the silence layered over the street sounds and faint music that rose from below.

"Why did you come back, Cali?"

His question took me by surprise. "The reunion, of course."

"You didn't come back for the tenth."

"I wasn't ready. But this year, I wanted to find out what happened to everyone. To you."

"Then why pretend to be someone else?" He shifted in his chair. Our knees touched, and he didn't move his away, so I didn't move mine, either. He reached for my hand.

"That was an accident," I said. "I was mistaken for the filmmaker and played along."

"How's it going to end? Are you going to 'fess up?"

I shook my head. "Maybe. It's been a surprising night so far." I tried not to sound grumpy about it. "Actually, I came back to confront Alma and Jen, but I changed my mind."

"So you said." He looked puzzled. "What did you want to talk about that was so scary?"

"You know, what they said about us in the cafeteria at lunch. On senior picture day."

He shook his head. "Us? You mean you and me?"

I started to tell him, then stopped. He didn't remember, and it would sound silly, petty almost, after all these years. How could someone be upset for fifteen years about a taunt in the cafeteria line? I had to solve my own problem, and I had to hurry before the night dissolved into total chaos. Then again, it might be too late.

I stood up, a little unsteady in my bare feet. I stepped away from the roof's edge and walked to the other side of the bench, aware of his eyes on me. "I need to go."

He stood, too. "Please don't go. Ask me why *I* came to the reunion."

"Because you're a pillar of the community?"

"Ask me."

His eyes were warm, and he looked straight into mine. I felt exposed, but not afraid. "Okay, why did you come?"

"Because there's something I never got to do in high school, and I've thought about it for fifteen years." His face moved closer.

"Yeah?" My voice sounded thin and breathy. "What?"

"This." And then his lips closed over mine, and we were in each other's arms again.

Chapter Seven

Rick led me back to the bench, still kissing me. His lips moved lightly over my face, then down to my collarbone. He moved aside the leather jacket that was draped over my shoulders and gently bit my bare skin, catching the thin strap of my dress in his teeth. My breath was coming in ragged pants, from anticipation as to what he'd do next, and from restless desire.

Rick was here, with me. I never thought I'd live out this fantasy, so even if it was just for tonight, I was going to enjoy every second.

Rick muttered hoarse endearments as he caressed my back, kissing my shoulders, returning to my mouth, getting closer to my breasts. I was dizzy with rum and lust.

The thought that I needed to be careful flitted through my head, but I didn't allow it to distract me. My friends had outfitted my purse with enough contraceptives that neither prospect concerned me.

"Cali," he sighed. "You are just as I imagined you." He rubbed his lips across my cheek, my chin, then reclaimed my lips, which felt swollen now from all the attention.

I tugged on his shirt, and he stopped my hands, trapping my wrists against my waist. His lips traveled up my shoulder, nibbled at my throat, and worked their way back to my mouth.

"Are you sure about this, Cali? We can stop."

"Are you insane?" I whispered. "We can't stop now." I pulled my hands free and tugged on his shirt, exposing a muscular chest. I put my hands on his flat stomach and ran them up to his chest.

His turn to moan. He pulled me close, rubbing against me. The music from downstairs filtered through the windows below, providing a passionate beat.

Behind me, the door opened. We jumped apart, and I scrambled to straighten out my dress.

"Oops, sorry." The woman in the doorway didn't move away. Her mascaraed eyes watched us both avidly, as if we were putting on a public show. I guess we were, now.

"Sara, go back downstairs. And close the door," Rick said. He seemed unperturbed, damn it.

"Whoa, it's the documentary chick," Sara the Snoop said.

"No kidding?" A man's voice came from over her shoulder.

His head popped out through the doorway. We interrupting something?" His face brightened. "Hey, there's a table out here. You allowed to smoke out here?"

Rick put his hand on my shoulder. "Cali—"

"I'm Dorothy," I hissed.

His eyes narrowed. "Has it occurred to you that this charade is ridiculous and unnecessary?"

"Well, it's *my* ridiculous and unnecessary life you're messing with." I pushed past Sara and her leering companion and down the crowded steps, shoes in hand. I wished I'd worn flats. *Flats and black glasses,* my inner demon snickered. *Flats and a unibrow.*

Rick did not understand. Fueled by embarrassment and righteous anger, I headed downstairs to the bar. It was probably less crowded than the upstairs room, where the action seemed centered on the pool tables.

I sat on one of the vacant barstools, and Zack put a glass in front of me.

"A *mojito* for the *señorita,*" he said.

"Could you make it just Coke?"

His eyebrows rose. "Sure, babe." He swept the glass away.

"Did you really go to Elmwood Park High? I was told to interview you."

"No. But if it gets me bigger tips, I'll say I want to Harvard. I don't care." He grinned as he placed a fresh glass on the bar.

A tentative sip proved it was just Coke. Relieved, I drank half of it. Sexual frustration obviously made me thirsty. I glanced toward the stairs. No sign of Rick. He was still upstairs.

I cursed myself for checking the stairs every few seconds, hoping to see Rick. I should just march up there and tell him what I wanted. And I would, as soon as I figured it out. I put my shoes on and tried to stand up. *Ouch.* Off they came again, which was just as well. I didn't want to ruin them by getting the insides dirty.

A moment later I felt Rick's hand on my shoulder. Above us Taylor Dane pleaded for her lover to "Tell It To My Heart." Yeah, right.

He sat on the stool next to me. "Sorry I took so long. I got held up by a little situation." His face looked grim.

"Is something wrong?"

He shrugged and leaned forward. "Tell me about Jen and Alma, Cali. You said they were responsible for some awful event, but from your description it was embarrassing, not life-changing."

"I guess when you're eighteen and shy, embarrassment that profound *is* life-changing." It had certainly hurt enough.

"So you went to college and really changed your life." He reached out and tucked my hair behind my ear, his finger tickling my jaw, warm against my skin. I shivered.

"I wouldn't go so far as to say that I owe Alma and Jen my gratitude for triggering the change," I said defensively. "I've worked hard to get where I am today."

He nodded. "I'm sure. But I see the same Cali that I knew. Smart and funny. You could look at someone and size them up in a minute." He laughed softly. "Too bad you couldn't do the same in the mirror."

I straightened. "What's that supposed to mean?"

His right shoulder came up in a familiar half shrug. "Nothing against you. I guess we're all unsure of ourselves, until the moment comes when you see the path clearly. The right choice is obvious."

"Is that how you felt when your father died?"

"Not at first. I rebelled, but yeah. Zack's family invited me to dinner after Dad died, and it was an epiphany. I realized how much my old man meant to them. The jobs, the station. And his old customers all came by just to tell me how they trusted him with their cars." He was silent for a moment, staring into space.

I put my hand over his. "So you stayed."

He nodded. "And your path was clear, too, wasn't it?"

"Actually, I sort of fell into my career. It's exciting, but I'm still looking for—" I started to say satisfaction, but the word had taken on new meaning tonight.

I remembered who I was. Forthright Cali. Blunt New Yorker and assertive businesswoman. I also remembered that Rick was still married, even if it was over. What was I doing? I put my hand back on the bar.

"Why didn't you think it was worth mentioning that you're married to Jen?"

His brows knit, then smoothed out. "I should have. I was planning to, but you looked just the same, and I wanted you to see me the same way. You may as well know what happened upstairs just now. Jen was making out on the couch with some guy. It was embarrassing for everyone, not just me. She saw me and went nuts."

"She does that so well," I murmured.

"No kidding. She also said she's filing for a divorce." He ran his hand through his hair. "She wanted me to feel bad, but all I could feel was relieved. We should have split up long ago."

"And you didn't think you needed to tell me?"

"It's not worth mentioning. It's over." He braced an arm on the wall above my head, all sexy and Brando-like.

In that moment I realized how much I'd changed. I didn't need to confront Jen or Alma. And I didn't care that he hadn't told me. We both yearned to go back to that moment when there was no Jen, when it was just Rick and Cali in the library, and Rick had said that he wanted me, that he thought I was beautiful. Those were the words that had changed my life. If he thought I was beautiful, anything was possible.

"Remember I agreed with you when you said Jen was responsible for the worst day of your life?" he asked. "Well, for me it was the worst seven years of my life. I think I've got you beat."

"I'm surprised you survived." He was close enough for his intoxicating scent to affect me, but I kept edging away. "I guess we have a lot of catching up to do."

His face drew closer. "Yes, on so many levels. I want to know what you read, what you eat. What's your favorite food?"

I laughed. It was so off-topic. "Food? It's a toss-up. Mussels marinara and Cuban-style black beans and rice. Yours?"

"Prime rib and baked ziti," he said. "I'll have to add Cali's skin to favorite tastes."

My internal thermostat, already cranked high at his closeness, ratcheted up another five notches. I swallowed, remembering his kisses, the feel of his hot breath on my bare skin.

"Speechless, Cali?" His tone was teasing, but his eyes were serious.

"What can I say?" My voice was hoarse. I swallowed again, but it didn't help. "This is crazy, Rick. Teasing each other serves no purpose. On Sunday, I'll head back to New York and my life, and you'll go back to yours."

He leaned in further, and his lips grazed my cheek. "Who's teasing? Don't you wonder what it would be like, Cali? Didn't you think about this?"

I turned my face, catching his lips with mine. Our kiss was long, lips barely touching, prolonging the moment; until finally we deepened it, tongues exploring, and our bodies closed the space between us.

Lost in the kiss, in the feel of his body pressed against mine, I didn't care who saw. I wanted Rick, and he wanted me. Sunday seemed very far away.

A commotion on the stairs drew our attention. It sounded as if a fight had started upstairs and was moving downstairs. A couple of people jumped down the last few stairs and immediately turned around. Not anxious to get away, just angling for a better view.

Chip Alstead tumbled headfirst down the carpeted treads and landed in a crumpled heap on the landing. Before anyone could check to see if he was okay, he leaped up and headed toward the bar's door. His shirt was torn and a bloody scratch marred one side of his smooth chest.

He didn't glance to either side as he strode out, banging the door open with the flats of his palms. The door swung shut silently behind him.

"And stay out," Jen screeched. She sounded like a cartoon demon. I turned, astonished, to see if she'd sprouted a tail and horns. Her hair was mussed, but other than swaying to stay upright, she seemed fine.

She looked around proudly at her audience, which had grown since Chip had run outside.

"See, I told you I'd get him. No one screws over Jen Petersen."

Alma appeared at her elbow and started trying to tug her into the other room. "Come on, Jen. You've had one too many."

"No, I haven't," she shouted. She spotted me and weaved over. "Rick and Dorothy. How sweet. You two book a hotel room for the night, or you just going to do it on the bar?"

Rick cut his eyes toward me, which I took to be a nonverbal warning to be still. I was fine with that.

"Come on, Jen. Let's get you home."

"No way. I want to talk to Dorothy."

"Get her out of here," Zack commanded, and Alma grabbed her friend and led her away.

I watched, remembering a day when I was eighteen, standing in line at the cafeteria, shuffling forward with the crowd, waiting for the servers to toss overcooked broccoli and stiff chicken fingers onto my tray.

Alma and Jen had come straight to me, which was unusual enough to make me look up. They were giggling, falling into each other with laughter.

"Cali's in love," they'd chanted. "Cali's in love with Rick."

Then Jen had reached out and whispered, "I heard you two have sex in the library all the time."

I'd stood there, shocked and mortified, wondering if it would be all over school. Rumors travel fast through school corridors. My barely there romance with Rick would probably be over before lunch period was done.

Jen had smiled triumphantly, then smacked her hand into the bottom of my tray, sending my salad and opened carton of milk sailing up and onto my white blouse. It was Picture Day, and I'd hidden, crying and stained with milk and Thousand Island dressing, in the art department's faraway girls' bathroom while everyone had their photos taken. I'd vowed never to cry in front of them again, and I hadn't.

From that moment, Jen and Alma were my enemies. I could still hear the laughter that chased me down the hall. Not just Alma and Jen. Everyone had laughed. I went from invisibility to senior class joke with a flip of Jen's hand.

Just remembering made my cheeks burn, and the heat made me sympathize with Sue Ann. Strange how something that had happened fifteen years before could still cause a strong physical reaction. Like Rick's fingers, I thought, although that was a totally different feeling.

Rick's mouth on mine, his fingers caressing my face, the heat of his body through our clothes, his hardness pressed against my back. Now *that* was a memory. A definite keeper, even though nothing had happened after that. Graduation day came, and my parents flew me to Miami for a huge family reunion.

Thinking of him made me restless. I wondered where he was, and whether we could finish what we'd started. Moments like that were impossible to recreate. An oppressive sadness came over me.

I slid from the barstool and went to the other room. The floor was even more disgusting in my bare feet.

The room was crowded with women, friends of Alma and Jen standing around the booth where Alma hiccuped and mopped her eyes. Crammed into the booth with them were several others, including the woman from my hotel, the flu lady. She looked better, although it was hard to tell if her eyes were bright with curiousity or fever.

I went to them, wondering what to say.

Alma looked up, and her face crumpled when she saw who stood over her. Jen, on her left, sat straighter and stared at me warily.

"Alma—" I started.

"Please," she said, voice choked. "Don't start. I don't know what I can say to make you keep this quiet. It's embarrassing enough that everyone saw. I wouldn't be surprised if it's in the papers tomorrow."

Jen put a consoling arm around her friend. She looked

up at me. "I'm sorry I let my feelings get carried away. Can you just forget everything that happened?"

"I wonder if I can," I said. "It's not as if I thought about it all the time, but it's not something you just forget, either." I glanced back at Sue Ann, who was talking to the big raw-boned blonde. The woman turned to look at me and I realized it was Jane, the famous cook.

"I'm sure you're amused by all this," Jen said, voice tight. "But we're all parents, and business people. Consider the impact on our kids."

I must have looked as confused as I felt.

"Please, Dorothy," Alma pleaded.

"What?" The word came out of my mouth, but an echo came from the woman next to Alma.

"What did you say?" she said.

"Dorothy Kalucheck?" I asked, pretty sure of the answer.

"Yeah." Her eyes focused on me. "Hey, it's my Good Samaritan. Got an aspirin? My head is still pounding."

Alma and Jen looked from Dorothy to me.

"I thought you were Dorothy Kalucheck," Alma said, pointing at me. "If she's Dorothy, who are you?"

"I'm Cali Montalvo." I waited for her reaction. Her eyebrows rose, but she didn't immediately spit on the ground and throw up her fingers in an evil eye countersign. Beside her, Jen moved suddenly, as if startled.

"Cali?" She thought for a moment. "Oh, you worked in the library, right? Why did you say you were Dorothy?"

"I didn't. You did. I just didn't correct you." I swallowed

my pride. "I'm sorry I lied. I guess I wanted to know if anyone recognized me."

Alma shrugged. "I didn't, sorry. But you look great." She actually sounded sincere.

Jen's frown deepened. "No wonder Rick was all over you."

"Rick was all over her?" Alma looked me up and down. "Well, well." She stared down at my shoes, which dangled from my left hand. "Are your shoes Jimmy Choos? Can I try them on?" She stood up and I held them out.

"Does Rick know it's you?" Jen demanded. She stood, too. She was a lot taller than me, especially now that I was barefoot.

I stood straighter. "He recognized me right away. So did Sue Ann."

Alma looked across the room at her. "She was always observant. She's a journalist now, you know."

"She told me."

Alma steadied herself on the booth back as she slipped into my shoes. "Wow, they hurt. How can you wear them?"

I shrugged. "Practice. They don't hurt so much if you're used to wearing stilettos."

Alma giggled. "I have a pair of stilettos, but I wear them for five minutes max. And only for my husband."

I stared down at Alma's feet, crammed into my five-hundred-dollar shoes. Every woman needs a pair of sex-only shoes, but I felt faint at the vision that came to mind. Maybe I'd retire this pair.

Alma stepped out of my shoes. "Thanks. I can die happy."

"This is terrific stuff," Dorothy said.

"I thought I put you to bed," I said.

"I had a job to do. Had to get to the pre-reunion party," she said. "I feel like crap, though."

"She has the flu," I explained to Alma, ignoring Jen. I told her how I'd helped Dorothy to bed before coming to the party. "But we didn't do the name thing. I was in a rush to get here."

"Let's sit down. I'm exhausted," Alma said. She leaned her head back, wary eyes on Dorothy.

I sat in the booth next to my former archenemies.

"So explain again why you pretended to be Dorothy," Alma said, looking puzzled.

"Not that we mind," Jen said, whispering. "Since it means that the real Dorothy didn't really see what happened."

"She can hear every word you say, Jen." Alma looked disgusted with life.

"But she can't name names," Jen said confidently. "It'll be a footnote in the documentary. If she decides to do it," she added.

"I'd say a public marital meltdown makes a compelling story," I said.

"Nobody noticed, believe me," Jen said, waving a hand erratically. "They're all drunk."

"Speaking of compelling stories, there's the one about the fake Dorothy," Alma leaned forward. "Well?"

"It was because of you guys." I lowered my voice. I was close to resolving fifteen years' worth of angst, but I didn't want to share it with every female in our class.

"A practical joke?" Alma suggested, looking pissed off. I couldn't blame her. I'd had my fill of those tonight, too.

"No, it's because of what you guys did to me on Picture Day senior year."

Alma looked blank, but Jen's lips lifted at the corners in an evil smile.

"In the lunchroom," she said. "You were so funny."

Remembering brought a red flush to Alma's neck and face.

"Wow, Cali. I'd forgotten about that," she said. "I'm so sorry. Kids can be mean, can't they?"

"Yes, they can," I said. Interesting how she'd distanced herself, saying 'kids' instead of 'I.' At least she'd apologized. I turned to Jen.

She waved a hand in front of her. "Hey, no tearful confessions here, Cali."

"No apology, either, I see." I kept my eyes locked on hers. She looked away first.

"I didn't think it required an apology."

"Jen—," Alma said, frowning.

She turned. "Shut up, Alma. Just shut up. You can be such a wimp."

Alma stepped back, eyes wide.

"Whoa. I think Jen's going high school on us," Sue Ann said behind us.

I looked around. The women in the room were all intent on our conversation, especially Dorothy, who was taking notes furiously.

Jen stared at each of the women. "What are all of you

looking at?" Her chin lifted. "Oh, I get it. If I'm going high school, well you are, too. None of you is any different than Cali here. Expensive clothes, cheap insides."

"What is that supposed to mean?" I took a step closer. She didn't move, but I could see the pulse jumping in her scrawny neck. She was scared.

"Just that. You were nothing more than trash, always were. What you are now is just fashionable trash. But fashions change. I never knew what Rick saw in you. You were pathetic, *California*." She sneered my name, as if it were another insult.

I didn't know I'd slapped her until the sound echoed off the walls and my handprint was a red imprint on her cheek. I stared at it, horrified, and she stared back. Around us, women were leaping to their feet.

"Jen, oh my God—" I started to stretch out a hand, to say I was sorry, but never got the chance. She bared her teeth like an angry German shepherd and launched herself at me, knocking us both down onto Dorothy Kalucheck, who'd stood for a better view.

"Oh no, you don't, Jennifer Peterson." A hand grabbed Jen's blond hair and tugged back, hauling her to her feet. It was Alma, looking like the Italian Avenger.

"You are not screwing this up," she hissed, her eyes sliding down toward me. I wondered what she meant, until I realized she wasn't looking at me. She was looking at Dorothy Kalucheck, who was on the floor next to me, watching the proceedings with amusement.

I was helped to my feet, and except for the fact that

everyone had gotten a good look at my panties when my dress flew up, my dignity was intact.

Alma signaled to one of the guys in the other room, who frog-marched Jen toward the front door of Scooters.

I sat down next to Dorothy. Alma, who had watched Jen's removal, slipped in on her other side and started to apply damage control techniques. From Dorothy's disbelieving look, the spin wasn't working.

"Thank goodness we all grew up," I said. "Some of us just have a little extra baggage."

Alma's eyebrows lifted. "You can say that again. Jen always thought she was a little better than everyone else."

"Jen said something awful to me that day, Alma. She said she knew Rick and I were having sex in the library, and that was so not true. I was sure the whole school would think it was, though."

Alma's expression was thoughtful. "Rick really liked you. It drove Jen crazy. She was used to getting what she wanted, and the guy she wanted spent all his time with . . . you."

"With a unibrowed geek?"

She looked embarrassed and nodded, sliding in next to Dorothy. "You've changed a lot, Cali." She turned to Dorothy. "Maybe it would be better if you picked another school for your movie. I mean, you feel sick and all. Maybe you should go home and rest."

Dorothy cackled like the Wicked Witch of the West. "Are you kidding? This is rich. There's enough material here for three films."

Alma sighed and leaned her head back against the upholstered booth back. "I know."

She seemed vulnerable, and I spotted an opportunity to get the *la pura verdad*. The absolute truth. "Alma, why did Rick marry Jen?"

She moved restlessly. "Because he came back into town when his Dad was dying, and he was sad and lonely and pissed off, and Jen was persistent. When he got his head together again, he saw he'd married a woman who never left her living room except to go to the mall. Jen's not like you."

My chest tightened. Jen had lied. No surprise there, but for once I was glad. He really didn't love her.

Chapter Eight

Rick was outside, shoulders hunched against the chill. I still had his jacket.

"You look like you could use a drink," I said.

He lifted a rueful eyebrow. "I may never drink again."

I took his hand and squeezed it. "Are you going to be okay?"

"Sure. My divorce announcement could've been more private, but at least everyone will have plenty to talk about at the reunion tomorrow."

A taxi driver at the curb popped out of his car. "You guys coming or what?"

"You called a taxi?"

"Yes," he murmured, fingering the strap of my dress. "I've

had a couple of drinks, and I keep an apartment in the city."

"Is that an invitation?" I laughed and his arms went around me. I felt at home again. "What is it about you," I asked. "I feel so comfortable when you hold me."

He pulled back and looked at me, and for once he wasn't smiling. "I think I know what you mean. It feels like being in your most comfortable chair, right?"

I lifted an eyebrow. "Not the most romantic image, but yes, that's it. And not just the chair. The chair, and a really good book that you can't wait to read."

"Anticipation," he said, agreeing. "Comfort and anticipation." He nuzzled my throat. "What does that mean, do you think?"

"Fifteen wasted years," I said.

He laughed and stepped back. "Right on the money, California." He ducked my playful slap and danced away, keeping out of reach, then bowed by the cab.

"Your carriage, milady."

"I'm not sure," I said. I glanced back. Scooters' upstairs windows were still filled with people dancing and shooting pool. I never got to beat Rick at eight ball.

"Let's get away from this place," he said, his gaze following mine. "I've had enough for one night."

"First sense you've made in a while," I said.

He held the door for me, then frowned, noticing my bare feet.

"I'm not sure I'm ready for your apartment," I told him. "But you can come with me to my hotel room."

"I don't want to slink out of your hotel room in the morning. Come to my apartment. I've got a king-sized bed," he wheedled.

"I don't know." Sex was one thing, but getting cozy on his turf was giving up power. And had Jen slept there with him? I hated the image that came to mind.

"Three hundred-thread count Egyptian cotton bedsheets."

"Hmmm . . ."

"Huge whirlpool garden tub. Custom bath salts."

"Well—"

"What do you say, Cali? Come to my place. I'll treat you like a queen."

His eyes shone with sincerity, and something else. I looked away, unable to give it a name. I wanted him so much. Not for the sex, although so far it had been incredible, but because Rick Capaldi was like a piece missing from my soul, from my heart. A piece that I hadn't realized was missing until I was made whole.

"Okay, I'll come with you," I said. I wanted to spend every second I could in his company. Forty-eight hours left.

With a boyish whoop and a grin, he scooped me up into his arms and tucked me into the waiting cab.

I woke up at noon the next day, still aching from the intense pleasure of our lovemaking. Within seconds of walking into his apartment, I had been back in his arms. I thought it might be awkward to start again, but it seemed natural, as if our bodies were made to fit perfectly together.

He moaned, and pulled me close again, rubbing against me. He'd turned on music, a jazzy salsa that provided a counterpoint to our heartbeats.

"I want to feel your skin against mine," he murmured, and pulled up the hem of my dress. It floated over my head and onto the floor next to his truly huge bed.

The three little shirt buttons by his neck thwarted me for only a couple of seconds. I undid them, blessing the manufacturer as each easily slipped free of its buttonhole. He pulled it over his head while I undid the waistband of his pants.

My bra had somehow come unfastened, and Rick's hands slipped up my torso to cup my freed breasts. His fingers caressed my nipples, and they saluted him in appreciation.

"It better not be fifteen years before the next time," he growled. He pulled my bra off and tossed it aside, then dipped his head to allow his tongue to flick the engorged tips of my breasts. "You are so beautiful, Cali. I never felt so close to anyone else, when we were kids. This is what it would have been like if you never left."

Right, I thought, not believing him, but this was my fantasy, too, and I was going to feed my dreams while I could. I rubbed my hands on his bare back, enjoying the muscles that roiled under his smooth skin.

His arms tightened around my shoulders, and he picked me up, surprising me. He'd done that earlier, too. I'd never been carried before and the sense of powerlessness was frightening. I buried my face in his chest, and he held me tightly for a moment, as if he didn't want to let me go, then carried me to his huge bed and gently laid me down. My senses were overwhelmed with the combination of his scent and mine, the perfect blend of ourselves. I wanted to cry.

Rick knelt at the foot of the bed, admiring me, as if I were a buffet laid out for his pleasure. His eyes half-closed from desire, he stood, hooked his thumbs in the waistband of his pants and pulled them down.

The sight took my breath away. In that moment I so understood sexual addiction. I could do this every day for the rest of eternity. When he had discarded his socks and shoes, I arched my back, expecting more yummy attention on my breasts, but he went lower, stopping only to swipe my belly with his tongue before he hit his true target.

I almost added my voice to the night's chorus, gritting my teeth and groaning instead. "Stop," I panted. "Rick, too much."

The feelings were so intense I thought I'd pass out. I pulled on his hair, trying to get him to stop, but his tongue continued, exploring, stroking, and hitting true every time.

I felt my orgasm build, and cried out as it broke, a wave of pleasure that left me limp.

He rose and lay across me, his weight a soothing counterpoint to the lighter-than-air exhilaration he'd just caused.

After a moment I regained my voice. I didn't speak immediately, not because I didn't have anything good to say, but because I was afraid I'd babble.

"Rick. Wow." Okay, so wit eluded me just then.

His face was against my neck, and I heard a satisfied laugh. My hands traced nerveless fingers across his back, feeling his muscles, touching him lightly. I wanted to give him as much pleasure as he'd given me.

I wondered if he would have felt so strong or so manly when he was eighteen and I had first wanted him. I loved the rebel then, and didn't know enough about life to appreciate the person behind the façade they present to the world. And in high school, we're all about façades. This was the real Rick, grown up and full of life. Some things are worth waiting for, and sex with Rick was definitely on that list.

When he finally rose onto his elbows, the tip of him poised at the juncture of my legs, I looked into his eyes and gasped, not because he was big and hard and about to drive into my wetness, but because his eyes, the color of molten honey, were looking straight into mine. Suddenly, it was real, not fantasy.

I felt as if I could look into his eyes forever. I revised my sexual addiction decision. I could do this every day, forever, but only with Rick. I couldn't be this intimate with anyone else, ever.

We'd changed the sheets before sleeping, even though we could barely stay awake. The bed had been wet from sweat and lovemaking, but even in the new, crisp sheets, every bit as luxurious as Rick had promised, the musky smell of our lovemaking clung, like an aphrodisiac made only for us.

I stretched like a lazy cat, enjoying the feel of the soft sheets and down pillows. I turned over to look at Rick.

He slept on his back, arms over his head. His strong

profile was unchanged. I'd fallen in love with his Roman nose when I was sixteen, and now, at thirty-three, I fell in love all over again.

It was love, all right, and I was stupid to have put myself into this situation. I'd come here looking for Rick, looking for closure, and all I'd leave with was pain. We had no future, so any emotion I invested in Rick would be a hurtful waste.

I ran my fingertips lightly over his bare chest, twirling them in the thick hair between his nipples, which hardened into pinkish brown pebbles that needed to be kissed.

I leaned on one elbow and licked the closest one, flicking my tongue over the warm nub. A sigh ruffled my hair.

I looked up and met his eyes, warm and smiling.

"You can wake me up like that every day, if you want." His voice rumbled, low and sexy. His left arm pushed under and around me, pulling me against him.

I wanted to snuggle, but that could come later. "Make love to me," I said.

"Oh, yeah," Rick said. "Exactly what I had in mind."

"Making love" is a vague and euphemistic term. Rick and I had wild, aching, throbbing, orgasmic monkey sex.

We licked and sucked every bit of each other's bodies, exploring territory we'd only wondered about for fifteen years, and when we finally rested, side by side on our backs on his bedroom carpet, our calves and lower legs on his bed, we held hands.

"Cali, I'm part owner of this apartment building," he said, playing with my fingers.

I hummed, eyes closed.

"It would be perfect for an office for you. You could have one of the downstairs apartments. It's got an exclusive address; your business would be a fit for the neighborhood."

I opened my eyes. "What are you talking about?"

"Your design business. You said you were tired of doing someone else's designs. Sue Ann told me about your Cali E business. Hang your shingle here." He was on his side, his head held up on one hand, the other stroking me lightly.

"I'm not going back to Elmwood Park."

"Chicago's not a small town, Cali. You can be in Manhattan in two hours. Can't you email or fax your designs from here? Line up your distributors from here?"

I'd never thought about it. There was an immediacy to living in New York that I could not duplicate in Chicago, but everything he said was true. But—move back? I shook my head.

"I'd come to you, Cali, but I can't run my businesses long-distance. You can. Come home, Cali. Come to me."

I looked at him, handsome and disheveled, the sweat of our lovemaking glowing on his skin. In the low light he looked like a burnished god.

"I have to go back to Manhattan. That's where my life is."

He lay back down, staring at the ceiling. "I understand," he said. "I understand, but I don't accept it."

He rolled back over, and pulled me closer. With a moan, I surrendered, looking into his eyes as he entered me, our gazes locked even as our bodies found the rhythm.

This is as honest as it gets, I thought, and then he was in me, and I couldn't think anymore. Our bodies strained against each other, our faces cheek to cheek, and the feeling was incredible. I'd never felt such intimacy.

Sex had always been a lukewarm exercise, the few times I'd had the dubious pleasure. From now on it could only be a painful chore, because after today I would never have Rick, and Rick was the only one who had ever made me feel this way, who had ever gotten this close to my heart.

I felt my orgasm build, surprised again that it was even there, and held my breath, afraid I might frighten it off. But stroke after stroke, Rick drove me higher, until I grabbed his shoulders, tight, and jammed my mouth into his arm to keep from crying out loud. Then, the feelings too intense, I wrapped my legs around him to stop his movements. He didn't stop. His breathing grew ragged, and with strokes so deep they almost hurt, he came, too.

No one else had taken me this far, not my body, not my heart. The phone rang, and he shot me an apologetic look and answered, still panting.

He listened for a moment. "Okay, be right there." He hung up. "It's the shop on Cicero. I need to run out there. I can drop you off at your hotel so you can get ready for tonight."

Tonight. The reunion. Damn.

"Sure," I said, and started to gather my clothes. I bit my lip. Lovemaking this intense was supposed to be followed by tender words, gentle caresses. We'd had some of that, but this abrupt departure cheapened the moment.

It didn't help that I'd decided to leave. I couldn't stay, couldn't spend more time with Rick, followed by a painful good-bye.

It was ironic. I'd made my peace with Elmwood Park, and Rick, my sole friend fifteen years ago, my first love, was now the reason I had to go.

Chapter Nine

The nine o'clock flight to LaGuardia out of O'Hare would be crowded. I sat in the packed passenger lounge, wondering if my old school chums were over their hangovers.

I smiled as I remembered the crazy night, especially the finale. The smile faded as I thought of the future Rick and I would never have.

Maybe I'd email him in a couple of weeks—I'd picked up one of his cards from his dresser. I owed him an apology.

My row was called and I stood and trudged toward the jetway. Behind me a man muttered an oath. I glanced at the long, grim line behind me. Someone was making a scene, shoving his way forward. A security guard came out from behind the gate attendants' desk.

I hoped it wasn't a nut. I didn't want to sit on the ground any more than I had to. Now that I'd come this far, I wanted to be home.

"Excuse me, sir," the guard said to someone behind me.

I faced forward, maintaining my New York detachment, but part of me wanted to know what was going on.

"Sir? If you'd step this way?" The guard waited impassively while the unruly passenger stepped out of line. He grinned at me as he passed. It was Rick.

I felt my mouth drop open. "Rick?"

The guard stopped. "Are you two traveling together?"

"No," I said.

"Yes," Rick said at the same time.

I glared at him. "You are not. What are you up to?"

He shrugged, ignoring the curious looks of our fellow passengers, all eavesdropping like *Inquirer* reporters. "I figured if you were going to miss the reunion party, there wasn't any point in my being there, so I decided to come with you."

"Did I invite you?" Never mind I'd deserted him without any explanation.

"New York is a big city," he said with a condescending smile. "I don't need your permission to travel, Princess Cali."

Rick in New York. The thought was exciting. "What about the reunion?"

He shrugged again. "I figure they got enough excitement out of me last night. The question is, did you?"

I felt myself turn red. Twenty pairs of curious eyes turned to me.

Rick reached into his jacket and pulled out a clear plastic

corsage box. He opened it and lifted a creamy orchid from the inside.

He held out the corsage. I felt light-headed. I'd thought it was the aftermath of too much rum, but it was the dreadful, teenage feeling. Longing and uncertainty back full force.

"Don't leave, Cali. Let's get to know each other again. Remember how we used to talk?"

I nodded. "You don't think it's too late?"

"Heck, no. And now that everyone knows who you are, you'll have lots of fun."

"They'll think I'm a dork. Still a dork," I revised.

Rick pinned the corsage on my lapel. "What is it, Ms. Montalvo, reunion or New York? Either way, it'll work out."

We could be friends again. Every relationship didn't have to end in marriage. But I studied him, wondering what it would be like to be married to him, to see him every day, sleep at his side every night. Damn marvelous, that's what.

His arm went around me. "Did I ever tell you about Nona, my psychic grandmother?"

"Don't think you did," I said, enjoying the weight of his arm, the feel of his chest against me.

"She said I'd marry a Latina. Warned me against hot *Cubanitas*."

"Really?" I pretended to consider it. "Well, how will you know if you're in trouble?"

His lips closed over mine. Long seconds later, I came up for air. He was looking at me when I opened my eyes.

"Well?"

"Peligro," I whispered. "You are in such danger, mister."

The security guard led us back out of the terminal, to the cheers of Aisles Twenty-five through Forty-three.

It had turned out to be one hot, crazy Friday night. And the whole weekend loomed large. Yeah, baby.

The More Things Change

• ● •

SOFIA QUINTERO

The call caught me in the midst of a grant-writing frenzy. At four o'clock, I still hadn't reined in the budget, added relevant statistics to the needs statement, or collected updated résumés, and we had to messenger the damned proposal to the mayor's office by close of business. I only picked up the telephone because I thought my financial officer was calling with the latest figures.

"Yes."

"Ricky?"

No one had called me Ricky since college. I wouldn't allow it. A woman doesn't spend six years and ninety thousand dollars to acquire a Ph.D. only to let people outside her family call her by a nickname from her stint as a scabby-kneed tomboy.

"Who's this?"

The voice on the other end sang, "It's Lisa!"

"No way!"

"Yes!"

Lisa Pacheco was my best friend at Barnard College. The housing lottery threw us into a double during our first year, but I couldn't have chosen a better roommate. Despite all the hoopla over affirmative action, it isn't every day that a Dominicana from Washington Heights enrolls at such a prestigious (read: expensive) university, and I dreaded rooming with some valley girl who claimed an affinity toward Latinos because Rosie Perez was, like, way cool and who owned every album by Miami Sound Machine. The dorm goddess smiled upon me because the housing office matched me with Lisa, a Boricua from Brooklyn who loathed Rosie Perez and couldn't care less about Gloria Estefan with or without her Sound Machine. Just like me, Lisa clung to freestyle music, felt safer walking down noisy, bodega-lined Amsterdam Avenue than past the eerily still luxury apartments along Riverside Drive, and loved baseball (although the poor girl was a Mets fan. I never held that against her. She can't help the way she was raised). After graduation Lisa headed to Georgetown to attend medical school, and we fell out of touch.

"Look at you, *diosa*, running your own agency, serving the people. But I'm not surprised," said Lisa. "So are you married, Ricky? Any kids?"

"Married, yes. Kids, no." Funny, Lisa would ask me if I married, since in college I vowed more than once that I would never—how'd I put it?—*submit to such patriarchal bondage.* Hoping to preempt some serious teasing I didn't have the time or stomach for, I rushed to ask, "What about you, Lisa? When'd you come back to the city?"

Lisa sighed. "Actually, I just came back a few months ago. You know . . . after a bad breakup."

"Oh. I'm so sorry to hear that, Lis," I said. "How long were you married?"

"We weren't."

"Kids?"

"No. We talked about it but . . ."

Shit. It had been way too long. I refused to strike out. "Aw, Lis, all I can say is that anyone who'd let you go isn't worthy of you."

"Thanks, Ricky," Lisa said, her voice mixed with appreciation and doubt. Then it perked up. "But guess who's getting married next weekend?"

I gave her question some thought. "Not Gladys?"

"Uh, huh."

"Get out!" *No way, get out* . . . one phone call from a college friend and I had regressed into a silly coed. Gladys Arroyo and Miriam Sánchez became our roommates sophomore year. Although they're both from Corona, Queens, they had not met until high school where they were the only two Latinas in their class at Our Lady of Perpetual Grace in Woodside. On their college applications, each requested to room with the other. During their first year, they shared a double at Brooks Hall but the following year somehow wound up in a suite with two other women; one they didn't know from

Eve, and the other they knew they would murder before the semester ended. The housing lottery was less kind to Lisa and me. We got tossed in a Columbia College suite with two male juniors. Neither of us were opposed to living in a coed dorm; we just weren't keen on sharing the same suite with two men. When Lis and I went to the housing office to complain about our assignment, Gladys and Miriam were already at the window creating a scene. Lisa and I propositioned them about a switch, and they agreed. We tracked down the other two women, and the six of us marched to the housing office and demanded a swap. Gladys, Miriam, Lisa, and I landed a quad on Claremont Avenue and remained there until we graduated.

So Lisa and I gambled that sharing a suite with two other Latinas from New York would work better than rooming with two *blanquitas* from God knows where. It did, but not after we spent a semester wondering if we had made a huge mistake. No drama, mind you, we just didn't click right away. As close as Lisa and I were, we tried not to be cliquish. We were both at the top of our classes at lousy high schools and had suffered four years of SLS — Smart Latina Syndrome. That's when the guidance counselor calls you a credit to your race yet only recommends you apply to "colleges" that advertise on the back of matchbooks. Meanwhile, your classmates accuse you of acting white even though you're fluent in Ebonics and know the lyrics to every rap song on the radio. For Lisa and I, attending a prestigious school like Barnard had nothing to do with joining the elite, becoming wealthy, or distancing ourselves from our communities. We just wanted to do what we had to do to be in a position to be who we wanted to be.

Like my parents, Gladys's parents settled in Washington Heights before she was born. By the time she was five years old, they managed to buy a modest house in Corona, Queens, and worked two jobs apiece to put her and her two siblings through private school from K through twelve. Just before Miriam turned eight years old, her mother packed Miriam and her brother, Pablo, left Colombia (and Miriam's father), and settled in Corona with her sister and her son.

Miriam and Gladys, however, fell right into the elite mind-set as readily as Lisa and I shunned it. If that television show *Clueless* were set in Queens, Gladys and Miriam would be Cher and Dionne. Same bourgie attitude, lower tax bracket. Much lower. Still, the way they sashayed about the suite wearing clay masks and practicing French—which neither majored in—you'd think they'd cashed in their western Queens street cred for an account at Chanel. Sometimes, to mess with them, Lisa and I would start speaking in what we called Franglais (which, now that I think about it, was actually invented by Pepe le Pew). Miriam would huff, "OK, you guys are so not funny," and Gladys would add, "Yeah," while barely holding back a monster giggle.

Finals have a way of making college roommates bond, and it happened to the four of us in a big way. Two o'clock in the morning on the day of my last big exam and Lisa's deadline for a twenty-page term paper she had only started seven hours earlier, we decided to take a break to eat. The two of us usually kept to ourselves, but as we headed out the door we found Gladys and Miriam suffering in the living room. Gladys had chewed her usually perfect manicure down to the cuticles as she hunched over a massive economics text, while Miriam seemed on the verge of tears as she stared at the blinking cursor on the blank computer screen. So Lisa and I asked Gladys and Miriam if they wanted us to bring them back anything. Gladys kept changing her order until I finally said, "Look, just come with us." So the four of us headed out to Tom's Diner (which then was still a cool grease joint and not the chichi wannabe spawned by Suzanne Vega and Jerry Seinfeld).

Before you know it, we're talking and bonding over the challenges of being a working-class Latina at an expensive Ivy League university. How people smiled at us like a circus monkey when you said something insightful in class. How we busted our asses at off-the-books jobs during breaks in addition to our work-study gigs, praying to earn enough to pay what our student loans could not cover in time to register for the next semester. How we resented that there were few if any Latinos represented in the core curriculum, but you could always find a goddamn Margarita Night somewhere on campus. How every time we spotted another Latina notorious for trying to pass for white, we had to fight the urge to holler across College Walk, *"¡Miras tu con las manchas de plátanos!"* How it killed us when other Latino students— whether they went to a public high school, a private school on their parents' aching backs, or even to a New England boarding school on scholarship—came from neighborhoods just like ours, yet averted their eyes when the cafeteria or maintenance workers went on strike even though they could easily be our kin or neighbors. I remembered like yesterday walking out of Tom's, catching Lisa's eye and knowing she had the same thought. *These chicas are all right.*

Our conversation over scrambled eggs and home fries was enough, but what happened on the way back home sealed the deal. Nothing unusual happened; we just didn't expect the ordinary to go down like it did. Gladys and Miriam walked ahead of Lisa and me when they were passed by two 'hood rats who had one blunt too many. One said something so nasty to Gladys, she stopped in her tracks to stare at him as if she could not believe a stranger had been so vulgar. Next thing we know, Miriam is going off on him like cuckolded trailer trash on *Jerry Springer.* "¡Canto de mieRRRda, tetra hijue-puta! ¡Vete apuñala al mico, güevón! ¡Remalparido!" The Corona really came out in her (the neighborhood, not the beer). Instead of extracting his friend from the situation, 'Hood Rat No. 2 decides to add his half cent, which, of course, meant Lisa and I had to get involved. Next thing you know the four of us have Potty Mouth and Copy Cat surrounded, abusing them in two and a half languages, one of them in three dialects (lucky for them Gladys is Dominican, too).

You'd think four budding feminists at a prestigious women's college would go home and rage all night over being harassed on the street by strange men. Not us. We stopped at an all-night bodega, bought some wine coolers, and celebrated the way we handled those idiots with much pride and laughter. Lisa even raised her bottle and said, "I propose a toast to Miriam . . ."

"Relieved to know ya still have it in ya," I finished.

Although Gladys and Miriam both put much energy into repressing it, just knowing that they remained Latina *Nuyorquinos* at heart proved enough for Lisa and me. When their upper-crust aspirations got the best of us, all it took to revert them was a pitcher of sangria and freestyle night at the Latin Quarter. In turn, Lisa and I even let Gladys and Miriam ply us with French fashion tips, some of which I still use to this day.

Now after all these years, Lisa called to tell me that Gladys was getting married.

"To whom?" I asked. "Miriam?"

"No, silly!" Lisa laughed. "Her brother, Pablo."

"Oh!" That made sense. Sort of. He and Gladys dated on and off for years. Not in that tumultuous kind of way relationships at that age can be. More like they drifted in and out of each other's lives. Gladys had a different crush every semester, but I never saw her with anyone besides Pablo, who stayed over at our place whenever he visited from U Penn where he was prelaw. The ongoing relationship between Gladys and Pablo always seemed so dispassionate yet inevitable. I guessed somewhere along the way they were able to discover the fire without getting burned. "So how'd you find this out?"

"I bumped into Miriam in the Village outside of Saint Vincent's where I'm doing my residency. . . ."

"And where she was shopping."

"Of course. So Miriam tells me that Gladys is marrying her brother next weekend, and that although her sister gave her a fabulous bridal shower, Gladys still feels a little cheated because Pablo's best man threw him a wild bachelor party, but that she doesn't dare ask for a bachelorette party, let alone so close to the wedding . . . Finally, I say, look, let's take her to one of those male revues this Friday. And Miriam goes, 'Yeah, and let's track down Ricky so it can be the four of us again. A bachelorette party, a reunion, it'll be perfect.' I called Barnard's alumni office, and here I am. I know it's short notice, but it's a special occasion and I'd love to see you. Please tell me you'll go with us."

While I have nothing against it, a male revue is just not my scene. I warned my own sister, Mena, that if a stripper showed up at my bridal shower, I'd lock myself in the bedroom until he left. The crotchless panty hose, flavored lubricant, and other racy gifts I received were cool (and quickly put to use, I admit). But I had just learned that my agency's board of directors had me at the top of their short list to replace the outgoing executive director. I had to draw the line at some strange guy dry-humping me, especially in front of my coworkers and potentially future subordinates, who were invited to the shower. Besides, Eduardo and I passed on a lavish church wedding to exchange vows in the backyard of our new house. When you dispense with that kind of tradition in favor of such practicality, paying several hundred bucks to a man with less body hair than a newborn rat to grope me just didn't make sense.

So my own bridal shower consisted only of relatives and colleagues. Between finishing my doctorate, tending to my relationship with Eduardo, and building my career, I had little time to maintain old friendships or cultivate new ones. I had been so busy with other aspects of my life that I hadn't even had the time to miss having girlfriends. And now Lisa called and the void in my gut ran so deep, my legs ached under the weight of its emptiness.

"I'd love to go."

I admit it bothered me for a second when Miriam nixed the idea of meeting at Tom's for dinner when we touched base by phone on Friday afternoon. I caught her before she had to run into a business meeting, so catching up had to wait until dinner in favor of planning Gladys's special night.

"Did you buy her gift yet?"

"No," I said, hoping my shame went undetected.

"Great. Don't. After dinner let's take her to one of those sex shops so she can pick whatever she wants."

I loved that Miriam was still such a take-charge gal, especially when it got me off the hook. "And then let's have dinner at Tom's."

"That dive?" You'd think I recommended Burger King. "*Ay,* no, no, no . . ." Miriam insisted we take Gladys to Il Mulino for dinner and then to the ten o'clock show at Studs. I understood wanting to take Gladys to a nice place, especially one near the club. But I thought Tom's would be perfect even if it doesn't have a Tokyo location, a sommelier, or reservation list. "We have to take Gladys someplace special," she said.

Tom's is special, I thought, but I bit my tongue. Instead I said, "Il Mulino's it is." Like I went there all the time even though I had never heard of it before Miriam recommended it.

"Gladys does not pay a cent for anything."

"Of course."

"And whatever happens with us tonight, stays with us tonight."

"Absolutely."

"I'm serious, Ricky. You can't say a word to your husband. God forbid, we're all having dinner together some night, and he slips. The less he knows, the better."

I envisioned all of us having dinner together at my house. Eduardo and I, Gladys and Pablo, Miriam and her husband, and even Lisa happy again with a fellow worthy of her, sitting around our dining room table, the white wine and Barnard stories flowing. We tease each other and shock our men with our college escapades, all of us falling in love with one another all over again. Yet through it all, Gladys, Lisa, Miriam, and I smile at each other knowing that we had saved the best memories for our private reminiscences.

"You got it, Miriam," I said. "Girls only."

For the first time in months, I left work early. I headed to Fifth Avenue and walked into a random boutique and quickly scoured the sales rack for a dress cheap enough to fit my budget, yet pricey enough to fool Miriam's discerning eye. Then I remembered one of her tips. *Choose black. It always looks expensive. Always have one little black dress.* Only an hour later when I was under the dryer at my favorite hair salon in El Barrio, while the manicurist filed my nails, did I feel a pang of guilt. When was the last time I bought a new dress or did my hair for Eduardo? Then I remembered that he preferred it when I wore my hair in its natural curl and walked around in his A-Rod jersey. Which only made me feel more guilty. Even though I hoped that this reunion with Gladys, Lisa, and Miriam would lead to more girls' nights out, I vowed that I would plan something extra special for Eduardo next weekend. Actually, the following weekend. Next weekend was Gladys's wedding, and I knew after tonight, she would extend an invitation which Eduardo and I would accept, of course.

That night Eduardo pretended to be fine with my going until the last minute. Just as I stepped out of the shower and began to apply my makeup, he snuck up behind me and planted a wet kiss on my neck. I knew what he was up to and that it wouldn't work. But we hadn't had sex in over a week while I worked ten-hour days over that proposal, and now I was set to skip out the door and into the hands of muscle-bound men in G-strings. *Bendito,* how could I deny him (or myself).

After convincing me that he had spent the past week curling weights with his tongue, he finally came out with it in that way men who are in denial about their jealousy usually do. 'Uardo propped himself up on an elbow and said, "I can't believe you want to go to this thing. You haven't seen any of these women in years. Now all of sudden you're going clubbing with them."

Not wanting to squelch the fading waves of pleasure before their time with too much movement, I stayed put with my eyes closed. "We're not going clubbing, honey." I couldn't resist. Hey, the more you love a man, the less willing you should be to let him take you for granted. "We're going to a male strip joint. Stuuuuuds." That earned me a gentle tug on my hair. "Ow!" I yelped, exaggerating the damage.

"I didn't marry you for your sense of humor."

I opened my eyes and rolled over to face him. Right past that nonchalant smirk, I saw the same uneasy smile that accompanied Eduardo on our first date eight years ago. Nestling under his chin I said, "When's the last time you hung out with the guys?" I felt his neck stiffen and laughed. "It's not a trick question, I promise."

"On Sunday I went over to Dave's, and we watched the baseball game."

"And when's the last time you saw Dave and the fellas before that?"

"I dunno."

I drew away from him and sat up. "You guys drove out to Jersey to check out that SUV he read about in the paper, remember?"

Eduardo snickered. "That wasn't exactly a guys' night out, Ricky. Dave just saw the ad, decided to check it out, and asked me to tag along for the hell of it."

"The last time I had a girlfriend call me and ask me to tag

along on any errand just for the hell of it . . ." I couldn't even remember. Not even if I counted my sister. I looked at Eduardo to see if he was following where I was headed. He stared at me with such a longing to understand, it frightened me that he just might. I leapt out of bed, walked over to the dresser, and spritzed my hair. "I mean, who would I call if you go do something stupid, and I have to put you out?"

I watched Eduardo's reflection as he folded his hands behind his head and leaned back against his pillows. "In other words, 'Don't worry, 'Uardo. I have no intention of running off with a stripper or doing anything crazy like that while running the streets with my homegirls tonight.'"

So we met at Il Mulino at seven. When I arrived, Gladys and Miriam were already seated and halfway through a carafe of red wine. During the entire drive to the restaurant, I worried that I would walk into the restaurant and not be able to recognize them. That Gladys and Miriam would have changed so much I would not be able to spot them in a roomful of pantsuits and updos. Yet there they sat almost like I remembered them with nothing but changes for the better.

Gladys put on a few pounds and looked fabulous for it. She chopped her straight, dark hair into a sleek bob, and as always, her makeup was flawless. Gladys opted for a black V-neck blouse, a flared ankle-length skirt and boots with tiny heels.

Miriam looked exactly the same except she dyed her hair a honey blond and shimmied her still petite yet curvaceous frame into a low-cut dress the color of a maraschino cherry. While I had no doubt that Miriam had her hair done at Oribe's and that what she spent for her entire outfit would cover my mortgage, her new look shocked me. In fact, it seemed like Miriam and Gladys had exchanged looks over the years where Miriam turned up the volume on hers while Gladys toned down hers. I decided to take this as a good omen and hoped that they would see a similar, positive change in me.

"Ricarda Durán!" Miriam called, and soon the three of us huddled in the middle of the restaurant in a screechy group hug. That, too, made me feel better as the uncomfortable vision of them greeting me with fingertip handshakes and air kisses also crossed my mind. Before we broke, we heard, "*¡Diosas!*" in that familiar voice. Lisa entered the restaurant and rushed over to join us.

Of the four of us, Lisa was the one you didn't want your boyfriend to meet. Not because she would ever betray you — she's the one friend you knew would never do that — but because you were scared to death he would develop a not-so-secret crush on her. For a poor medical student who had just gotten off call, Lisa still radiated that natural beauty that makeup did more to cover than enhance. She had grown out her auburn hair to shoulder length and cut it in bouncy layers. Her crème-colored pantsuit and taupe slingbacks added to her modelesque stature. I just knew that Lisa had spent her afternoon as I did mine — rushing around trying to pull her look together, and I loved her for it.

Our circle was complete. We all took our seats, and Lisa

and I ordered drinks and appetizers. Then Miriam fired off a question that came off more like an accusation.

"Ricky, what's this about you getting married?" she asked.

Taken aback by her tone, I hesitated to answer. Lisa said, "She finally found a guy who'll play footsie with her without complaining that she's too competitive." Gladys and Miriam laughed, and I flashed Lisa an appreciative smile.

Miriam said, "Really though. What's his name? What does he do?"

"His name's Eduardo and he's a senior development officer at the Putnam Foundation. He heads up the division that makes grants to youth programs and senior centers."

"So you two met because he funded your agency," Gladys guessed. "Oh, sounds like a scandal waiting to happen."

I feigned horror at the thought. "Actually, about eight years ago, I applied for a position as a program officer at Putnam even though I kinda suspected that I didn't have enough experience . . ."

Gladys gasped. "You slept with him to get the job!"

"No, I never even met with him while I was interviewing!" I knew my getting married would send them reeling, but that was no reason to presume I had changed so much as to pimp myself for a job. "I did manage to get an interview and even aced it, or so I thought. But two weeks later, I get the thanks-but-fuck-you letter, you know, so I threw it out and moved on. The very next day, I get a call from Eduardo." I pretended to pick up my telephone. " 'Hello, Ms. Durán, this is Eduardo Cordero. I'm calling to see if you received our letter.' I recognize his name from the research I did to prepare for my interview and I thought, oh, wow, they were really impressed with me. They told the head of the division about me and passed on my résumé, he's calling to offer me some other position. So I tell him that I did receive the letter and that I was so disappointed because I wanted very much to work for Putnam, and so on and so on. All of sudden, the man starts stuttering. 'Well, uh, Ms. Durán, uh, I actually am happy you're not qualified to work here. I just happened to notice you when you came for your interview, and I desperately wanted to ask you out, but that would've been inappropriate at the time and impossible if you had gotten the job, but since you won't be coming to work for us. Not that that's why you didn't get the job! I mean, without a doubt, you're completely underqualified, Ms. Durán. Quite frankly, I don't even know why they brought you in for an interview . . .' "

Lisa erupted into that enthusiastic snort that always got me laughing, too. Gladys joined us while Miriam sneered and sipped at her wine. "What an awesome story," Gladys said.

I thought so, too. I loved telling that story. But this night was supposed to be about Gladys. "What about you, Gladys?"

"Show 'em the rock," Miriam said. Gladys obliged, thrusting her left hand in the middle of the table. We all leaned forward to admire the shimmering mushroom sitting on Gladys's hand. I don't know anything about diamonds except that the half karat on my own ring finger almost kept Eduardo and me from qualifying for the loan to buy our brownstone, and we tormented ourselves about possibly re-turning it when our mortgage broker called with the good news. Gladys's diamond reigned over her hand like it had been born there and the other four fingers were hired to do its bidding. As we fawned over her engagement ring, I no-ticed that Miriam's wedding band was no shy runner-up but a contemporary platinum number that looked just like a doll's tiara with quite the sparkler at its peak.

"Pablo says he started saving for it years ago. Claims that he put money in his savings even those months when we seemed to be through," said Gladys as she contemplated her ring finger. Then she dropped her hand in her lap and rolled her eyes. "Probably just forgot to stop the deposits."

I nudged her in the arm to reprimand her. "There's gotta be a story there," I said. "After all these years you wind up marrying the proverbial guy next door."

"Especially after all the back-and-forth you did during college," added Lisa.

"So tell us about that moment when you realized that what you'd been looking for was right . . ."

But Gladys waved her hand and said, "Oh, we just hooked up, you know. I finished business school, got a con-sulting gig with PaineWebber . . . It was time." She shrugged and refilled her wineglass. "I want to finish having kids by thirty-five."

Then Miriam said, "*¡Ay, nena,* don't rush! Don't get me wrong. I adore my son. But when he's not the only thing keeping me sane, he's driving me crazy. Like father, like son." She laughed and took another sip of wine.

"You have a son?" Lisa said. "I know you have pictures. Show us, show us." Miriam reached into her Kate Spade pocketbook for the matching wallet and showed us the photo of an adorable toddler with spiky black hair, golden skin, and Asiatic eyes. He looked nothing like Miriam. Yet something told me not to inquire about his father.

But Miriam volunteered answers to more questions than I had. "It's like his father spit and it grew limbs, and before you know it, it's a boy, ha, ha, ha! I didn't want to name the baby after my ex. In fact, I wanted to name him after Pablo, but Larry insisted we make him Junior. 'Why name him after your brother?' he says. 'He doesn't look like him. He doesn't look like anyone in your family. He doesn't even look like you and you're his mother.' And to think I never cheated on the sonofabitch when I had the chance."

Her remarks tugged at my loyalties. On the one hand, I wanted to grill Miriam about Larry like a detective so I could have enough information to track him down and kick his rotten ass. If any one of us was going to be that rare woman who had it all, it would be Miriam. She would devote as much attention to her husband and children as she did her career. Whoever this Larry was, he obviously was too much of a self-absorbed sonofabitch to not know what he had in her. On the other, I found myself wanting to defend ... fidelity. God knows I didn't want to come off like a preachy convert to the religion of marriage, especially when I didn't know what exactly had occurred between Miriam and Sonofabitch. If I asked, however, I risked putting a damper on our reunion. Sure, I burned with curiosity to know Miriam's whole story, but I knew she would be all too eager to tell us and become the glum center of attention. And as much as I wanted to console her, I knew I couldn't pretend to commiserate with an outlook I did not share.

Thankfully, the waiter came by to take our orders and gave me an opportunity to think. By the time the waiter collected our menus and left for the kitchen, I had a proposal. I raised my water glass and said, "I say that tonight not only we bid farewell to Gladys's singlehood in honor of her upcoming nuptials, we also celebrate Miriam's liberation from Watsisface."

"Larry," said Lisa.

"Nah, I like Watsisface," Miriam said, laughing and lifting her wineglass in the air. Lisa and Gladys joined us and we clinked. "To my re-bachelorette-ization!"

"Cheers!" I yelled, proud of my proposal.

Then Gladys turned to Lisa and said, "Where are you in all this?"

It took a few seconds for Lisa to figure what she meant, but then she replied, "Oh, I'm single, too. Again. I mean, we were never married, but . . ." She gave Miriam a commiserating smile. "You know, a hard breakup."

"Are there any other kind?" said Miriam.

"Anybody we know?" asked Gladys.

Lisa reached for a sesame breadstick, and her hesitancy gave her away.

Gladys gasped. "It *is* someone we know," Gladys said. "Who?"

Lisa kept her eye on the breadstick as she twiddled it like a cigar. "You guys remember Celina Ferrer?"

"Who could forget her?" Miriam grumbled. "The bitch was perfect." I burst out laughing because I thought the very same thing. Bad enough Celina Ferrer was gorgeous and brilliant, she didn't have the decency to be a stuck-up bitch so we could be righteous in our envy. Think Mary Ann's sweet demeanor in Ginger's smoking bod. But Celina's boyfriend, Mark Osario, was no Gilligan.

Gladys scraped her chair forward so hard, I thought she would prostrate herself across the breadbasket. "Oh my God, when'd you start going out with Mark Osario?" she asked.

Celina dated Mark all throughout college. She chaired Alianza Latina Americana, the pan-Latino student organization for Columbia undergrads, and even founded Boriqueñas at Barnard. Mark headed the Charles Drew Society, the group for premed students of color and eventually became captain of the crew team. Celina and Mark broke up for a semester during our junior year, and no one would touch either of them. As beautiful as each of them were, they were stunning together. Only a big dreamer with a strong heart and a healthy esteem would dare challenge fate on that reconciliation. I don't blame Gladys for assuming Lisa won over Mark though, because if any woman on campus had a chance, it would be her.

Gladys slapped Miriam's hand. "Can you believe it? Lisa nabbed Mark Osario! Was he as good as he looked?"

"He'd be the first," Miriam said.

"Like you wouldn't have jumped him if you had the chance." Gladys turned back to Lisa. "Remember that stupid little swim test they make you take in order to graduate? I went to the pool to take mine, and Mark and some of the other guys on the crew team were leaving, and oh my God!" She didn't need to say more. Not a single Latina at Columbia (and I'd say a high percentage of all the women of other races, too) failed to pine for Mark Osario. Yours truly included, even though my attractions usually veered toward the guys that women overlooked for their flashier buddies. I even bragged about it. Most women favored Hutch; I liked Starsky. When they drooled at Bo, I stared at Luke. While everyone swooned over Johnny Depp on *21 Jump Street,* I fantasized about having a ménage à trois with Dustin Nguyen and the older black man who played the captain (although that crush I kept to myself). I could never tell a soul that Ricarda Who-Needs-a-Man Durán was a secret member of the bandwagon known as the Mark Osario Fan Club. Not until our junior year did I admit to Lisa in one of our 'til-the-break-of-dawn conversations in our double that if I could have one night with Mark where no one had to know or get hurt, I'd do it. I remember that Lisa just smiled and nodded like she felt the same way, but instead of feeling jealous or threatened, I felt closer to her than ever. I didn't mind sharing my secret or my crush with Lisa.

"You know, that time when he and Celina were broken up? He flirted with me once in the dining hall," said Gladys. "It's true, ask Miriam." Miriam nodded half-heartedly, rolled her eyes, and went back to her drink. "But I was so scared 'cause you know how it was. When you're a minority at a school like that, there's just no way you can see someone and not have everyone in your business."

Miriam added, "No way you can date someone of the same race and not end up sleeping with someone's ex. If it's not someone who lives in your dorm, it's someone in your class. If not in your class, in your club . . ."

". . . and believe it or not, I was still virgin."

Lisa and I were both shocked to hear that. "All those times Pablo came over and spent the night, you never . . ."

Gladys shook her head and continued, "And Mark seemed so much like a . . . a . . . man." Gladys grabbed Lisa's hand. "Tell us, tell us! How'd you and Mark get together?"

"We didn't," Lisa said. I heard the annoyance in her voice. "But you said . . ."

"I said, 'You guys remember Celina Ferrer?'"

"So why mention Celina Ferrer if . . ."

Then it hit me. I shouted, "Because it *was* Celina Ferrer!" All the other restaurant patrons snapped their necks in our direction. I even heard the man at the next table whisper to his date, *Is that the one they call the Hispanic Oprah?* I slapped my hand over my mouth and just as quickly yanked it away. I hoped Lisa would understand that my embarrassment was over my outburst and not about her revelation.

"Celina's the one I just broke up with before moving back to New York," she said. "When we realized that we were both headed to Georgetown, we decided to look for an apartment together. . . ."

Miriam asked, "Is that when you guys got together? In medical school?"

"Actually, it happened that semester when she and Mark broke up for that spell. We'd always been good friends, and I dropped by her dorm room to see how she was doing. Eventually, Celina told me that she broke up with Mark because not only was she questioning her sexual orientation, she was questioning it because of me. Then Celina said that she was only admitting this to me because somehow she sensed that I was, too. And she was right. So we got together. Secretly, of course."

"So what happened?" I asked.

"She got scared about coming out and went back to Mark."

"So you're . . . like . . . " Gladys stuttered.

"Yes, Gladys, I'm, like . . . " Lisa joked.

"Oh." Gladys sat as still as a statue. Had we chosen a sidewalk café, I'm sure a pigeon—or as we native New Yorkers lovingly call them, rats with wings—would have made himself at home on her head.

We all sat perfectly still. No one even took a sip or picked up her fork. What do you say when your best friend from college reveals she just ended her first lesbian relationship with the campus goddess? Being the closest to Lisa, I felt particularly terrible about my loss for words. First Miriam, now her. I neglected my friendships to study social work only to have lost my counselor's touch now that I needed it the most.

"I wish I was gay!" Miriam said suddenly. "Better selection, less drama. . . ."

I reached for my drink. "I seriously doubt that." Within minutes of reuniting with her after all these years, it became obvious that by her petite lonesome, Miriam offered more drama than a Greek tragedy.

Lisa chuckled at my dig which made me feel better about my not having the perfect words to express acceptance of her sexuality and sympathy over her breakup with Celina. But my crack flew over Miriam's head faster than a Boeing. "Another woman would understand me. She'd be in better tune with my wants and needs. And if she weren't, at least she'd freakin' ask."

I turned to Lisa and said, "C'mon, Lis, is it really all that easier?"

"No!" she said, clearly relieved that someone finally bothered to ask. "It's not harder, it's not easier, it's just different. Like, what's tough about being with men?" She paused to find an example, and thankfully she did before Miriam began reciting a litany.

"You know how we complain that men don't want to communicate? Well, when you're with another woman, everything needs to be processed to death. Doesn't matter how small or big the issue is. Whether it's about choosing a place to live or deciding who's going to walk the dog, it's gotta be a conference. And God help you if it's a disagreement because automatically it's never about what it's about, it's gotta be about something else. Something bigger, something deeper.

And that means it takes a thousand conversations to resolve the matter. I mean, sometimes you've just had a hard day and need some time to yourself and that's it. You just want to say, 'Can you just leave me the hell alone right now?' and not have her read something more into it that's just not there, like 'I hate you' or 'You suck.' All I said was, 'Leave me alone right now,' and all I meant was 'Leave me alone right now.' Nothing more, nothing less."

"OK, I get it," Miriam said. "You were the guy in the relationship. Gotcha."

Lisa didn't even hear her. She poured herself more wine and softly said, "And when things are right . . . "

Lisa's voice trailed as she slipped into a private remembrance of what right was like. The look on her face told me "right" actually hadn't been all that different for Lisa and Celina than it was between Eduardo and me. They finished each other's sentences, shared comfortable silences, and knew when a peck on the cheek or squeeze to the shoulder at the right moment was nothing less than tossing a lifeline. Like anyone reeling from the loss of her soul mate, Lisa was trying hard to convince herself that the hard times with Celina were worse than they really were because that's how damned good the easy times were.

I reached over and placed my hand over Lisa's. "Women," I said. And she cut loose with another snorty laugh. That got Miriam started, too.

Gladys, however, remained parked in Heteroville. "So . . . like . . . how long have you known you were . . . you know. . . . "

Even Miriam saw through that question. "¡*Ay*, give it a rest, Gladys! Lisa was not checkin' out your scrawny behind while we lived together at Barnard, OK? I mean, the woman had Celina Ferrer. Why would she bother with you?"

Although she tried to fight it, Gladys had to laugh, too. "To hear this bitch talk, you'd never know I was marrying her brother in a week."

"So are you nervous about the wedding?" Lisa asked.

Gladys zeroed in on a mushroom abandoned on her plate. "Not really."

"It's perfectly natural, you know," I said.

Gladys turned to me and said, "OK, I know this is such a *telenovela* thing to ask, but seriously, Ricky. How did you know? I mean, you never even considered marriage and then you meet this guy and you dove right into it so . . . "

"No, I didn't dive in, trust me," I said. I thought of saying more, but I didn't want to move the focus off Gladys. "I won't lie and say I was a hundred percent sure. No one ever is. The only thing you're really sure about is the risk . . . "

"Amen," said Miriam.

" . . . and whether you love someone enough to take it."

Lisa raised her glass and said, "Even I can drink to that."

I lifted my glass, too, and said, "To Gladys y *pobre Pablo*."

Giggling, Miriam and Gladys followed suit, and the four of us repeated, "*Y pobre Pablo*." As I sipped, I thought, *this is going to be an unforgettable night*. Damn it, if I weren't right. Poor Pablo indeed.

When we arrived at the Sin Bin, Lisa dragged Gladys off to the lingerie rack while Miriam and I perused the lotion aisle. Every once in a while I would peek over at Gladys and Lisa to see how they were faring. I knew Lisa wanted some time alone with Gladys in the hopes that she eventually would grow comfortable with her again, but I wanted to keep an eye on them so I could swoop in at the first sign of awkwardness. More for Lisa's sake than Gladys's.

"I swore to God it'd be you," said Miriam.

"What?"

"If I thought anyone was going to come out tonight, it'd be you. You were the one that was so anti-male. . . . "

"I was not anti-male," I said. "I was anti-male chauvinism. . . . "

" . . . and nothing could be more pro-male than marriage. Remember how you used to say that all the time." Miriam read the label on a tube of something called Slicky Dicky and dropped it into our shopping basket. "Something else you once said actually helped me get through my divorce."

So it was officially over with Watsisface. "Really? What was that?"

"That studies showed that the most content and healthy people were single women. Followed by married men. So whenever I got really down, I'd remember that and think, 'Hey, now that the sonofabitch is gone, I'm finally better off than he is.'" She gave this unconvincing laugh and moved down the aisle to the edible underwear.

I didn't know what to say to that. Was Miriam sincere when she said that remembering my words helped her through the divorce by reminding her that she was better off single than in a bad marriage? Or was she hinting that I was some kind of hypocrite for giving marriage a chance? Seeing that we had not seen each other in so long and had some reacquainting to do, I chose to give her the benefit of the doubt.

"I think the reason why single women are generally happier than married men is because women are still pressured into marriage for its own sake," I said. "You know, instead of doing it on their own terms the way men are encouraged to do." ⟍

"Well, I married Larry on my own terms," said Miriam. "No one pressured me into marrying him. I certainly didn't need to marry him. I made just as much money as he did. I owned my own house, my own car when I met him. And it didn't matter to me one way or the other if I had kids or not, so the ol' biological clock wasn't a factor. So Dr. Durán, you tell me why after getting married on my terms, I'm fighting with my now ex-husband about not having his little girlfriend stay over on the weekends he has our son?"

Sounds like love wasn't a part of your terms, I thought. But as defensive as I felt, I didn't say it. First of all, Miriam'd probably say, *Love isn't enough.* And she'd be right, so spewing out a superficial response like that would only make me sound like a pop-psych phony. And I didn't want to get off the defensive by putting her on it. For whatever reasons, Miriam was already there and desperately wanted company. But as much as he seemed like a bona fide heel, talking shit about Larry when I didn't know him wasn't the answer. After all, Miriam married the man and bore his child. I could only criticize him so much without passing judgment on her. Besides, absolving Miriam of any culpability in the failure of their relationship—especially when I knew so little about it—went against everything I knew about being an effective social worker. Or a good friend because despite my own professional experience, I only had to look at my own personal history for examples of failed relationships with no clear victim or villain.

"I can't tell you that, Miriam," I finally said. "I mean, with the little I know about your particular situation, anything I'd say right now would just be go-girl-fuck-him bullshit. Then what kind of friend would I be?"

Miriam stared at me as she weighed what I had said. She walked toward me and dropped a pair of cherry-flavored edible panties into the shopping basket. "You're right. You wouldn't know. Sorry for putting you on the spot."

Was that resignation or sarcasm? I wouldn't know because we haven't been in touch all these years? Or I wouldn't know because I didn't know the first thing about relationships, let alone marriage? Before I could ask her, Gladys came running over with a purple teddy in one hand and a turquoise baby doll in the other.

"Which one should I get?" she asked.

Lisa caught up to her. "I say the turquoise, but what do I know?" She seemed frustrated. I started to wonder if her conversation with Gladys carried a similar theme.

"Definitely the turquoise," I said.

Gladys looked to Miriam for the final verdict.

"*Ay*, of course, the turquoise," she said. "That purple thing's so cheesy. I can't believe you even considered it." Miriam snatched the hanger from her and marched back to the lingerie rack. "Now if you can get this baby doll in royal, that'd be perfect."

"Pablo likes royal?" asked Gladys.

Miriam squinted at her. "You asking me?"

Lisa and I hesitated to follow them. "Let me guess," I said. "You lesbians don't know the first thing about lingerie."

"Apparently."

"Good thing you didn't take her to the vibrator section." I thought that would at least make her smile, but I was wrong. "Give her time."

"And a couple of drinks."

"Served by a dude with big, oily pecs."

Lisa finally grinned. "Is Miriam having fun yet?"

"I'm starting to think she needs this a lot more than Gladys does."

"OK, let's get this party started."

We arrived at Studs early enough to grab one of the tables in front of the stage. I must have been expecting something like the set of *Soul Train* because I was struck at how small the club was. *The better to see them with, my dear.* At the front of the room, the stage resembled a wide catwalk. Simple tables and chairs surrounded the perimeter and filled toward the back to a very long bar. On either side of the room toward the front were staircases that led up to a balcony. The balcony overlooked the stage but seats were available only on the extreme right and left. In fact, some parties of women had already nabbed seats on the right side of the balcony. The left side remained dark and empty.

From what I could tell, at least five other bachelorette parties were there for the show. Lisa pointed out one bride-to-be with her Furla friends sitting diagonally across from us on the other side of the stage. "Is she even old enough to get married?" she asked. The Jessica Simpson look-alike in a red plaid micromini, white knee-hi socks and Mary Janes pranced around with a veiled tiara on her head, a pink garter around her thigh and a shot glass in her hand. She threw back her drink, slammed the glass on the table, pulled a bill out of I-don't-want-to-think-about-where, and hollered for the server to bring her another one. One of her guests teased her to save her money for the dancers to which the nubile bride slurred, "Oh, fush the huck up!"

"That pisses me off," I said. "All these politicians running around trying to quote unquote preserve the sanctity of marriage by banning gays from doing it. You want to protect the institution of marriage? Keep rich, straight chicks like Britney Spears, J. Lo, and Tammy Tequila over there from doing it."

Lisa grinned at me. "Ricky, quit trying so hard." She put her arm around my shoulder and hugged me.

My belly tumbled with embarrassment. "I'm serious!"

"I know you are." Lisa stood up and said, "This first round's on me. Who wants what?"

Gladys pointed at Tammy Tequila. "Whatever she's having."

Miriam said, "I'll have a merlot."

"You can't be serious. We're in a goddamn strip club," I said, "Get her an apple martini, and bring me a cosmo."

Of course, the second Lisa turned her back, Gladys and Miriam bombarded me with questions. How did I feel having shared a room with Lisa all those years? Did I have the slightest clue that Lisa was lesbian? Did I ever suspect her having a secret affair with anyone let alone a woman like Celina Ferrer? Why the hell would she agree to go to a show at Studs, let alone suggest it? Was Lisa thinking about going back to men?

"None of that matters. Look at how thoughtful and sentimental she is," I said. "She's still the same Lisa we've known and loved all these years. Which means she's more broken up over Celina than she'll ever let on 'cause she doesn't want to spoil Gladys's night. That means we have to look out for her and make sure she's having a good time, too."

"How?" asked Gladys.

"We can offer the drunken schoolgirl over there cash to give Lisa a lap dance," Miriam cracked.

"Bright, Miriam, real bright," I said. One of the things I always adored about Miriam was her quick lip. She was the only person I ever knew who could outdo me with the snappy comeback, and back in college a line like that would make me brim with admiration and even some envy. When did I become so hypersensitive to see malice where none probably existed? After all, Miriam was the first to say something affirming about Lisa's sexuality at the restaurant. It may have been based on stereotypes about gay relationships, but her heart was in the right place. I had to chill out and not assume her bitterness over her divorce colored everything she said and did. So I backpedaled into a joke. "Pay that skinny white girl to give Lisa a lap dance? Miriam, please. She's so not Lisa's type."

No sooner than Lisa returned with our drinks and took her seat, the house lights dimmed. The DJ played Corina's "Temptation" as a masculine shadow made his way to the center of the stage, and the women screamed and applauded. A spotlight zoomed over the crowd as Corina sang.

> *Temptation is a part of life*
> *It doesn't matter if it's wrong or right.*

Gladys dug her nails into my arm and shrieked in my ear like a kid at her first circus. Miriam stood to her feet, raised her arms over her head, and clapped so hard I thought she might burst into flames. Even Lisa looked over her shoulder to grin at me with anticipation. I polished off my cosmo, waved over a server and told him, "Bring us four tequilas, keep the rounds coming, and give me change for this twenty."

"Singles?"

"You got it, papa!"

The spotlight finally settled on the figure on stage revealing the boyish MC. He looked to be in his late twenties and wore a navy suit and black T-shirt. While a few of the women welcomed him with polite cheers, most of the crowd booed his attire. For such a handsome guy to be dressed so smartly, he obviously did not look like he had any intentions of getting naked, and these women were not going for it.

"*'Dito,*" said Lisa.

"*'Dito,* my ass," yelled Miriam. "TAKE IT OFF!"

The crowd joined her chant. *"TAKE IT OFF! TAKE IT OFF! TAKE IT OFF!"*

The MC grinned and shrugged his jacket off one shoulder. The women roared, and he laughed. He motioned for them to settle down as the DJ faded out "Temptation."

"Ladies, I want to welcome you to Studs. All our regulars know that we're pretty laid back here."

"Whoo, hoo!" someone in the balcony yelled.

"We want you to have a great time with us, and in order to do that, we ask you to follow a few rules. First of all, we ask that you not throw anything on the stage at any time. . . ."

"What about money?" the balcony heckler asked.

"Only if it's bills, honey," answered the MC and everyone applauded.

"Why's he just the MC?" grumbled Gladys. "He's so cute."

"Ladies, we also ask that you do not take pictures during the show." The crowd protested and the MC had to wait until they quieted down. "I know, but believe me, these guys work hard to put on a great show for you, and cameras are a distraction. If you like what you see, just come back!" The audience cheered that suggestion. "And finally, at times a lucky lady is invited by a dancer to join him on the stage for a special performance. . . ."

"Ooh, ooh!" cooed the balcony heckler.

"If she's so damned enthusiastic," I said, "why the hell is she sitting all the way up there in the first place?"

"I was beginning to wonder the same thing myself," said Lisa.

Miriam smirked. "Maybe she's getting a private show up there."

"That'd explain all the hootin' and hollerin'," I said.

"If you happen to be one of those lucky ladies, Studs ask that for your own safety, you set your drink on the table before you take the stage."

"No more damned rules!" yelled You-Know-Who.

"Now, now, there's one last rule, and that's, have a fabulous time! Without further delay, please welcome your first dancer of the night. He's a *mucho* macho from Massachusetts. Ladies, give it for him, and he'll give it up for you . . . ULTIMO!"

Dressed in combat boots and a camouflage set with a matching cap pulled over his eyes, Ultimo strutted toward his appreciative audience to that annoying Nah-Nah-Nah-Nah-Nah song by Kaylie, Kylie . . . you know the skinny bitch I'm talking about. He grabbed the bill of his cap and flicked it off, revealing tawny skin, dark curly hair and an aquiline nose.

Gladys lost her mind. She jumped to her feet and

screamed, "Oh, my God, he looks just like Benjamin Bratt!" Lisa and I looked at each other and giggled. No, he didn't. Still, we were thrilled that Gladys had wasted no time in getting her fantasy on. After all, she was the reason why we were here.

I shoved a few of my singles into Gladys's hand. "Get 'im, girl!"

Gladys rushed to the edge of the stage waving the bills, but Tammy Tequila and her entourage had beaten her to the punch so Ultimo gyrated his way over to their side of the stage. The server came with our tequila and set them before us. I grabbed the salt shaker, sprinkled a small mound on the back of my hand, and then looked to pass it to Miriam. She was peering at Ultimo as if trying to locate him through a fog. I nudged Lisa, passed the salt shaker to her, and then pointed at Miriam.

Lisa cupped her hand over her mouth and called her. When Miriam turned, Lisa said, "If you'd stop being so vain and put on your glasses, you'd get a better look."

Miriam stuck her tongue out at her and leaned toward us across the table. "I'm almost positive I've seen that guy somewhere before."

"Damn, how often do you go to these kind of places?" I teased.

Lisa said, "You know, the same guys who do these revues often work bachelorette parties. Maybe that's where you saw him."

"Or maybe she saw him in a porno," I said. The tequila warmed me up so much so fast, I started wriggling to

Kylie's bass line and singing *Nah-Nah-Nah* along with her.

"I remember!" Miriam yelled with recognition. "It was a bachelorette party! For Gladys's sister."

"Hold the phone," I said. "Her sister got a stripper for her bachelorette party, and she turns around and throws Gladys a sedate little bridal shower. Whatta bitch!"

"Now you see why I wanted to do this for her."

"Good call." I raised my palm and Miriam gave me a high five.

"Am I a good friend or am I a good friend?" she said.

"You're a damned good friend." I even grabbed Gladys's tequila, toasted Miriam, and then downed it.

Lisa motioned toward Gladys and said, "Did she react to him like that at her sister's party?"

Miriam said, "No, the poor thing was too busy playing hostess to really get into the show."

"Oh, maybe that's why she doesn't recognize him."

As if on cue, Gladys turned around, her face flushed with frustration. "I need a hand here, guys, or else I'm never gonna get Ben away from that skank in the plaid skirt." Then she turned back to the stage and started banging on it with one hand while waving her single with the other. "Ben! Over here! Beeen!"

"It's Ultimo, *loca*!" I said, laughing. Although our rivals had managed to tuck quite a few bills into Ultimo's waistband, he had only taken off his shirt, which Tammy wasted no time in draping over her bony shoulders. I started to count off several singles from the batch the server gave me, but then I had a better idea. I grabbed my purse and scoured it until I found a five-dollar bill. I joined Gladys at the stage, pressed the five into her hand, and banged the stage along with her. "UL-TI-MOOOOO!" Lisa and Miriam did the same and sure enough, we made enough of a racket to grab his attention. "Later for the cheap tricks and their chump change, baby. Come to mama!" Spotting the five in my hand, Ultimo flashed a perfect smile and shimmied over to our side.

Gladys jumped and hooted as if she had won the lottery. "He's coming!"

Miriam yelled, "Make him earn it. He's gotta take off something."

"That's right," I agreed.

Like an obedient protégé, Gladys nodded. She waved the fiver at Ultimo, who planted himself right in front of her. He pivoted to show off his muscular tush and then bumped downward to the music into a squat. He bounced his ass, suggesting that Gladys tuck the bill inside his waistband. Instead she responded with swift slap across his butt. "Ow!" The four of us screamed in laughter.

Both hurt and impressed, Gladys said, "It's like he's got rocks in there."

"Do you, Ultimo?" I said. "Let's see what ya got." I reached into my purse for another five and waved at him to show him I meant business. No stripping, no tipping.

Ultimo got the message. He grabbed his camouflage pants at the hips and gave a hard yank. Quicker than you can say Velcro, Ultimo's pants were in his hands and his ass on display. Only a sliver of army green fabric stood between the four of us and his firm rump. For the first time I found myself embarrassed. I quickly tucked my bill into Ultimo's G-string at the safe crook of his well-defined hip.

Lisa gave me a playful shove. "You talk so much shit!"

"Shut up. I'm a happily married woman."

"Yeah, yeah, yeah." She poked her bill into Ultimo's thong and threw her arm around me. "C'mon, if anyone knows how to loosen up without losing control, it's you."

Lisa's teasing made me laugh at my own self-consciousness. I came here to show my friends a good time, and that pretty much required that I have one myself. So long as I didn't do anything that would upset me had Eduardo done it, and I had no intention of doing that.

Miriam pulled back Ultimo's thong so Gladys could slap her bill right on his tailbone. Despite all this appreciation, his hungry eyes already had caught a wave of Hamiltons beckoning him to the opposite side of the stage. So with his cable bill paid, off he went to entertain the wealthier bachelorette party and earn his rent. A man's gotta do what a man's gotta do.

The four of us sat down and had another round of tequilas. Miriam told Gladys, "Don't you remember your new boyfriend? He's the same guy who danced at your sister's bachelorette party."

Gladys was still wincing from the shot. "Really?"

"I swear to God, it's the same guy."

"It's not like I walked into some modeling agency and picked his picture out of a stack of headshots. I just called a number I found in the Yellow Pages and prayed they would send me a stud!" Gladys squealed at her wordplay. "God, how did I miss him?"

Miriam said, "You were in the kitchen most of the time, remember? Mixing piña coladas and warming up hors d'oeuvres."

"No, I was in the kitchen on the phone," Gladys said. "Fighting with your brother over God knows what."

"Well, I know someone who's getting army fatigues from his bride on their wedding night."

"Pablo would never wear them," said Gladys. "Especially if he knew where I got the idea."

Lisa, Miriam, and I yelled in unison. "So don't tell him!" We cackled and pointed at each other.

"And if he really gets bent out of shape just tell him . . ." Lisa started but then she stopped herself. "Forget it."

"What?"

"No, we're having fun, and I don't want to spoil anyone's time. It's not important."

"What?"

"It's stupid."

"WHAT?"

"A lot of the guys who do this are . . . you know . . . gay."

"No way!" Gladys face dropped so fast I thought her chin would hit the table and shatter.

"Not all of them, but . . ." Lisa shifted in her seat.

Gladys huffed in disbelief. She clapped her hands, stomped her feet and cheered Ultimo's name. "My Ben is not gay."

"Come to think of it, that makes perfect sense," I said.

"It's OK, Ricky," Lisa said. "Let it go."

Seeing how uncomfortable Lisa had become, the last thing I wanted to do was let it go. We came to Studs to get buzzed and pay gorgeous men to strip to their thongs while we ogled them. Fait accompli. Give Ultimo his money, bring another round of drinks, and send out the next hunk. Gladys was getting hitched, I already was, Lisa was gay, and Miriam wished she were. It should not matter to a single one of us who Ultimo/Ben curled up with after the show.

"No, think about it," I continued. "How does a guy get felt up by all these horny women and not get excited? I doubt while he's up there shaking his thang, he's reciting baseball stats to himself. And how many straight men you know would go to such lengths to trim their nose hairs let alone get a razor that close to their balls? I mean, if my husband shaved under his arms even once, I'd shove singles down his pants, too."

Miriam whooped at my remark—louder than she ever did for Ultimo—and I wished I could take it back. I said it for laughs but not one of that kind. Yes, I genuinely wished Eduardo would shave under his arms. I also wanted him to cancel the subscription to the Playboy channel, hang out less with that Neanderthal Dave and more with his coworker Greg, and do more chores around the house without my having to harangue him to do it. Most of all, I wanted to be able to gripe freely about these things to a girlfriend without feeling like I was betraying Eduardo because she secretly took pleasure in his imperfections. Like she was rooting for our discord to be something worse than the typical marital squabbles. I found myself getting angry at Miriam.

"Excuse me, I have to go to the bathroom," I said.

Lisa grabbed her purse, too. "I'll go with you." She threw some cash on the table. "Why don't you guys order us another round."

I asked a woman at the next table where the bathroom was, and she told us to head up the stairs to the balcony and make a right. Lisa and I made our way to the staircase that led to the second level. "What the hell . . . ?"

"I'm sorry. It's my fault. I never should've said what I did," said Lisa.

"Stop apologizing. You didn't do anything wrong." We found the line into the ladies' room and joined it. "First of all, what does Gladys care if some dancer she'll probably never see again is gay?"

"Well, this was the second time . . ."

"Lisa, stop it! She didn't even remember him. And she's getting married to her college sweetheart next weekend. Her best friend's brother! Why the hell's she so disappointed?" I realized the women ahead of me were eavesdropping on our conversation, so I lowered my voice. "And Miriam? I don't know about you, but she's starting to scare me, and she's not even drunk yet."

"Did you hear what she said about her son in the restaurant? You'd think she'd wish she never had him. All because his father turned out to be a moron."

"No, what threw me for a loop was when she said, 'I should've cheated on him when I had the chance.' What was that about?"

"And she's supposedly cool with my being gay, but it's because she sees me as the stereotypical man-hating dyke. At first, I thought she was really OK with it, but now . . ." Lisa looked over the balcony and her eyes fell on Gladys and Miriam in the crowd below us. Gladys folded her arms tightly across her chest while Miriam wagged her finger in her face about something Gladys clearly had heard many times before. "I feel so bad. First time in years since we've seen each other, and here we are talking about them behind their backs."

I thought about that for a moment. "So?"

"So?"

"You don't think they're fuckin' talking about us right now?" I rested my elbows on the rail of the balcony and said in my squeakiest voice, 'Lisa doesn't even like men anymore, OK, so how would she know if one was gay? And how come she knows so much about strip clubs? You know, a lot of these guys do this, a lot of these guys do that? Oh, my God, Lisa Pacheco's a lesbian!' "

Lisa laughed and came back to me as Miriam. " '¡Ay, can you blame her? And Ricky's either losing her mind or lying through her ass. She's not married. This Eduardo probably doesn't even exist.' "

Then I tried Miriam on for size. " 'I mean, look at her, Gladys. I know she's some nonprofit crusader, but c'mon! Hasn't she ever heard of Century Twenty-one? Isn't that the same dress she wore to our graduation?' "

" 'I didn't notice,' " Lisa as Gladys said. " 'I was too busy making sure Lisa wasn't trying to check me out.' "

And we laughed like we used to in our dorm room late at night. The kind of laughter that's rooted in who you really are and can only be released by another soul grown from the same soil. I laughed like this with 'Uardo, but I have to say, there was something special about doing it again with a woman who knew me from a previous lifetime.

After exiting the stall, I elbowed my way to the mirror and touched up my makeup. I looked around for Lisa and then quickly pulled my cell phone from my purse. I opened it, and sighed with relief. Eduardo had called and left me a message.

"Busted!" Lisa propped her chin on my shoulder. "You miss your hubby, you miss your hubby." She moved to the sink next to me and pumped soap into her palm.

"Shut up."

"How many times did he call?"

"Just once."

Lisa stopped washing her hands to coo. "Aw, that's so perfect," she said with utmost sincerity. "Often enough to show he cares yet infrequent enough to show he trusts. He's a keeper."

With such an enthusiastic endorsement, I stopped resisting the urge to dial my voicemail. "Let me check the message to be sure there's no emergency." *Hey, sweetie. It's your husband. Eduardo. Cordero. Remember? I'm kidding! Just checking in, hoping everything's going well. Anyway, when you're done shoving dollars down some guy's pants, call me back and tell me how bored you were. Love you.*

"Everything OK at home?"

"Everything's fine."

When we finished in the ladies' room and returned to the table, the next dancer—a black guy so beautiful he made Tyson the model look like Tyson the boxer—had already taken the stage. Dressed as a construction worker from his hard hat to tool belt, he wound his hips with his back to the crowd to Amber's "Sexual":

> *It can't be intellectual*
> *The way I feel is sexual.*

Then Tyson Squared stepped aside and in the center of the stage sat Tammy Tequila, grasping a twenty-dollar bill between her teeth. He straddled Tammy's thighs and grinded his way onto her lap. The women roared. Tossing back another shot of tequila, Gladys slammed the glass onto the table and joined the din while Miriam forced a smile and took a long sip of her fresh apple martini.

"I get it now," Lisa said. Then she grabbed my hand and pulled away from our table and toward backstage. "Come with me. I've got an idea."

Gladys paid us no mind, but Miriam asked, "Where are you two going?"

"Forgot something."

We wove through the crowd of chanting bodies until we reached the door that led backstage. There we found the show's MC standing guard. Lisa tapped him on the shoulder, and he turned. "Sorry, ladies, no one's allowed back here.

Employees only. You'll have to wait until after the show if you want an autograph."

"We just want to make sure someone special gives our friend some undivided attention," Lisa said as she fished into her purse. She pulled out a fifty and held it up for him to see it. "Think you might be able to help us?"

The MC took the bill and said, "I can see to that person-ally."

"You strip, too?" I said. Then I chided myself for being politically incorrect. "I mean, you're a dancer?"

"They save the best for last," he grinned. "Which one is your friend?" Lisa and I pointed toward our table. "The lit-tle blonde with the red dress?"

"No, the other one."

"Oh," he said, his eyes opening wide. "She's a hottie. The pleasure will be all mine."

"What's your name?" Lisa asked.

"I'm Frank, but the DJ will introduce me as the Gen-eral. I'll be dressed as a naval officer." Then he winked at us. "And a gentleman."

Lisa and I squealed like teenyboppers. *An Officer and a Gentleman.* It had to be a sign that we made the perfect deci-sion. Gladys loved that movie! Not only did she play that soundtrack over and over again, she once dragged us to a downtown indie theatre having a Richard Gere retrospective so we could "see it on the big screen the way it was meant to be seen." I mean, the guy's a good actor and easy on the eyes, but Gregory Peck or Raul Julia, he ain't.

"And, Frank, we want this act to be just a duet," said Lisa. "Get it."

"Got it."

We thanked him and rushed back to our table. "Gladys will pay us libations for the rest of her days," I said.

Lisa stopped in her tracks. "I know this is her night, but maybe we should have someone show some love to Miriam, too."

"You took care of Gladys, so leave Miriam to me," I said, "She doesn't want a hard-bodied man. What she needs is a stiff drink."

When we arrived at our table, it took all our willpower to play nonchalant. Lisa kept the singles in Gladys's fist and I, the martinis down Miriam's throat. It tickled us to watch Gladys's eyes burn with envious outrage as bride after bride—and the occasional committed single who came out of her own pocket for the honor—had an opportunity to costar with every hunk that took the stage. One dancer dressed as a firefighter carried his charge—a stunning black girl who seemed more at place at a cotillion than a night club—on the stage, gently laid her on the floor, eased her legs open, and mimed oral sex. The poor thing just buried her face in her hands and shook her head back and forth. If she were as lucky as she were adorable, her husband-to-be would produce the same effect with the real thing on their wedding night. Even a middle-aged Filipina had her way with a stripper in a doctor's costume, wasting no time showing the doctor what ailed her. He led her to the chair at the center of the stage, but instead of taking a seat, Ms. Thang immediately

bent over the back of the chair and braced herself for an enthusiastic spanking. Even Miriam felt compelled to raise her
fourth apple martini in reverence to her mettle.

But it really irked Gladys when Tammy Tequila wob-
bled on stage for a second round with Bull the Matador to
Pajama Party's *"Over And Over."* Bull moved the chair aside
and laid his cape along the floor. He offered Tammy his
hand, motioning for her to sit on the cape with her back
facing the audience. The way she slumped onto the floor, I
thought she would never get up again. First, Bull palmed
her head, pumped his hips into her face and rolled back his
head with feigned pleasure.

> *Touch me, over and over*
> *Move me, over and over*
> *Love me, over and over*
> *I need more of you*

Going along with the pantomime, Tammy clamped her hands
on his hips and bobbed her blond head like she was paid to.
Not to be outdone by this drunken amateur, Bull ordered her
to turn around to face the hollering audience. No sooner had
Tammy scampered around to face us than he placed his hand
on her shoulder and pushed her forward. Then he grabbed her ankles, pulled them to his waist and pounded away.
Tammy flopped around like an X-rated Raggedy Ann, the
hem of her plaid micromini flapping against ribs and exposing her baby-pink thong. Tammy drummed the stage and
tossed her flaxen locks to the rhythm of the song.

Oh, touch me, over and over
Move me, over and over
Love me, over and over
I need more of you

"I fuckin' hate her," Gladys whined.

"Ricky, when are you going up there?" Miriam said.

I've barely got enough money to buy gas to get home after water-ing your sour ass all night. "I'm having a good time right here," I said.

"*¡Ay,* you know you want to! Been married long enough."

"After you, *muñeca.*" And that settled it as I knew it would. I couldn't even imagine a happily married Miriam carrying on like Tammy Tequila behind closed doors, let alone going through the motions in front of an enthusiastic audience. Then again, I couldn't imagine a happily married Miriam at all.

The song ended, and pouting Tammy crawled back to her friends who had to peel her from the stage to the floor limb by limb. Bull made his way across the stage, collecting pieces of his cast-off costume as well as scattered dollar bills and taking the occasional bow as the women showered him with applause. Lisa looked at her watch, then showed it to me: a quarter to twelve. The final performance—the one she paid to land Gladys the role of leading lady—had to be next.

Then the stage darkened and the DJ's voice came over the loudspeaker. "Ladies, we're almost at the end of to-night's show . . ." The women in the crowd moaned in unison and the DJ chuckled. "Well, you'll just have to come back and visit us again here at Studs real soon, won't you?" The crowd cheered for that idea. As I applauded, I looked around the room and recognized every face that would be there next week if not the following night. Eduardo and I often talked about investing in some kind of business in our neighborhood so I began to wonder . . . "To close the show we have the officer and the gentleman you've been waiting all night to see . . ."

As the DJ played the opening bars of Joe Cocker's "Up Where We Belong," the Studs regulars began to chant. "General, General, General . . ."

"Show him your love and he'll show you his. . . ."

"General, General, General . . ."

"Ladies, put your hands together for THE GENERAL!" The women rocked the club with their screams as the MC Frank dressed in a white naval uniform sauntered down the stage. He moved deliberately, first mimicking the precise moves of an enlisted man, then posing in time to the ballad as it wafted over the applause and cheers.

Who knows what tomorrow brings

"Oh. My. God," Gladys said. "I love this song."

In a world where few hearts survive?

Maybe it was the corniness of it all. Of the anticipation over what Lisa and I had in store for Gladys. Or the tequila took the express vein right to my funny bone. I just doubled over in a fit of giggles. Lisa lightly patted me on the back of the shoulder. "You all right?" Her eyes shone with the excitement to ensue which only made me giggle even harder. I felt so wicked and delicious. "OK, Ricky, no more for you."

Gladys whipped around in her seat, surveying the remaining competition. To her right, the feisty Filipina waved a single bill back and forth like a candle at a vigil while the Southern belle chatted away with a girlfriend as if they were in a sewing circle instead of strip club. But then Gladys spun to her left and gasped with rage. While a woozy Tammy leaned against the stage serenading the General, her friends scraped the bottom of their pocketbooks and piled bills on the center of the table to buy her one last trip to heaven.

Gladys whirled around to face us. "Cash! Guys, I need more cash," she yelled as she rifled through the few bills she had in hand. "He's not gonna give me a second look for seven dollars." She leaped to her feet and planted herself at the edge of the stage, her face contorting for a scheme to get the General's attention while we coughed up some dough. Suddenly, Gladys shoved her pinkies in her mouth and whistled strong and high. All these years, and I never knew she could do that!

It served as a battle cry because other women swarmed toward the stage and waved their bills for the General's attention. "Shit," said Miriam as she fumbled through her purse. She opened her wallet to the empty billfold and then yanked out a credit card. "Maybe I can just swipe this down his ass, you think?" she slurred.

But the General was a man of his word. He fixed his
eyes on Gladys and headed toward her. She gazed up at
him as if the heavens opened, God had smiled down upon
her, and God looked exactly like a young Richard Gere.
Then Gladys looked in horror at the singles crammed into
her upraised fist. She spun around to face us.

"Money!" she demanded. "Give me money, I need more
money. Quick, before Booby Spears over there takes him
from me."

Lisa and I fell over in laughter while Miriam tried to hand
Gladys her credit card. The noise in the room soared into a
collective howl. When Gladys turned around, she found the
General right in front of her, hunkering down and offering
her his hand.

"He picked me!"

"Go, girl, go!" Miriam yelled. "And remember. Make him
earn it."

I leaned over to Lisa and whispered, "Our plan's working. Three drinks ago it would've been 'Make his ass pay.'
And we both know what that would've meant." Lisa and I
shook hands, congratulating ourselves.

Gladys slipped her hand into the General's and he pulled
her onto the stage. Not only did Tammy Tequila sulk, she
shoved her bill into her bra and sank back in her seat. One
of her friends—the cash's true owner—extended her hand
in silent but adamant request for the return of her money.
Tammy pouted and slapped the bill into her hand. Her
guest shoved the money into her jacket pocket, motioned
for two other women, and they left right then.

As the General led Gladys to her throne in the center of the stage, Miriam clapped heartily and cheered, and for the first time that night, it felt like old times. At that moment we had managed to come together and reveled in each other's company. We took joy in Gladys's pleasure no less than had it been our own.

The General removed his white cap and gently placed it on Gladys's head. She adjusted the fit and ran her fingers across the gold braid as if she had no intention of returning it. Then the General sashayed behind her and peeled off his white gloves, sliding them off one finger at a time. Gladys bounced her knees and watched his every move like a little girl watching her birthday cake being carried to the table.

"General, General, General . . ."

Heeding the call of his fans, the General opened his jacket, caressing every button as Gladys's eyes followed his hands. He popped the last button, and the lapels of the jacket fell away revealing his tanned, bulging pecs. Then he took Gladys's hands and placed them on his chest.

Lisa stood up. "You guys have any more singles?"

"Are you serious?"

"I got another idea." I found a few bills tucked inside a zippered pocket in my pocketbook and handed her one. "Watch this," said Lisa. Then she climbed onto the stage.

Miriam gasped. "What's Lisa doing?"

"I don't know." But I knew it was going to be good.

Lisa scuttled across the stage and wedged the single into Gladys's cleavage, and the crowd roared its approval. Except for Tammy Tequila who was too busy fumbling into her jacket and trying to tear her mesmerized guests away from the onstage action. The General caressed Gladys's cheek as he grazed his lips above her temple, down her neck, and across her chest. He cupped his palms under her breasts, and like a windup doll, Gladys threw her arms in the air and arched her back. The General buried his face into her bosom, while the crowd thundered and Gladys pumped her fists. Then the General emerged from his foray into her cleavage with the single between his teeth.

As if to raise the stakes, the DJ switched to Usher's "Yeah." The General flexed his muscular arms over his head as he popped his hips to the syncopation. Everyone in the crowd rose to her feet to sing and clap along with the music.

She's saying come get me, come get me. Yeah.

Inspired by Lisa's move, I grabbed a dollar bill and rushed across the stage. With the audience cheering me on, I tucked it into the front of Gladys's waistband. "I'm gonna get you, bitch!" she laughed. I blew her a kiss and climbed off the stage.

When I got back to the table, Lisa greeted me with a high five. But Miriam shook her head and grabbed her purse. "You guys are wusses," she said. Brandishing a ten-dollar bill from I don't know where, Miriam stormed the stage.

"And y'all call me competitive," I said. As Miriam drew near, the General spotted the bill in her hand. He approached her, extending his hand to request she dance with him. I jumped to my feet to throw a fit. "Uh uh, Franky! You promised!"

Lisa yanked at my arm and pulled me back into my seat. "C'mon, Ricky. At least, it's Miriam."

"I don't care. Now that he's finally paying Gladys attention, she wants to jump in her spotlight? You gave him fifty dollars to dance for Gladys and Gladys only."

I spoke too soon because Miriam just smirked and brushed past the General. Then she laid the ten-dollar bill across Gladys's crotch. I thought Gladys might draw the line and grab the bill and place it someplace tamer. Instead, she showed her consent by tilting her hips and giving the General a come-hither stare that I never knew she had in her.

Next thing I knew she was all up on me screaming yeah, yeah, yeah!

The crowd almost blew off the roof with its stomps and hollers, and when Miriam passed the General on her way off the stage, she gave him a sharp look. *Earn it.*

Miriam returned to our table. "That's how you take care of a friend."

Lisa raised her drink to her. "Hear, hear." I lifted my glass as well and we toasted her. Still ashamed that I had thought the worst of Miriam, I squeezed her hand and planted a kiss on her cheek. Then I thought back to my tame bridal shower with prudish regret.

I especially felt guilty driving my poor sister, Mena, crazy trying to find party ideas with all my limitations, genuine and invented. First, I waited until the last minute to give her permission to throw a party for me. I vacillated over my schedule for weeks before my wedding, making Mena skittish about setting a date for fear that I would cancel at the last minute over some work-related matter or fail to show up altogether at my own party. When I finally agreed to let Mena have the party—well, she kept calling it a party; I insisted on calling it a shower—she had no time to track down old friends like Lisa, Miriam, and Gladys. My "friends" were coworkers and colleagues and for that reason I nixed the stripper. Although at that time I claimed to do it out of respect for Eduardo. Mena knew damned well 'Uardo would not care so long as I did nothing I might kill him for doing at his bachelor party. She later told me that she stopped short of asking Eduardo to give me his blessing to party on. When I asked her why, she said, "'Cause after I thought about it, I realized that I might create trouble between the two of you if I asked him to do that. I knew that if I did, he'd do it, and that just made me love him all the more. I didn't want the poor man to think otherwise by being so gung ho about your bachelorette party so I decided to let it go."

In fact, when Mena suggested a girls' night out on the town, I vetoed that as well. I knew that could be just as wild, if not more than hiring a stripper. Instead of having a roomful of women sharing one man behind closed doors, I could find myself having to interact with a string of strange men on the street. Bridal showers that took to the streets became scavenger hunts for scandals. No thanks.

So as I watched the General give Gladys a lap dance, I

wished I had let my sister hire a stripper. It would have been a much more memorable night. And maybe more girls' nights would have followed.

"Ricky, look!" Lisa snapped me out of my thoughts in time to watch the General grab Gladys's legs, push them behind her head, and bury his face between them. The club trembled with howls and applause as he shook his head like a grizzly fishing for salmon in a stream. Gladys threw back her head and ran her fingers in his hair.

"Go, Gladys, get busy," chanted Miriam. "Go, Gladys, get busy."

Lisa and I chimed in and soon the entire club did, too.

Go, Gladys, get busy. Go, Gladys, get busy.

And soon women from all corners of the club brought their final singles to the stage to donate them to Gladys's cause. Oh, quite a few took the opportunity to put their hands on the General if only for a few seconds, but no one attempted to divert his attention from the star bride. They wedged their singles into Gladys's cleavage, along her waistband, and even—don't ask me how they kept them put— behind her ears. By the time the song ended, Gladys looked like a grinning pine tree.

The DJ switched to Nice & Wild's "Diamond Girl." The General took that as his cue to launch his finale. When he emerged from Gladys's crotch with the final batch of singles between his teeth, he grabbed her hands and planted them on his grinding hips. Gladys ran her hands down his outer thighs.

Diamond girl, tu me haces sentir como estoy en fuego junto a ti
Tu me captivas con tu amor, te quiero dar todo mi calor

Ever the cheerleader, Miriam yelled, "Take it off, take it off!"

Take it off, take it off!

Gladys's hands made their way back to the General's waist. She looked up at him, and he nodded. With that permission, she yanked and tore his costume pants down to his knees. I gasped at what I saw bulging from his pristine white G-string.

"Jesus, I think he's . . ." Even after all we had witnessed together that night, I still could not bring myself to be that explicit. ". . . excited."

For the first time all night, Miriam giggled uncontrollably. *"¡Ay, ay, ay!"*

"*Ay, ay, ay,* my ass! I'm not trying to be Polly Puritan here, but are they, like, allowed to do that?" I said. "I mean, all the other guys managed to keep themselves in check, and they all can't be gay."

"Don't worry, it's probably not real," said Lisa. "Some of the smaller guys compensate by putting dildos in their thongs, that's all."

"How the hell *do* you know these things?" But I did relax a bit.

Miriam scoffed. "After what I paid, that thing had better be real!"

"After what *Lisa* paid, it had better *not* be real!"

"Ricky, what the hell are you talking about?"

Just as I was about to tell Miriam exactly what the hell I was talking about, Lisa stepped between us. "All that matter is that Gladys is having a great time."

"Exactly," said Miriam.

"Gladys. Not him!" I shot back.

"You two knock it off. The show's going to end any minute now. Everyone had a blast and no one got hurt. Right?"

I knew Lisa was right, but something about Miriam's casual attitude toward Gladys's comfort and safety bothered me. I could not imagine that even Studs regulars would be comfortable with an erect stripper humping them in public, let alone understand why a woman slated to marry in a week would not mind. Especially with her fiancé's sister in a front-row seat.

The music stopped and the DJ's voice boomed over the speakers. "Ladies, thank you for visiting Studs, and we hope that you'll come again real soon."

"Let's find a nice café somewhere for some dessert and coffee," Lisa said.

Now that the show had ended and Gladys would rejoin us soon, I had no choice but to let the matter go. "That sounds cool."

Miriam said, "Great."

"OK, let's get the blushing bride and get out of here," said Lisa. We looked toward the now dark and empty stage. "She was there a minute ago."

"Maybe she went to the bathroom," said Miriam. "Where is it again?"

"Up the stairs and to your right."

"I have to go myself so I'll go find her and bring her down." She took off and Lisa and I sat down at our table to wait. We watched as the young black girl and her friends put on their jackets and collected their purses. She held a giant lollipop in the shape of a chocolate penis, still wrapped in clear plastic and tied with a red bow. One of her guest spotted Tyson Squared—now fully dressed in denim overalls and a matching jacket—reached into her purse for a camera and called him over to their table. Grinning, he sauntered over and posed with the bride-to-be while everyone gathered around them with their cameras. Then he posed good-naturedly with every guest who wanted to take a picture with him while the bride obliged and snapped photos. When they were finished, Tyson Squared took the bride's hand and kissed it, teasing her about the massive rock on her tiny finger and wishing her a long and happy marriage. Then he bid the party a safe trip home and walked out the side exit.

"How sweet," said Lisa.

"Yeah." I chided myself for overreacting about the General's stuffed G-string. I looked up toward the balcony toward the ladies' room. From what I could see, the line had whittled down to only three women so I figured Miriam and Gladys had made it inside and would rejoin us soon. Club employees milled about us, sweeping gift wrap and multicolored confetti into neat mounds, returning tables to their proper places and placing chairs on top of the tables. A server came by to wipe down our table and pile the glasses onto a tray. When he finished and left, I said, "I didn't mean to get all paranoid and rain on the parade."

Lisa smiled. "You didn't. You were just being you." Then she chuckled. "Remember that big fight you and Miriam got into at the Latin Quarter our senior year?"

"Don't remind me."

During our last year at Barnard, the four of us caught a bad case of senioritis. After Lisa triumphed over her last final, we headed to the Latin Quarter on Broadway at 96th Street. Until that night we had an unspoken code that wherever the four of us went together, we left together. Or so I thought because it had never been different. Nor did we ever wander out of each other's sight for too long or leave any of the others alone with someone she had just met. That night at the Latin Quarter, however, Miriam met a guy and changed the game plan.

After going without sleep for almost three nights, I barely danced with my seat that night. If it had been up to me, we would've just stayed in our dorm room and celebrated by ourselves. Besides staying up late to finish papers and study for exams, I lost sleep at the thought of moving out of our two-bedroom apartment on Claremont into a tiny studio on West 115th Street.

A little after midnight, the four of us agreed to leave at one. Soon after, this older guy approached Miriam and asked her to salsa. With our blessing, she headed to the dance floor with him. One moment we saw Miriam's partner twirl her around, the next she disappeared. From where we sat we scanned the dance floor, but no Miriam. Gladys convinced me that Miriam was fine, but Lisa agreed to go dance with me so we could look for her. We spent a half hour on the dance floor and still no Miriam. Now Lisa began to worry, too. We went back to our table, and Gladys said, "Oh, Miriam stopped by. She said if we want to leave, go ahead. She'll be fine."

Well, I wasn't fine with that. "Where the hell is she now?"

"Last I saw her, she and I-Forgot-His-Name were headed to the bar. She's coming right back though. I asked her to bring me a Coke."

So Lisa and I sat. Or more like Lisa sat and I seethed. Miriam returned, all snuggled up with her newfound friend. She introduced him to us, but his name went in one ear and out the other. She placed Gladys's soda on the table and asked, "So you guys are heading out at one, right?"

"No, we're staying," I said.

"We are?" asked Lisa.

"We can't leave Miriam by herself."

"Oh, go ahead. I can take a cab." She gazed at I-Forgot-His-Name-Too. Clearly, he had promised to cover her carfare back to the dorm.

"We'll wait," I said.

That was when Miriam whispered something in the guy's ear. He nodded and headed back to the bar. When he walked out of earshot, Miriam whirled around to me and said, "What's the deal, Ricky? You guys agreed to go home at one, and I want to stay a little while longer. I'm cool with . . ."

"No, Miriam. *We* agreed to leave at one. And if you insist on staying, we have to stay here with you. . . ."

"You don't have to anything. In fact, I want you to go . . ."

". . . about to leave you alone in a crowded club with some guy you just met, you must be out of your fuckin' . . ."

". . . home, Ricky! Just fuckin' go home already!" Miriam spun around and stormed away from me.

And I pursued her. Not knowing what else to do, Lisa and Gladys followed me. At the bar, I saw Miriam giggling and drinking while I-Forgot-His-Name-Too whispered in her ear. "Don't go over there and embarrass her," Gladys begged.

"*Calmate*, I'm not going to go over there." Instead I planted myself at the bar around the corner from where Miriam sat. "We're just going sit here and keep on eye on her until she's ready to leave."

"What's the difference if we stay one more hour?" Lisa said as she slid into the stool next to me. "The place closes at two."

"I don't want to sit around waiting for another hour," whined Gladys.

"Then go dance."

"No one's asked me."

"Then ask somebody."

"I want to go home."

"We all stay or we all go."

So Gladys marched over to Miriam. Without excusing herself, she walked in between Miriam and her "date" and told her something that apparently required a whole lot of head rolling and finger swaying to thoroughly convey. Miriam responded with a quizzical look, and Gladys pointed to where Lisa and I sat. Or more like where Lisa sat and I fumed. Gladys stormed away from Miriam and headed back toward us.

Meanwhile, Miriam whispered into her dance partner's ear. He reached for a matchbook with one hand and inside his jacket for a pen with the other. He tore the matchbook cover in half and scribbled across one piece. Then Miriam took the pen from his hand and scribbled across the other. They exchanged scraps, she kissed him on the cheek, and then barreled toward the exit without giving the rest of us another glance.

When we hit the street, I jogged a few paces to catch up to Miriam. We trotted a block in silence. Then I finally said, "I don't know why you couldn't just take his number down in the first place."

Miriam came to a halt, spun around to face me, and hollered, "How dare you embarrass me like that!"

And then we had it out like we never had before right there on the corner of 97th Street and Broadway. Gladys and Lisa knew better than to interfere. The best they could hope for was that Miriam and I would shout at each other to the point of fatigue before a cop arrived.

"How dare you abandon your friends in a club over some guy you barely know?" I have to admit that at the time I felt like a whiny teenager. *You flat-left me.*

"But I told you to go. How many times did I say, 'Leave'? You think because you live with me, you're entitled to know my business and invade my privacy *cada vez te da la* fuckin' *gana?* You're not my mother, Ricky!"

"No, I'm just your friend."

"Friends don't cock-block!"

"Cock-block? If that's what you think I was doing, then to hell with you, Miriam. You don't know what the hell a friend is. And you know what? Fuck me, too, for wanting to make sure you didn't get raped or worse!"

I started back up the street. Within seconds, I heard Miriam say, "Ricky, hold up," and run toward me. I ignored her now more out of hurt than anger. After years of enduring her teasing—Miriam loved to call me the Amazon of Washington Heights—she truly thought I insisted on waiting for her at the club out of some twisted jealousy.

I felt Miriam grab my arm and I yanked it away. "C'mon, Ricky, let's stop acting like we're in junior high school and talk this thing out. We're graduating in a few days, and I don't want this festering between us when we might not . . ." For the first time I realized that I wasn't the only one who was anxious about the potential permanence of our impending separation. "I don't even want to wait until we get home to deal with it. Instead of bringing all this anger back to our apartment, let's just find a café or a park bench or wherever and talk."

Gladys and Lisa caught up to us. "There's an all-night diner right up the street. Gladys and I can go home, leave you two alone."

"No," Miriam said.

I nodded. "Stay."

So the four of us went to that all-night diner and sat down, and Miriam and I hashed out our disagreement like adults. I apologized for treating Miriam like a child and being rude to her "date." She apologized for acting like a child and being rude to us. The four of us hugged, cried, and told one another that we loved each other and vowed to be friends for life.

Then graduation came, and we went our separate ways. I moved into that Columbia-owned studio on West 115th Street while I attended the School of Social Work. Lisa headed to medical school in Georgetown. Gladys left for Illinois to get her MBA at Northwestern, and Miriam moved back to her mother and aunt's house in Queens and took a job at a fashion house. For the first few years after graduation, we managed to stay in touch and saw each other in pairs over the holiday season and summer months. In the mail, I received an announcement about Lisa's graduation from medical school and an invitation to Miriam's wedding. It so happened that her wedding took place somewhere on Long Island the weekend before I had to defend my dissertation, and I decided I could not afford the risk of losing a day's preparation time. We never managed to get together as a foursome, and eventually the telephone calls became emails, the emails dwindled into Christmas and birthday cards, and finally the cards faded into prolonged bouts of silence. That is, until this Friday night.

I looked down at my watch. "Where the hell are those two?"

"I was just wondering the same thing," said Lisa. "We'd better go get them. You know how those two can be when they get in front of a mirror."

I laughed at that truth, and we collected our things and headed up the staircase. But when we arrived at the bathroom, we found a handful of women primping for the next escapade on their evening's itinerary and a Studs employee emptying the trash bin. Lisa even checked under the stalls for Miriam's Valentino sandals while I called their names. We walked out of the ladies' room and back down to the main floor. Pockets of stragglers made their way toward the exit, but we saw no sign of Miriam or Gladys.

"Let's check the bar," said Lisa.

When we got to the bar, we found no one but barmaids cleaning up for the night. One even said, "Sorry, ladies, we're closed."

"We're just looking for our friends. Is there another bathroom here besides the one upstairs?"

"No, ma'am, the only other bathroom is backstage and for employees only."

Lisa and I exchanged dumbfounded looks. "Maybe they went outside."

I wanted to believe that but instinctively knew that wasn't the case. "Will you go look?"

"OK, but they may not let me back in, so if I don't come back . . ."

"Then let me go with you."

Lisa and I walked to the exit. A bouncer stood at the door bidding patrons farewell while handing out fliers for an upcoming event. Lisa walked over to him and said, "Listen, we're looking for some friends of ours. Do you mind if I just stepped outside for a moment to see if they're out there and come back inside if they're not?"

"No, miss, I wish I could let you do that, but once you leave, I can't let you back in. Club policy."

"C'mon, she just wants to take a peek and not get stuck out there alone if they're not out there," I said.

"I understand that, but I can't let you do it. Club policy."

"What do you think she's trying to do? Smuggle in a sleeping bag and spend the night here?"

The bouncer sneered. "Oh, you'd be surprised what some of you women would do after a show like this."

Then I heard Miriam call my name. Lisa and I turned, and my stomach sank to see her alone. "Where's Gladys?"

"Last time I saw her she was with the General," she practically sang. "Lord lift us up where we belong!"

The bouncer snickered and shook his head. "Aw, man. Fuckin' Frank."

"What do you mean the last time you saw her she was with the General?"

"We were on our way out of the ladies' room when the DJ came up to us and said that Frank wanted to talk to Gladys. I could tell that she really wanted to go see him one last time so I said, 'Hey, tonight is your night. You go have fun and whatever happens here stays here.' Just like we agreed."

Lisa surprised me when she yelled, "You let her walk off with him and you don't know where the hell they went?" She pushed past Miriam and stormed toward the main floor. "Show me where you saw her last."

Miriam froze at Lisa's sudden abruptness, so I gave her

a gentle push to follow her. "The DJ said something about a VIP room."

Lisa walked up to an employee sweeping the floor. "Where's the VIP room?"

He looked up and pointed to the opposite side of the balcony. "It's not a room really. Just a section we curtain off sometimes for . . ."

"Thanks," Lisa said and headed up the staircase. I stayed on her heels and Miriam struggled to keep on mine. We reached the balcony in time to see a short guy in a baseball cap emerge from behind the curtain.

"That's the guy I spoke to, that's the DJ," said Miriam. Then she scrambled in front of Lisa. "C'mon, what are you doing?"

"We just want to make sure that Gladys is OK," I answered.

"Why wouldn't she be OK?"

"You can't be serious?"

Lisa marched right around Miriam and past the DJ toward the curtain. He stopped to watch us and when he saw where we were headed, he dashed past Lisa and planted himself in front of the curtain.

"I'm sorry, ladies, no one is allowed past this point."

"Is this the VIP section?" I asked.

"Yes, it is, that's why . . ."

"A friend of ours is supposed to be here," said Lisa, "and we just want to make sure she's all right."

"I can't let you go back there." Lisa tried to push past him, but he blocked her path. "What does your friend look like?"

Miriam started to describe Gladys, but I cut in, "Look, we're not going anywhere until we see her."

"Then I'm gonna have to call security," he said.

"Yeah, why don't you do us all a favor and do that," I replied, calling his bluff.

The DJ flustered. "Just wait right here," and disappeared behind the curtain.

Miriam called behind him, "Tell her that we'll be waiting for her out . . ."

"Right here," Lisa and I said.

Lisa and I exchanged one look, then at the same time, we each reached for opposite sides of the curtain. For some crazy reason, Miriam tried to stop us, but together we were too strong for her. Lisa and I jerked back the curtain with such a force, the rod trembled and several of the hooks popped off and bounced across the floor.

In a corner on a sofa, Gladys sat on Frank's lap. He cooed in her ear as his hand disappeared up her skirt. Both were fully dressed (or at least that's what I believed at the time) and oblivious to the fact that their private party had been crashed.

The DJ bounded out of a dark corner and over to us. "I said y'all are not allowed back here."

Ignoring him Lisa yelled, "Gladys!" She finally looked up and saw us. Embarrassment flooded her face. Gladys slowly climbed off Frank's lap and straightened her dress. He stood up and turned his back to us, presumably to tuck away his manhood and close his zipper.

The DJ said, "Y'all need to get out of here now."

"As soon as we get our friend," I said.

"She's a big girl and can take care of herself."

No. He. Didn't. "You don't know the first thing about her, *puñeto*," I yelled. "So mind your fuckin' business and get out the way before you get hurt."

When he heard that, Frank finally turned around to intervene. "Hey, hey, hey, everyone calm down here." He looked at me and said, "Look, you don't have to disrespect my DJ like that."

"Disrespect your DJ?" said Lisa. "Your DJ's disrespecting us. You want somebody to calm down, you talk to him." Then she looked at Gladys and said, "Let's go. Now!" Gladys knew better than to argue with Lisa now that her patience had run low. She scooped her purse off the sofa and trotted over like an obedient puppy without even a glance at Frank.

"See, all this is unnecessary," he said. "Like my man said, she's a grown woman and can make her own decisions."

"He's not a man," said Lisa. "And neither are you." She grabbed Gladys by the arm and dragged her through the curtain. Miriam gave an apologetic shrug and followed them.

I lingered to give Frank one last piece of my mind. "The next time your girlfriend goes out, you'd better hope she's with friends just like us." His DJ opened his mouth and I said, "Go 'head, say something. Give me the reason to go straight to your manager. And if you think he'll let you get away with this, wait until he gets his copy of my letter to the state liquor authority." Both of them kept their mouths shut, and when I turned around to leave, Lisa was standing there waiting for me. She had returned to make sure I was OK.

"Where are Paris and Nicole?" I said.

"Outside. Look, Ricky, I know this is a lot to ask, especially after all that's just happened, but would you mind terribly driving them home?" asked Lisa. "We'll go to Raffaella's first for some coffee. . . ."

"Yeah, yeah."

"Are you sure? It's OK to say no."

"No, it's not a problem."

"I just want to make sure that they get home without any more incidents."

I put my arm around Lisa's shoulder. "For you, yes."

Lisa put her arm around my waist. "It's so good to see you, Ricky." We both exhaled and fled Studs.

We got my car out of the parking garage and drove to Raffaella's in complete silence, each of us brewing in her own thoughts about what had occurred. Thank God, it only took ten minutes to arrive and settle in at the café. We each placed our orders and then the silence returned.

Finally Gladys made a surprising announcement. "I have to tell Pablo."

Not only was telling Pablo the last thing I thought she would even consider, I found myself oddly touched that she would share the possibility with us. She knew that Lisa and I did not approve of her behavior at Studs, and it crossed my mind that she merely tossed out that idea in the hopes that we would talk her out of it.

"I think that's the right thing to do," I said.

"Me, too," said Lisa.

Miriam shook her head. "I personally don't think that's necessary, but whatever you decide to do, you have my support."

"You don't think I should tell him?" Gladys seemed genuinely shocked by Miriam's nonchalance.

"Tell him what, Gladys? You didn't do anything."

"Because we stopped her," Lisa said. She looked to me for support.

"Gladys, you honestly can't say that if we hadn't shown up when we did, nothing would have happened."

Gladys shook her head. "No, I can't say that." The server arrived with our orders and we paused until he finished and left. "But it's not what you guys think. I mean, nothing would have happened that I didn't want to happen. I'm not that drunk."

"It doesn't matter," I said. "You're drunk enough for him to have taken advantage of you. And he would have, had we not barged in."

"Frank was a doll," Gladys said, batting her eyes like a teenager gushing over her crush. "He wasn't going to do anything to me. If I had wanted to stop, he would've stopped." She paused as if she wanted to say more, but instead added a third packet of sugar to her latte.

Lisa scoffed. "You don't know him or what he's capable of. You don't know if he would've slipped something in your drink."

"Exactly."

"You don't know how many times he's done this before with other women."

"Probably does it all the fuckin' time."

"You don't know if he has a disease."

"Or if his little friend would've wanted to do more than be a lookout."

"No! Frank's a sweetheart. Nothing like that was going to happen."

Miriam said, "The bottom line is, thank God, nothing did happen. And that's why there's nothing to tell Pablo. Whatever happened at the club, stays at the club."

"No, I have to tell him."

"Tell him what? That you kissed a stripper? For what?"

"Because we're getting married next week, and if I can't tell him that, maybe we shouldn't get married."

Why did it take that long for me to realize that Gladys was having such serious doubts about the wedding? Not the ordinary nerves that engaged couples have the eve before their walk down their aisle like I surely had. She disappeared with Frank not because she felt entitled to one last fling before she married Pablo, but because she was deathly afraid that perhaps she should not marry him.

"¡Ay, Gladys, you're acting like you cheated on him!"

"Didn't she?" said Lisa.

"No, of course not!"

"It really doesn't matter whether we think she did or didn't," I interjected. "The point is—and Gladys, tell me if I'm wrong here—whatever you did do was something that if

Pablo did at his bachelor party, you would want him to tell you."

With a somber slant to her lips, Gladys nodded. Miriam gasped as if Gladys had lost her mind right before her eyes. "Kissing? If he had kissed a stripper he's never likely to see again, you would want him to tell you?"

"We did a little more than that." The three of us shut up and leaned in for the scoop. "Frank has my panties."

"What?"

"At one point, he took them off, and I guess I left them behind at the club. But that's all he did, I swear to God."

"You left your panties behind at the club?"

"I checked my purse, and I don't have them."

"And you're going to tell Pablo *that*?" Miriam asked. She murmured and then took a long sip of her cappuccino.

"You don't think I should? I mean, if I were in his shoes, I would want to know."

Lisa reached across the table and put her hand over Gladys's. "It's your decision, but I think you should tell him," she said. "If you're going to go through with this marriage, you want to get it to an honest start. If you can't tell Pablo what happened and work through it, you have to ask yourself whether you should be getting married. Yes, a lot worse could have happened that didn't, but something *did* happen."

"My brother's not going to call off the wedding just because you flirted with some stripper," said Miriam.

"You don't think so?" My social worker's ear caught a hint of disappointment in Gladys's tone, but my experience told me that if Pablo did not call off the wedding, she would go through with it.

"I know so," said Miriam. "Besides women need to stop feeling guilty about doing things that men do all the time without a second thought."

"Not all men," I said.

"That's right. Your husband's perfect," Miriam said.

"Far from it, but I know that. You, on the other hand, don't, so don't go there."

"I'm not saying anything about your husband in particular, Ricky, I'm talking about men in general. Including Pablo, who I know that if he were in Gladys's position, not only would he not say shit, he'd never think about it again. So she shouldn't beat herself up over what *almost* happened. And just for argument's sake . . ."

"Please no more arguments," said Gladys as she fiddled with the crumbs of her coffee cake.

". . . Let's just say something had happened. So what? It's your bachelorette party. It's one night. It's before your wedding. Big deal, let it go."

"So you're saying if Gladys had fucked that guy, you wouldn't tell your brother?" Lisa asked.

"No, I wouldn't tell him. He's my brother, but she's my friend. All I wanted is for Gladys to have fun tonight, and if that meant one last fling before she got married, so be it. If Pablo weren't my brother, I wouldn't feel any differently, so why should I change my tune just because he is?"

We fell silent, chewing on our pastries and Miriam's rationalizations. I tried to remember what I knew of Miriam's relationship with her brother Pablo. They never struck me as particularly close. Then again, they never appeared unusually antagonistic either. Back in our college days, Miriam and Pablo just . . . were. But I had to remind myself that I had not talked to Miriam in years, and I had no idea what might have occurred between them for her to become so casual about his emotional welfare. Something involving her ex-husband, Larry, maybe. Perhaps something that Pablo knew about and, out of a twisted sense of fraternity, kept from Miriam to protect Larry. Or maybe he meant to protect Miriam although she didn't see it that way.

Then I considered the possibility that nothing had happened between Miriam and Pablo at all. More like something had happened to her. Larry did something to her. Or maybe Miriam did something to herself. Along the way she made a choice—to act out, to settle, to look the other way. Some poor choice that demanded she be less than honest with herself. And now Miriam had to experience the miserable consequences and would be damned if everyone did not suffer along with her, including her best friend and brother.

I could have asked Miriam and found out what that was, but I felt it'd be too much, too late. Not because of what happened at Studs, but because it was one of those things where I had to have been there all along in order to understand. To be helpful. To be a friend. And then I began to feel some responsibility for what had occurred at the club.

"I gotta get going," I said. I reached for my purse and motioned for our server to bring our bill.

"Do you guys need a ride?" Lisa asked. She nudged me

to remind me of what I had agreed to at the club. I had not
forgotten nor did I intend to renege. Still, I wish she had let
me out of it considering the recent conversation.

"No, we can take a cab into Brooklyn," said Miriam.
"Gladys is staying with me."

Lucky Gladys. "I insist," I said.

"Don't you live in El Barrio? It's out of your way."

"Where do you live? Park Slope? That's nothing from
here, especially at this hour. Lisa, where are you?"

"I'm on the Lower East Side. Nice night like this, I could
walk if I wanted to."

"At this hour, like hell you will. Just come with me to
take them to Brooklyn. Keep me company on the way back
into Manhattan. Unless you're tired . . ."

"No, I'd like that."

"You're sure?"

"Totally."

Gladys started one more fight before we left Raffaella's
when she insisted on picking up the tab. Ordinarily, it
would have been a silly argument, and we would have had a
riot having it. But we all knew she made the offer as a way
to apologize for her behavior earlier that night, and it all
just seemed so sad.

During the drive to Brooklyn. Miriam hinted that she and
Gladys find some neighborhood bar or lounge for a nightcap.
Gladys said she was tired and just wanted to go to bed. She
pulled out her cell phone and dialed a number. "I bet Pablo's
not even home yet." As soon as Gladys said that, her head
snapped back against the car seat. "Hey, honey, where are

you?" she droned into the telephone. "Already? Oh. Well, did you have fun? 'Cause . . . you sound real . . . sober. Yeah, me, too. Wait until you see the presents the girls got us."

I waited for Gladys to hint that something critical had happened that night that they needed to discuss. I waited for her to get off the telephone and ask us for our advice on how to handle the discussion and all its possible consequences. I waited for an opportunity to counsel Gladys that if she had such deep reservations about marrying Pablo, she owed it to herself to cancel the wedding despite whatever pressures others may impose on her.

"I guess I can go back and exchange it for the purple one."

When Lisa and I dropped off Miriam and Gladys at Miriam's Park Slope apartment, the four of us climbed out of my car to exchange hugs and numbers. Suddenly Gladys said, "You guys know you're invited to the wedding, right? I mean, I know it's last minute and all, but of course, I'd love to have you there. Ricky, feel free to bring, um . . ."

"Eduardo."

"Yeah, we'll make it work." She said nothing to Lisa about bringing a date, and I knew it had nothing to do with Lisa's recent return to singlehood.

"Oh, thank you, that's sweet," I said. "We can't make it though. 'Uardo has this big thing next Saturday so . . ."

"And I'm on call that weekend," said Lisa.

"Oh. OK. But let's the four of us get together when I come back from my honeymoon, yeah?"

We promised to stay in better touch, and then Lisa and I

climbed back into my car and drove off. The second I stopped at the first light, Lisa said, "What a night."

"You mean nightmare."

"I can't believe Gladys ran off with that stripper."

"At least she wanted to tell Pablo about it. I give her that. I mean, Miriam was encouraging her to lie to her own brother!"

"Let me tell you something, Ricky. When I came out, my brother took it hard. In fact, he was pretty fucked up to me, and for a while there I thought our relationship was over. We're great now, closer than ever, but you know what? Even then had I learned that his fiancée disappeared with some stripper, I'd tell the bitch, 'Do you want to tell him or should I?' And then I'd give her a deadline."

I snickered in agreement and pulled onto the Manhattan Bridge. "Even if it were me?"

"Especially if it were you."

"Me, too."

"You don't even have a brother," she teased.

"Even more the reason . . ." We had a good laugh over that and then suddenly Lisa grew so serious, I began to worry. "What?"

"It's my fault."

"What's your fault?"

"What happened tonight?"

"That Gladys ran off with that himbo? How you figure that's your fault?"

"I gave the pig fifty bucks so that he'd pay her special attention . . ."

"Lisa, stop! First of all, you did not pay him all *that* much. . . ."

"I just wanted her to have fun."

"And she was. We all were except for Miriam, who wasn't even really trying. The fun stopped when Gladys decided to take things too far."

"God, I'm just as bad as Miriam!"

"You are not! Lisa, you're talking as if you paid him to fuck her . . ."

"Jesus!"

". . . and you didn't. They hooked up because he wanted to, not because you slipped him an extra couple of bucks. They hooked up because *she* wanted to. She said it herself at the restaurant and again at the café. Gladys has no business getting married, and if she had asked me, I would've told her so."

Why did Gladys have to ask me? After all, we had been friends for years. But the Gladys who balked when strange men harassed her in the street, until her friends made her feel safe enough to fight back, had become a Gladys who disappeared on those friends with a horny stripper. Maybe because so much time had passed, I felt we needed permission to be the same with each other. Or actually to be different.

"Gladys went this far with the wedding out of some crazy notion that this is the right time and not because Pablo's the right man. That's why she did what she did tonight, and that's probably the real reason why she feels so compelled to tell him. A part of Gladys hopes he'll get upset and call off the wedding. None of this has anything to do with you. The way she was banging on that stage and waving that money, it probably would have happened even if you hadn't tipped Frank. And remember, Lisa, Gladys doesn't even know that you tipped him."

Lisa drew her hand to her mouth and gasped. "God, that's right. Imagine if she did! You know what they'd be saying about me right now."

"What?"

" 'Lisa, that big ol' man-bashing lesbo, paid that stripper to come on to you and sabotage your wedding.' "

"No!" I said and I truly meant it. "Miriam and Gladys might've gotten a little skanky over the years, but they're not that bad."

"You don't think?"

I gave it a second thought. "No. Miriam's in such a funky place toward men, had she known you had tipped Frank, she would've been all for it. Hell, she would've matched you dollar for dollar and thrown in the hotel room to boot. You saw her with that credit card." I forced a laugh.

"And to think, I almost didn't come tonight."

"Didn't feel like dealing with their reaction to your coming out?"

"Oh, no, not that at all. At this point in my life, the closet is locked. Whoever can't deal with it, that's their problem."

"Good for you!"

"It's just that I never got an invitation to the wedding. And I'm not so hard to find. I've been at the same address in D.C., and my parents are still in Brooklyn," said Lisa as she ran her fingers through her perfect hair. "If I hadn't bumped into Miriam in the Village last week, I never would've known about Gladys's wedding and that had nothing to do with my being gay because neither of them knew. I was so happy about the idea of all of us being together again, it never occurred to me until later that I had never received an invitation. I mean, did you?"

"No."

"So I started thinking why should I go? Obviously, Gladys felt so much time had passed since we spoke, the friendship no longer mattered. With all I'm going through right now with my crazy schedule and the breakup with Celina, why should I bother? But I started thinking about all the fun we had in college, the things we helped each other through. I really wanted to see everyone again, especially you."

Then it became my turn to grow quiet.

"What's the matter, Ricky?"

"Here you are blaming yourself for what happened tonight—which is totally stupid, by the way, and I don't want to hear anymore about it—but look at what I did. I knew Miriam had something going on, and instead of reaching out to her and trying to find a way to make her feel better, I made it worse."

"OK, now you're the one who needs to stop."

"Really. For God's sake, I'm a social worker, how could I have missed it? Miriam's depressed, and I kept plying her with apple martinis. You're a doctor. You know that makes it worse."

"Let's be honest. She started drinking way before we got to the club."

"Damn, that little thing can really hold it, too," I said with a hint of admiration.

"You just didn't want her to spoil Gladys's night. She did that all by herself."

"But getting her drunk wasn't the answer. I could've found a better way. Like talking to her. Asking questions. Just listening." We drove a few yards in silence and then I came clean. "I didn't want to hear it, Lis. I'm not in that place anymore, and I didn't want to go back, not even to help an old friend. Probably because I was afraid that if I did, I'd get stuck there."

"You having problems with Eduardo?"

"That's just it. I'm not. We have our spats like any mar . . . like any other couple." Lisa's smile told me that she caught my switch and that she appreciated it. "Even when I want to wring the man's neck—*y te lo juro,* that's every other day—I have no doubt that he loves me and that I love him. He fully accepts me for who I am, and I trust him implicitly. But it took me a long, hard time to get to a place where I could even imagine feeling like that about anyone. . . ."

"I remember."

". . . 'Uardo and I even broke up for almost a year because of my shit. . . ."

"Really?"

"We each had our own places, but we were practically living together, you know how that is. So he said, 'Ricky, it doesn't make any sense for us to be paying rent and utilities on two apartments, so why don't we just move in together?' And I'm like . . ."

". . . Just like a man to ask for an emotional commitment but make it sound like a practical decision."

Her response evoked mixed feelings in me. On the one hand, I felt heartened that Lisa recalled how I used to be without sounding at all invested in that person I no longer was. On the other, I felt deeply embarrassed to have a witness—no matter how sympathetic—that such a person ever existed in the first place. Lisa listened with such a selfless compassion, however, "heartened" won out and I continued sharing.

"Exactly. I'm thinking, *Eduardo, if you want to take our relationship to another level and move in together, then say, Ricky, I love you, I see us having a future together, I want to wake up to you every day, blah, blah, blah, let's move in together*. Don't fuckin' tell me how much money I can save, how much closer your apartment is to my job and all that shit."

"But you didn't say that."

"No. I said, 'Well, Eduardo, I've done the living-together thing, and it just doesn't work for me so I'm not going to do it anymore. The way I see it, people move in together to break up or get married . . .'"

"OK," Lisa agreed.

"'. . . One or the other is inevitable. I don't want us to move in together and start taking each other for granted. If I'm going to give up my apartment, it's because we're getting married.' That's what I told him."

"And you were bluffing."

"Totally."

We laughed and then Lisa's eyes widened. "He didn't?"

"He sure did."

"No."

"The sonofabitch said, 'So when do you want to get married?'"

"Get out. So what'd you say?"

"I didn't say anything." I paused as I remembered the pain on Eduardo's face when I responded to his proposal in silence, and he knew it had nothing to do with the fact that he had no ring or didn't get down on one knee. "He said to me, 'If you don't want to marry me, then I don't know what we're doing here.' He packed whatever things he had at my place, and then he walked out. I didn't see him for almost a year."

"So how'd you get back together?"

"I called him."

"You called him?"

"I called him and told him that I made a mistake and that if he'd still have me, I'd be honored to be his wife. And if you tell Miriam and Gladys, I'll never forgive you."

"Don't worry, I won't. As a matter of fact, you know what, Ricky?"

"What?"

"I'm off next weekend."

It took a moment for that statement to register with me as the confession she intended. "You mean you lied about being on call to avoid going to Gladys's wedding?"

344 • Sofia Quintero

"Yeah."

"So you're actually free next Saturday."

"I know. I'm terrible."

"Actually, I was thinking that if you're not on call, you're free to come over to my place for dinner." Lisa grinned at the realization that I had lied about my plans on Saturday, too. We drove for a while in silence until I found the courage to ask what I had been wanting to all night.

"So, Lisa, what's up with Celina these days? Do you know? Are you in touch?"

"Oh, yeah," she replied, trying to sound nonchalant. "Celina's back in New York, too," Lisa said. "She's doing her residency at Columbia Presbyterian."

"Lisa?"

"What?"

"Give me Celina's number. I'll call to invite her over to my place for dinner next Saturday, too."

Then Lisa gave that snorty laugh of hers, and I lost it like I always do.